Bookmarked for Murder

A Sebastian McCabe – Jeff Cody Mystery

Dan Andriacco

Paperback ISBN 9781780928944
ePub ISBN 9781780928951
PDF ISBN 9781780928968

Published in the UK by MX Publishing
335 Princess Park Manor, Royal Drive,
London, N11 3GX
www.mxpublishing.com
Cover design by www.staunch.com

This book is dedicated to

Carolmarie Stock

with fond memories of the Class of '66

CONTENTS

Chapter One
Poisoned Pens, Raised Voices

If you're going to find a body in a bookstore, I think it should happen in the mystery section—not romance. But maybe that's just me, Thomas Jefferson Cody.

Pages Gone By was the only used-book store in town (unless you count Beans & Books coffee house) and owner Noah Bartlett enjoyed playing host to various groups of literate folks. On the first Tuesday of the month, for example, you could find our good friend Sister Mary Margaret Malone (Triple M to me, and Sister Polly to most people) meeting there with her science-fiction book club. More than a few of the other members are citizens of dubious distinction that she first met in her volunteer job as chaplain for the city jail, but that's irrelevant to this story.

What matters is that on the fourth Monday in March I put in an appearance at the Poisoned Pens. This was a small circle of aspiring crime and mystery writers who also met monthly at Pages Gone By to critique each others' work and bolster each others' spirits. My attendance had been erratic since my marriage three years earlier. But this particular night I made it a point to show up.

"Dunbar Yates is going to be there," I informed my assistant, Aneliese Pokorny, that morning. "He's a friend of Mac's."

That did not by any means put the *New York Times* best-selling mystery writer in an exclusive category. My brother-in-law, Sebastian McCabe, maintains a vast network of friends far and wide, especially among his fellow mystery writers.

"In fact," I added, "he's staying with Mac for a few days while he does a round of mega-bookstore appearances in Cincinnati and Dayton. So I asked if he could stop by the Poisoned Pens and share some writing wisdom."

"I know somebody else who's going to be there," Popcorn said. Can a short, pleasingly plump woman in her early fifties with dyed blond hair look coy?

She certainly wasn't talking about herself. Popcorn's taste in literature runs almost exclusively to the racy romance novels of one Rosamund DeLacey, so mystery writing wouldn't be on her to-do list.

"I give up. Who?"

"A friend of mine. You'll see."

She took a pull on her mug of high-test coffee and left me to ponder that.

Anyone was welcome to show up at a meeting of the Pens, as at most writers' groups, so I gave her Sphinx act very little brainwork. *Probably one of her administrative assistant friends,* I thought. The grim Heidi Guildenstern would make a great writer of dark fiction, but she wouldn't lower herself to go near Mac, her former boss. It must be somebody else. Maybe Francine Cassorla in the classics department—she always wore black fingernail polish and purple eye shadow.

Popcorn and I labor in the communications office of St. Benignus College, where Mac's day job is as the Lorenzo Smythe Professor of Literature and head of the miniscule Popular Culture Department. In fact, she and I *are* the communications office, formerly known as the public relations office. The name changed about the time I managed to get Popcorn a promotion from administrative assistant to assistant, with a raise to match the title. In my book that was a bigger magic trick than Mac ever managed, even in his professional days on stage. He lost Heidi as his admin in the process, but they never got along anyway. Win-win!

After trying to imagine a few other campus characters as mystery mavens, I put the guessing game out of my mind and went back to working on a new college brochure with lots of fun facts and pictures of smiling students.

I was smiling myself that evening after a satisfying dinner of chicken cacciatore and mixed vegetables—healthful and delicious. Lynda Teal (Cody), journalist extraordinaire, is no slouch in the cooking department.

"I hate to drag myself away," I said, standing close to my beloved spouse. Even without heels she's just a few inches shorter than my six-one, quite curvy, with naturally curly honey-blond hair and a cutely crooked nose. She was wearing a flowered dress and her favorite perfume, the heart-stopping Cleopatra VII. Why *wouldn't* I want to stay?

"But you'll have fun," she said in her distractingly husky voice. "And I brought home work anyway, so I wouldn't be very good company." I gave her a skeptical look. She gave me a kiss, and not the hit-and-run variety. This didn't make me any more eager to leave.

"I'll wait up," she promised.

Pages Gone By, prominently located downtown on High Street, was a sizeable store divided maze-like by themed bookcases running in different directions. The mystery section, for example, was marked off by a silhouette of Sherlock Holmes and—a recent addition—a black statue of the Maltese Falcon.

Near the front of the store, within sight of the counter but on the other side of the room, was an open area with a coffee table and chairs. When I arrived that night, most of the chairs were already occupied.

"Good evening, Jefferson," Sebastian McCabe greeted me. Too broad of beam for one of the matching chairs, he was sitting in a wider model on wheels. Right next to him was his houseguest, Dunbar Yates, who gave me a "Hi, Jeff." We'd met briefly in Mac's office. I would have recognized him anyway from the photo that appears on the back of his Hector Gumm & Beauregard books—a broad, black face with a fringe of goatee not doing much to make up for the lack of hair on top. He was below medium height, say around five-six, with a paunch.

"It turns out that Dunbar knows our host," Mac rumbled.

"Not exactly," Yates corrected. "But I knew he looked familiar."

"From New York," Noah expounded. "When I worked at Crimes & Punishments Bookshop, Dunbar had a bunch of book signings there."

An Erin native who had moved back home about four years earlier, Noah Bartlett wasn't just host to the Poisoned Pens, but a member as well. A handsome man in his late fifties, graying hair always in need of cutting, he was in fact probably the best writer in the group. Years before he'd had several short stories published in *Ellery Queen's Mystery Magazine.* He'd often alluded to a novel he was working on, but so far as I know he'd never shown it to the group.

Several of the members were equally shy about sharing their work, promising they'd do it eventually. Connor O'Quinn, a muscular dude with a perennial three-day growth of beard, had never shown the group—or anyone else—a scrap of writing. I had Ashley Crutcher's word for that. Ashley had brought him into the fold, and I had a strong suspicion that his interest was more in her than in writing mysteries. Whether he'd even *read* one was up for grabs.

"I've been to New York," Connor commented *sotto voce* to Ashley in the wake of Noah's comment, as though he thought that was an accomplishment.

"I could never afford that," she said wistfully. Her expression brightened. "Though I guess I can now."

Ashley had slimmed down quite a bit since her estranged husband had been murdered a year and a half earlier, leaving her a six-figure insurance policy.[1] The jeans made that clear. Her face had lost its moon shape and she was paying more attention to her wavy brunette hair than she had in the days when she was married. The young widow appeared to be in the market for a mate. I didn't think she was serious about Connor O'Quinn, although they were, loosely speaking, a couple. According to Popcorn—who had observed the two engaged in conversation over the bar at Bobbie McGee's, where Connor worked—Connor was a lot more interested in her than she was in him.

Not so with the other couple in our little group, Roscoe Feldman and Mary Lou Springfield. Their admiration for each other was entirely mutual, and completely transparent. Roscoe had recently retired from teaching English at Bernardin High School. Mary Lou was still hanging on as the school librarian, even though she was well past the age to qualify for full Social Security benefits. They'd been going steady for eighteen or nineteen years. Rumor had it that Roscoe was slow to commit. I asked him once when he was going to pop the question and he said, "What question?"

"There's only one person missing," Mo Russert said, pointing to an empty chair on my right. It took me a minute to figure out that she hadn't miscounted chairs. All the regulars were there. But then I remembered that Popcorn had said a friend of hers would be joining us. Said friend was a no-show so far. "We might as well get started," Mo added.

---

[1] See "Dogs Don't Make Mistakes" in *Rogues Gallery*, MX Publishing, 2014.

I had a soft spot for Mo that had nothing to do with her pleasant face and dark bangs that made her look younger than her forty-plus years. We'd had a couple of dates before I married, just enough to establish that there were no sparks on either side. But I admired her spirit. She hadn't let the knocks she'd endured in life bury her dreams, the biggest of which was to start her own bookstore specializing in mysteries. For now, though, the former teacher worked part-time for Noah at Pages Gone By.

"We're really fortunate to have a speaker tonight who needs no introduction," she began. Predictably, she then gave him one anyway. Mo had the honor of doing this because, although the Poisoned Pens had no official president, she had founded the group and tried to herd us cats. Yates, seeming small next to Sebastian McCabe, tried to look both flattered and surprised as she said:

"Dunbar Yates is a native of New York City, where he still lives. After a twenty-year career in the U.S. Air Force, working in public affairs, he decided to give himself a year to see if he could complete and sell a mystery novel that he'd been working on." Mo glanced over at Yates, and then around the room. "We all know how that turned out. Dunbar's first Gumm & Beauregard novel, *Mudbugs and Murder*, sold well and won the Mystery Writers of America's Edgar Award that year for Best First Novel. He's written six more novels in the series, and they always move to the top of my to-read stack as soon as they come out. I'm half-way through *Bodies in the Bayou* right now."

A polite overstatement? Probably not. I'm a big fan of the series myself. Louisiana private eye Hector Gumm and his reliable partner, Beauregard, a Bluetick Coonhound, come across as real and likeable even when the plots leave something to be desired. The style is hard-boiled, my preferred subgenre, but with enough of a soft center to make the books popular with a lot of readers who also like cozies.

Mo said a few more words that I missed while I surreptitiously read an affectionate text message from Lynda on my smart phone. I messaged back, never mind what. I know that's boorish behavior, but at least I didn't check out the closing prices of various stock market indexes, which I was also tempted to do. With a goofy grin on my face, I put the phone away and tuned back in to the speaker. By now, that was Yates. I was sure I'd only missed a few innocuous platitudes.

"I'm grateful to all my readers, as every writer should be," he was saying. Yates was from the Big Apple, all right; you could hear that in his vowels. "I write for them and I enjoy meeting them as I travel around on these book tours. But I really love talking to my fellow writers, and I'm delighted that my friend Mac gave me this opportunity." He nodded toward my brother-in-law, who smiled benevolently. Mac told me later what he thought about Yates's comments: "Implying that an author of Dunbar's marked success was part of the same confraternity, as it were, with a group of mostly unpublished writers, was a gracious way to begin. It was even true."

Pleasantries dealt with, Yates proceeded to hold forth on his topic for the evening: the advantages and the pitfalls of the series sleuth.

"Edgar Allan Poe invented the concept of featuring the same detective in a series of short stories, as we all know." Actually, I was fairly sure this was breaking news to Connor O'Quinn and maybe one or two others. "But then, since he invented the detective story, everything that he did in the genre was groundbreaking."

Yates delivered all this in a casual way, speaking without notes, as befit a man wearing a denim shirt, sleeves rolled up, and khaki pants. His voice sounded like it was honed on cigarette smoke.

"The first detective story, 'The Murders in the Rue Morgue,' introduced the eccentric amateur detective C.

August Dupin and his nameless sidekick. The second, 'The Mystery of Marie Rogêt' made them series characters. Their third appearance, 'The Purloined Letter,' was the best story of the bunch and sealed the deal. Although Poe lived another five years, the series ended there. It was Arthur Conan Doyle's Sherlock Holmes who—"

And so forth. You know the story—how Holmes became so wildly successful as a series character, starring in a story a month in *The Strand* magazine for two years, that Conan Doyle committed literary sleuthicide so he could concentrate on what he thought was his more important work. But you can't keep a good shamus down, so Conan Doyle brought him back from death at the Reichenbach Falls a decade later and continued to write about him for another quarter of a century.

Even I knew all this, and I'm no Sherlockian. Yates was recycling it as background to some points he wanted to make. He was just about to get to said points when the front door opened. The store being closed for business on Monday nights, I deduced that the heralded new member of the Poisoned Pens had appeared at last.

"Sorry I'm late, folks. I got caught at the office."

My head jerked in the direction of the familiar voice. It belonged to an overweight specimen concealing his balding dome beneath a straw fedora. So this was Popcorn's "friend"—the guy she dated for months without telling me?

"Oscar! What are *you* doing here?"

Okay, I admit my question was rude, especially since Oscar is also a friend of mine and of Mac as well. But I'd just had the politeness startled out of me. Oscar Hummel, Erin's police chief, positively *scorns* mystery fiction.

"I'm writing a detective story," he said, almost haughtily. "A novel. I figure, if you can't beat 'em, join 'em."

"That is an admirable sentiment, if rather clichéd in expression," Mac boomed, a wide smile splitting his face above the beard. "I congratulate your enterprise, Oscar."

Myself, I wasn't so sure congrats were in order. Oscar used to make a minor hobby out of critiquing Mac's mysteries, which feature a magician named Damon Devlin as the amateur sleuth. The chief loved to point out how unrealistic the plots are, and how his cops would have solved the murders in no time. He hasn't said much along those lines ever since Mac managed in real life to solve some murders that resisted Oscar's police procedures. He'd even asked for Mac's help on occasion. But was he happy about it? I suspected not. And now he was venturing onto Mac's turf as Mac had onto his. Payback time, maybe?

Most of the locals knew Oscar, at least by reputation, but he probably didn't know all of them—certainly not Yates. Mac made the introductions all around.

"Pleasure," Yates said with a scowl that belied the word. "There's always room for one more, I suppose."

Actually, it's kind of tight in here.

I didn't blame Yates for the annoyance written all over his broad face. Who likes being interrupted? Not I.

"Well," Oscar murmured, "don't mind me, everybody. Carry on." He sat down next to me. Although Oscar's girth isn't of McCabean proportions, he deposited some overlap on each side of the wooden chair.

"Right," Yates said. He shifted back into lecture mode. "I've been discussing series detectives or, rather, series protagonists. Today you'll find continuing characters, and not all of them sleuths, in all the subgenres of mystery—hard-boiled, cozies, horror, romantic suspense, adventure, fantasy, you name it.

"Now, this has great advantages for the writer. He or she gets to know the character intimately, more than is possible in a single novel. That greatly simplifies plotting because the writer knows exactly how the hero will act in any given plot turn. The protagonist's personality may even generate the plot. And that character's love life or day job can provide fertile territory for subplots, some of which may extend over more than just one book. Those are some of the advantages for the writer of a series.

"Readers, for their part, seem to love following their favorite detectives, spies, or vampire slayers. So this is a great marketing tool for the writer, but it's also a double-edged sword. As first Arthur Conan Doyle and then Dorothy Sayers, Agatha Christie, and a lot of other successful mystery writers found out, familiarity with a popular character can breed contempt on the part of the creator. You could call it the Conan Doyle Curse."

This was a problem I would have loved to have had. Not even the first of my hard-hitting Max Cutter private eye novels ever found a publisher. Which reminds me: I need to get back to fiction writing.

"But let me tell you something." Yates chuckled. He'd probably given this same talk dozens of times to local chapters of Sisters in Crime or the Mystery Writers of America, always with that little chuckle at this point. "Any mystery writer would be damned lucky to be so cursed. I know I am.

"Any questions?"

Mary Lou Springfield, our white-haired school librarian, raised her hand first. Tall and thin, she looks like Miss Marple and writes like Mickey Spillane. "Conan Doyle killed off Holmes, or tried to. You wouldn't dare do that to Hector Gumm!" It was an admonition, not a question.

Yates shook his head. "Wouldn't dream of it. I love that guy. If I weren't me, that's who I'd be. It's the Coonhound that's a pain in the ass. In the original ending of *Later, Gator*, Beauregard got eaten by that alligator, not just bitten. I figured that after a few books of going solo, Hector could replace him with another dog with a better personality, probably call him Beauregard II. But my agent pitched a fit. Apparently it doesn't matter how many people you kill in a book, but you can't kill a domestic animal." He put up his hands in a comical "don't shoot me" gesture. "Hey, I'm okay with that. Beauregard stays."

"Do you ever run out of ideas?" Ashley asked. Connor O'Quinn looked at her like he had plenty of ideas, but not about writing.

"Ideas are a dime a dozen," Yates said. "You all have ideas, right?"

"A whole notebook full," Noah said—ruefully, I thought. Heads bobbed around the room in agreement.

"I've read a ton of lousy books that came from great ideas," Yates continued. "The trick is to turn a great idea into a great story. That doesn't come easy for me. It's hard work—the only kind of work I know how to do anymore. One of these days my wife may find my cold, dead hands on the keys of my computer and my last mystery unsolved." He shook his head. "But I won't run out of ideas."

"Anybody can tell you're a New Yorker a mile away, Dunbar," Noah said. "No offense." It was hard for me to imagine that Noah, with his small-town manners, had worked in Gotham. He must have been a fish out of water there. "So how did you come to write about Bossier City, Louisiana?"

Yates winced. "I was stationed there once when I was in the Air Force. I thought it would be a colorful setting for a private eye novel. And it was. The problem is, cities change. I have to visit the place every few years to keep up. Plus I follow the *Bossier Press-Tribune* online for local color."

The expression on Mo's face turned mischievous. She arched her eyebrows so that they almost touched her black bangs. "What question don't you like to be asked?"

"I'm not thrilled when people say, 'Do you write under your own name?'"

Cute.

Connor O'Quinn took his eyes off of Ashley long enough to ask, "Who's your favorite writer?"

"Paul Laurence Dunbar. But my mystery-writer hero is Hammett." He gestured toward the falcon statue perched on a bookshelf. "Nobody did it better."

Good answer. Dashiell Hammett, one of my favorites as well, wrote *The Maltese Falcon*, *The Thin Man*, three other novels, and dozens of short stories about a nameless private eye known as the Continental Op. He didn't invent the hard-boiled detective story, but he made it art.

"Hector never describes himself," Mac observed. "I have always wondered, Dunbar: Is he white or black?"

"Does it matter?" The way Yates fired back, I figured it was a question he was tired of being asked. "Erle Stanley Gardner never described Perry Mason. Maybe he was African-American. And maybe Hector Gumm is Hispanic. He could be."

"Touché!" Mac beamed as if he'd just scored a point instead of being scored on.

"Do you outline your books in advance?" Oscar asked. Until now he'd been unusually quiet for him, but the question didn't surprise me. Aspiring writers often ask professionals that.

Yates shook his head. "No, I'm a pantser—a seat-of-the-pants writer, not a plotter. I start out with the general situation and see what happens. Every day at the computer brings surprises. I figure if I don't know how the book's going to end, the reader won't either. Sometimes I know at the beginning whodunit, but not always. I pay a lot of attention to the motive, though. If the motive doesn't work, nothing works."

Mac looked as though he wanted to ask another question, but he closed his mouth when Roscoe Feldman hesitantly held up his hand.

"When do you write?" the retired teacher asked, peering at Yates through thick wire-rimmed glasses. He's been working for six years on a novel strongly influenced by the early work of John Dickson Carr and the later work of Mary Higgins Clark. I was fairly sure that if he ever saw a real gun he would faint.

"I like to start—"

A cell phone rang, one of those annoying jazzy saxophone ring tones. Noah popped up like a jack-in-the-box, looking at his phone. "I'd better take this." He disappeared into the office at the back of the store, saying "Hello" into the phone as he went.

"As I was saying," Yates went on, a look of annoyance passing swiftly over his features. "I like to write in the morning—two pages before breakfast. Then I write another two in the afternoon. So that's four finished pages a day. I polish as I go, so sometimes cocktail hour runs late."

Lynda wouldn't tolerate that.

"What's on your plate now?" Mo asked, looking up from the tablet on which she'd been typing.

"The eighth Gumm & Beauregard, *Magnolia Mayhem*, will be out in time for Christmas. I'm working on the ninth, no title yet, and thinking about maybe starting a new series."

Having listened all night without making my own contribution to all this shop talk, I was about to ask Yates what he was willing to tell us about this potential new series when we heard—

"You can't do that to me! You'll find out. This isn't over, no matter what you think."

It was Noah's voice, coming from inside his office. He seemed to be having what diplomats called a full and frank discussion with somebody. I thought I heard a raised voice on the other end, but I couldn't make out a word.

An awkward silence descended as some of us strained to hear more without appearing interested, and the more polite Poisoned Pens pretended that they'd heard nothing. This went on for maybe half a minute before Noah burst out of his office. His face red, he quickly resumed his seat and focused his attention on Yates.

Mac stroked his beard. I bet myself that he would be the first to speak. When he cleared his throat, I got ready to pay off. "You mentioned motives earlier, Dunbar. This is an aspect of detective fiction that has always fascinated me. Murder is not undertaken lightly. A killer—in plausible fiction, if not always in real life—must have a motive that is strong enough both to incite homicide and to override the fear of detection and punishment. And yet, this overpowering motive in most cases should not be obvious, for it is a major clue to the killer. This tension between the two obligatory aspects of the motive presents the author with a significant challenge. What is your favorite motive?"

Yates allowed himself a cynical smile. "You know my work, Mac, but I bet you never noticed this. I didn't notice it myself for years. In all my stuff, short stories and novellas included, I only use one of seven motives."

"Seven?" Oscar repeated. His eyebrows made a pair of question marks.

Yates nodded. "Yeah, the seven deadly sins—greed, pride, lust, envy, sloth, gluttony—"

"And wrath," Noah said before he could finish, "otherwise known as extreme anger or rage. I'd say that's a damned good reason to kill somebody."

Chapter Two
Job Security

"That doesn't sound like the mild-mannered book geek that I know," Lynda said the next morning, passing me the granola box.

"It's not the way he usually rolls," I agreed. "The brave new world of books and non-books must have him stressed out."

I knew from talking to Noah Bartlett that selling used books from a brick and mortar store was a tough gig these days, what with e-books making so many out-of-print titles available and online retailers simplifying the search for book collectors. But I still love bookstores. I look for them wherever I go, in big cities and in little towns.

Lynda, who does most of her reading on a screen, took a deep drink of caffeine-laced coffee. She hadn't had time to brew cappuccino. "Well, I hope he hangs in there."

My bride had waited up for me the night before, as promised, but we hadn't gotten around to discussing the Poisoned Pens meeting until breakfast. She wore a form-fitting bright yellow dress with a dragonfly pin. The jewelry had been a gift from the sultry actress Heather O'Toole, appropriately known in tabloid headlines as HO'T, whom we'd met in England.[2] Lynda and I often work out together in the morning at Nouveau Shape, but this wasn't going to

---

[2] See *The Disappearance of Mr. James Phillimore*, MX Publishing, 2013.

be one of those mornings. She had an early meeting with Megan Whitlock, her boss at Grier Ohio NewsGroup.

"The newspaper business isn't a growth industry these days, either," she added. Her pretty, oval-shaped face looked serious as she spread butter on her toast. At least it was whole wheat. "*Editor & Publisher* is gloomy reading. Every month it has stories of buyouts, layoffs, reduced publication schedules, and mergers of newspaper staffs under a single editor at the chain papers. More than 16,000 newspaper jobs were cut in the United States from 2003 to 2012, and the trend line since then is worse."

"What about digital? You're a whiz at that."

"None of our papers is meeting its goals for digital subscriptions."

I shifted gears. "There's always television." Grier was one of the last major media companies to keep broadcast and print together while others were spinning off the newspapers. As editorial director of Grier Ohio NewsGroup, Lynda works with all of the company's properties—on the air and on the newsstand. I think of her as a kind of circuit rider for news quality. She spends a lot more time on the road than I would like, with an office at the *Erin Observer & News-Ledger* as her home base.

"Grier is cutting back at the TV stations, too. Apparently the profit margins aren't high enough, whatever that means. I'm sure you know all about profit margins."

Her tone was just short of accusatory. *Is it a bad thing that I'm a knowledgeable investor?*

Considering her mood, I decided that this wasn't the time to point out that the non-profit sector wasn't immune from the budget axe. Ralph Pendergast had been slicing and dicing expenditures ever since his arrival at St. Benignus College as provost and vice president for academic affairs. That's why he'd been hired by the trustees—to wield a firmer hand on finances than our long-reigning president, the benevolent Father Joseph Pirelli. But after a half-decade of more cuts than a slasher film, the natives were getting restless. And by natives I mean alumni as well as students, faculty, and staff. The mood of the campus was not good. And the students didn't even know yet about the four percent tuition increase they (or their parents) were going to get hit with next year.

"If the bottom line is that almighty important," Lynda went on, not softly, "then I'm not sure Grier needs an editorial director to improve the quality of the news product. What does quality mean to number crunchers? Maybe that's what Megan wants to meet with me about. She wasn't specific, just said it was important. I could be searching Craigslist for a job tomorrow."

"Megan's not that stupid," I said stoutly. "Besides, she's your biggest fan—next to me, of course. She created that job and put you in it, which was brilliant on her part."

Lynda smiled and moved an errant honey-blond curl out of her eye. "That's very sweet, but Megan may not have a choice. I'm not sure her job is secure, either."

As president of Grier Ohio NewsGroup, Megan Whitlock directed all of the Buckeye State operations of the far-flung Grier Media empire from her office in Columbus. And she did it so well that I figured she'd eventually be hanging her chapeau at the Grier corporate headquarters in New York. If even her job wasn't safe, then times were tough indeed.

Whitlock had met with Lynda in Erin before, but rarely enough to make a hometown confab a major calendar item for Lynda.

Then it hit me. "You must have been worried about this yesterday and all night."

"I didn't sleep very well," she confessed.

"Why didn't you say something?" *You aren't the introvert in this relationship; that's my job.*

"I didn't want to worry you, too. I'm worried enough for both of us. And I didn't mean to bring this up now and then run off to work, either. It just kind of spilled out."

I held her hand. "I'm sure it will all work out, no matter what this meeting is about. Even if you got canned we'd be okay for quite a while. We have plenty of money." *Was that me talking? It didn't sound like me.* But in truth I had earned a few bucks during my thirty-seven years of bachelorhood, and invested a lot more of those bucks than I spent. "And we don't have any children depending on us."

The stupid comment was barely out of my mouth before I wished I could pull it back. The look on Lynda's face was a knife in my heart. *Oh, crap! Why did I say that?* "I mean for the time being. I'm sure we *will* have children. Any day now. Maybe you're too tense with all these work worries."

"Maybe."

Lynda poured herself a second cup of high-test java. *I really don't think that's going to relax you, Lyn.*

She evidently caught me watching this ritual. "You know, Jeff, the latest studies show that caffeine can actually be good for you."

Say what? "You're just messing with my head, right?"

"No, really. I'm not kidding. You can look it up."

"Well, that's interesting." *I'd like to read those so-called studies.* I stood up to put my cereal bowl in the dishwasher. "Anyway, be sure to text me and let me know what happens with Megan."

Since I didn't have a morning meeting with my boss that might determine—or end—my career, I spent forty-five minutes working out downtown at Nouveau Shape before I bicycled over to campus. The usual band of morning merry-makers sweated along with me, including a retired IRS employee, the county prosecutor, a young accountant with very athletic legs, and a couple of St. Benignus employees. I missed having Lynda there.

As I pumped my legs on the elliptical machine, I pondered how to play it with Popcorn when I got to the office. Should I be indignant that she hadn't told me that Oscar was the Poisoned Pens newbie? Or puzzled that she thought I would be surprised? Or happy that the chief had joined the dark side? This was trivial compared to what must have been going through Lynda's head at the same time, but that's how my mind works.

Deciding to play it casual, no big deal on the day after, I wished Popcorn a cheery "good morning" on my way to my desk. She responded in kind.

A few minutes later, she brought me a mug of defanged coffee and deposited herself in one of the chairs in front of my desk. "How was your Poisoned Pens meeting?"

"Enjoyable."

A pause.

"Well, did he show up?"

"Who?"

And so forth. I made her drag the details of the entire evening out of me. Call it payback. She and Oscar, both friends of mine, had dated on the sly for quite some time before going public with the relationship. I could understand them holding out on Oscar's possessive mother, but I was hurt that they hadn't told me. I'd had to figure it out on my own, and then wonder whether I was right. Asking would have been borderline prying. And I never pry. I leave that to Lynda, who does it professionally, and to Popcorn, who does it recreationally.

"Have you read that alleged mystery novel he says he's writing?" I said.

"I haven't had the pleasure." *Pleasure? You must really be in love.* She changed the subject. "I wonder who Noah was yelling at on the phone?"

"Beats me," I said. "Have you heard any good gossip about him?"

"Just that his store isn't doing very well and that somebody wants to grab up that particular piece of real estate for a brew pub."

The second part of that sentence was news to me. "Who is this prospective brewmeister?"

"I didn't hear that, Boss."

Microbreweries had been hot stuff for a few years now. I filed for future reference the intel that one might be coming to our quiet corner of the universe. Meanwhile, it was time to look busy. Sipping on my coffee, I fired up the computer on my desktop. Popcorn kept talking, as per our usual routine.

"You missed a call already," she said just as I typed the words "healthful effects of caffeine" into the search engine. Father Pirelli had advised me a long time ago to have my calls forwarded to Popcorn instead of dumping into voice mail. That didn't change when she got promoted to my assistant. I think it's a nice customer service touch, a rare one these days, to have a human being answer the phone in my absence.

She handed me a message form containing a vaguely familiar name, J. Randolph Smith, and his phone number.

"He's with *Higher Ed Insider*," Popcorn said. "He didn't want to tell me what it was about."

"That can't be good."

I abandoned my computer, which had turned up a dismaying number of positive health stories about caffeine, and called Smith. He sounded young and friendly. After the preliminary niceties, he said, "I was wondering whether you have any comments on the YouTube video of one of your professors, James Gregory Talton, that's gone viral."

Talton? Searching the Cody memory banks, I dimly recalled him as a history professor. He'd come to me once for help publicizing a book he wrote about Henry Clay. Surely a history professor couldn't be causing *that* much trouble. I mean, history is all old news, right?

"I don't know anything about Professor Talton and a YouTube video," I said.

"It's pretty riveting," Smith assured me. *Oh, joy.* "Professor Talton seems to be speaking to a small class, maybe a graduate seminar, and he's quite animated. He calls Abraham Lincoln a 'despot' who 'acted unconstitutionally' and caused the deaths of more than half a million people by fighting the Civil War, which Talton says was totally unnecessary. So, like I said, I wondered if the college would like to make a comment on that."

As I said, I thought absently, not *like I said.* Has the distinction been completely lost in American speech, even among educated people?

"Well, *as* I said, Randolph, I didn't know about this until just now. I'm going to have to get back to you later." *Never let them smell your fear.*

And I *was* afraid. Given Erin's proud history as a stop on the Underground Railroad—Mac's house had a small concealed room to prove it—dissing Abraham Lincoln wouldn't go over well with the locals. The other three hundred and sixteen million people in the United States who idolized our greatest president wouldn't be cheering either. A political aide to U.S. Sen. Rand Paul of Kentucky wisely resigned a few years ago after a ten-year-old blog post surfaced in which had written that "John Wilkes Booth's heart was in the right place."

The timing on this was terrible, too. The 150th anniversary of Lincoln's assassination, coming up on April 15, had not gone without notice in the media.

It could have been worse, though—and on other occasions it has been. Just six months earlier one of the art professors got caught showing one of his female students more than his etchings. That was a violation of Title IX, the federal law against sexual discrimination at any educational program receiving federal funds. Title IX cases can be messy, no-win affairs. A case in point was the ugly coverage by *Higher Ed Insider* the previous year about a theology professor upstate who had allegedly hit on a married couple. Fortunately, our art guy went quietly after only about a week of local headlines. Maybe Talton would do the same, I thought.

I should have known better.

Smith asked me to get back to him by the end of the day, either by phone or by e-mail, and let him know whether we had anything to say.

First order of business after hanging up the phone was to watch the YouTube video on my computer. It ran under five minutes, but seemed longer to me. A lot longer.

Just as I remembered, Talton was an African American with a big salt-and-pepper beard. He reminded me of a black Karl Marx with somewhat shorter hair. I later found out that he was in his late forties, but he looked a decade or so older. Speaking in a raspy voice right in the direction of the camera, he said incendiary things like: "Lincoln was a tyrant, a despot who acted unconstitutionally when he suspended the writ of habeas corpus . . . If he had lived, he should have had the honor of being the first president impeached rather than the hapless Andrew Johnson . . . The bloodiest war in our nation's history was all on his head."

Wasn't "tyrant" what Booth had called Lincoln after shooting him—"*sic semper tyrannis*" and all that? At least Talton hadn't actually mentioned Booth, unlike the former senatorial aide.

From internal evidence, it was hard to tell how old the video was. Talton's suit and tie were timeless—that is to say, unconventional classroom wear for a college prof any time in the last forty years. But how long ago he had made his comments really didn't matter; they were coming to light now and that made them news now. In the Internet age, no boneheaded statements ever go away. They're always still there somewhere beneath the surface, ready to be kicked over before the next deadline of some controversy-hungry news organization. Take my advice: Never blog, tweet, Facebook, e-mail, Pinterest, or Instagram anything you wouldn't want to read in a newspaper, see on television, or (worst of all) have admitted as evidence in court.

When the video mercifully ended, I tried to think where this might go. What usually happened when an academic said something that brought out the villagers with pitchforks? Gordon Gee, Ohio State University's bow-tied president, resigned under pressure after making a lame joke about Catholics. Larry Summers exited the president's office at Harvard after a no-confidence vote by his faculty, sparked in part by a speech in which he suggested the under-representation of women in science and engineering at elite universities could have to do with innate differences in aptitude between the sexes.

But those guys were just presidents, not professors. It's not only lonely at the top, it's also easy to get pushed off. Tenured professors, on the other hand, are harder to dislodge than a tree stump. And Talton was tenured. His bio in my files showed that he had come to St. Benignus fifteen years ago after taking degrees in economics from the University of Chicago and history from Notre Dame. He'd written four books and dozens of articles. With one of the most impressive résumés at our little college, there wasn't a snowball's chance in Haiti that he was going to be shown the door over this flap.

Still, I didn't want to read "St. Benignus College officials refused to comment" in J. Randolph Smith's story. So I spent a good chunk of the day drafting a statement and then waiting for people up the food chain to approve it— Professor Lesley Saylor-Mackie, head of the history department, and Ralph Pendergast, our beloved provost. Don't get the idea that I have to run everything I say past the grown-ups. That's not the case. But this was a national story, even though *Higher Ed Insider* doesn't have the readership of, say, *The New York Times.*

So I tried to higher-level input from Saylor-Mackie and Ralph before I began writing, but neither was around that morning. The professor was at a meeting at which she was wearing her other hat as mayor of Erin. Ralph was probably busy laying somebody off. So I just started writing. I made changes in word choice as I went along, then read it over several more times, making more changes until I had a version I thought Smith-worthy. Here's what I came up with:

> St. Benignus College fully appreciates that Professor James Gregory Talton's recently circulated negative comments about Abraham Lincoln, one of our nation's most beloved and admired presidents, will provoke vigorous debate. The exploration of ideas, even unpopular ones, is part of our mission as an institution of higher learning. While Professor Talton's opinions are his own, not those of St. Benignus, we cherish his academic freedom to present them.

At the end I was tempted to throw in something more explicit about free speech and the American way while I was heading in that direction, but why gild the lily? And shorter is better for reaction statements because it's harder to take part of it out of context.

Half of my job is putting out fires like this—the exciting half. It's also the challenging half. *But at least I have a job.* That reminded me. I pulled out my smartphone and texted Lynda:

Meeting over?

In a few minutes her response came back:

Yep. Just now. It's all good. Tell u tonite.

When I got home, Lynda was already in the kitchen fixing herself a Manhattan. I pulled a Caffeine-Free Diet Coke out of our state-of-the-art refrigerator. I couldn't let the girl drink alone, could I?

"So, how was your day?" she asked.

"Surprising."

My draft statement had been okayed without much trouble. I got the impression from Saylor-Mackie that Talton was a major hemorrhoid on his best day, but she approved of my approach—defend his rights, not his ideas. She turned down the opportunity to attribute the statement to her, or to add a quote from her. She tried to bring Talton into the loop when we talked about the statement, but being a full professor he couldn't be found before J. Randolph Smith's deadline. Ralph, as usual, didn't think that we should comment at all. No wonder Mac calls him our *bête-noir*, which I believe is French for pain in the ass. I finally talked Ralph into seeing it my way—wore him down, actually—and sent the statement off to *Higher Ed Insider* before quitting time.

Ralph used to own our house, by the way. We bought it from him. Sometimes I worry that his negative spirit haunts the place even though he's still alive. I'm much less bothered by the dead body that we found in the freezer when we first looked at the house.[3]

"What was the big pow-wow with Megan all about?" I said after I'd given Lynda the Cliffs Notes version of my day. It was warm for late March and we were sitting on our patio.

"Two words: Sweeps month."

This was a term I was only hazily familiar with, but Lynda filled me in: In February, May, July, and November, the Nielsen ratings service surveys television viewers to find

---

[3] See "A Cold Case" in *Rogues Gallery* (MX Publishing, 2014).

out what they're watching. So those are the months when TV stations pull out all the stops to attract more eyeballs so they can charge more for advertising. The news department was expected to do its bit by producing "you've got to see this" investigative stories.

"The February sweeps weren't so hot for any of the three Grier stations in Ohio," Lynda said. "So Megan wants me to coordinate one big project for all three stations, a series of stories they can all work on. Each station will have a local element for its market, but also a bigger picture. And we'll tie it all together on the web."

"Cool."

She nodded absently. "It would be cooler, though, if the next sweeps month wasn't May and if the Cleveland, Columbus, and Youngstown stations weren't already planning their own stories for that month. They're going to just love me coming in to tell them to rip up their playbooks because I have a better idea."

No pressure there.

"I'm sure your project will be better than what any of them had planned," I said, ever the supportive spouse. "What's the topic?"

Lynda frowned, making her face look even more oval, though no less lovely. "I'm still working on that. It's the first thing I have to figure out. I was thinking maybe the heroin epidemic."

How could I let her down gently? "Well, that's a big problem, all right. But hasn't that been given a lot of attention in the media? The Gannett papers did a five-part series last year. It would take a strong new angle to make it worth a TV series. I'm just speaking as a viewer here."

She stared into her empty Manhattan glass as if wishing it were a crystal ball. "Yeah, you're right. I knew that, but I needed you to tell me. There's no new angle possible on that one. I was also thinking about an investigation into legal gambling in the state. Ohio has four casinos now, plus a bunch of racinos, and I'm not sure that anybody's really explored all the implications of that. Have the local communities really benefited? Are the gambling addiction hotlines getting a workout?"

"Good questions," I said. "But Youngstown doesn't have a casino, so it would fall a little flat there." How do I remember this stuff? I don't even gamble. "But may I make a suggestion?"

"Sure." Lynda leaned forward at a most distracting angle. I almost forgot my suggestion.

"You intimated that the news directors or station managers or whoever won't be thrilled when you swoop in from corporate with this project directive, right?" She nodded. "Well, then, why don't you ask them for *their* ideas for a sweeps month series? I bet they'd be falling all over themselves to come up with something that would impress Megan as well as get viewers."

Her gold-flecked brown eyes lit up. "Jeff, that's a stellar idea! I know news, but I'm a print girl. Our TV people get what makes a good television story a lot better than I do. Plus, they'll appreciate that I asked and that will cause them to buy in."

I loved her excitement. I also loved the way she demonstrated her appreciation for my idea in a spousely way. After a while we ate a late dinner and read a bit before going to sleep. By lights out, Noah Bartlett and the conversation about him with which Lynda and I had begun our day was far from my thoughts.

That changed with a bang the following morning at the office. My cell phone rang just after Popcorn handed me a cup of neutered coffee. At first all I heard was a sobbing noise.

"Who is this?" I demanded. Mr. Sensitivity, that's me.

"Jeff?" One syllable wasn't enough for me to recognize the tear-filled female voice.

"Yeah."

"It's Mo. I just got here for work and I found Noah. He's—" She dissolved into sobbing again.

I gripped the phone harder. "Is he dead?"

She barely managed an affirmative response.

"But he seemed fine just the other night!" Everybody says stupid things like that in the face of death. Realizing just *how* stupid, I shut up and patiently let Mo cry on my virtual shoulder for a while.

"His head is smashed in," she finally choked out. "I think he must have been murdered."

Chapter Three
A Case for McCabe

I stared for a minute at the coffee mug in my hand. The message in bold letters seemed to mock me: **I'M NOT ALWAYS SARCASTIC—SOMETIMES I'M ASLEEP.**

"You've already called 911, right?"

"No."

That was a bad move—or lack of a move—but an understandable one. Oscar Hummel is a law enforcement veteran, a solid cop, but Mo's reading taste and her own mystery writing didn't run to police procedurals. In her mind, murder undoubtedly evoked visions of amateur detectives and private eyes.

"I don't know why," Mo went on, after a pause, "but I just thought of you."

That would have been a flattering comment if I hadn't known better. But I realized that Mo really meant she thought of Mac. She'd called me as a shortcut to my brother-in-law, although I admit that her subconscious may not have let her in on the secret.

"Have you touched anything except the door when you came in?"

"No, I don't think so. Not that I remember. I just now came into work and found Noah. He's all bloody. I didn't—" Her voice broke.

"Good. You're doing fine. Call 911 and don't let on to the operator, or to Oscar, or to anybody else that you called me first. Then just stand there until Oscar and his troops arrive. I'll mobilize Mac."

"All right. This is just awful, Jeff."

"I know. Try to hang on. You can fall apart later."

I disconnected.

"What happened?" Popcorn asked. I'd been only dimly aware of her standing outside my inner office the entire time.

"You don't know about that phone call because it never happened."

"What phone call?"

I love that woman.

"That was Maureen Russert. Apparently somebody bashed Noah Bartlett's head in. The body was waiting for her when she reported for work this morning." *Talk about getting the day off to a bad start.*

Popcorn's eyes approximated quarters. "You just saw Noah the other night. So did Oscar. He'll be on this case like flies on honey!"

"I'd rather he act like a cop on a murder."

My mind was spinning. I was still shocked about Noah, but not too shocked to be thanking my lucky stars that his killing—if that's what it was—didn't have anything to do with St. Benignus College. We had enough PR problems with our tenured professors.

"We must go to the scene!" Mac boomed.

Of course you would say so.

"I'm sure Mo would like that," I admitted. "But how can we just show up without spilling the beans that she called us first, which is probably illegal and definitely annoying to Oscar?"

Speaking of illegal, Mac lit a match and fired up a cigar, which is *verboten* everywhere on campus. "Ah, Jefferson, the one fixed point in a changing age! What you lack in optimism, you make up for in consistency. You are forever foreseeing obstacles where none exist." He spread his hands. "We are both frequent customers at Pages Gone By, old boy! Oscar knows that. We have even dragged him there in our attempts to improve his appreciation of sensational literature. What could be more natural than us just stopping by?"

That alone would be suspicious if Oscar had more imagination, because there's nothing natural—i.e., normal or ordinary—about Sebastian McCabe. I'd found him in his office watching a movie on his computer with the sound turned down. He'd been practicing lip reading, which he assured me would come in handy someday. At least he had the grace to look stunned when I dropped the news on him about Noah's murder. That lasted about two seconds before he went into rush-to-the-scene-of-the-crime mode.

He consulted his Sherlock Holmes watch. "No doubt Dunbar would be interested in this case as well. Unfortunately, however, for another thirty-two minutes he will be engaged in talking to Cynthia Torbeck's Creative Writing 201 class."

"Too bad," I said acidly. "Oscar will really regret not having one more amateur sleuth poking his nose into the crime scene."

Mac raised an eyebrow. "I am quite confident that Oscar will welcome our assistance . . . eventually."

"Not this morning," I said gloomily.

Chapter Four
Murder by Falcon

For the record, Mrs. Hummel's boy Oscar is nobody's fool. He understands full well that the strangely stuffed McCabe mind, honed as it is to perform magic and write mystery novels, is just the ticket for solving a small percentage of cases that prove immune to police procedure.

Sometimes he even admits it.

I just didn't think he'd want us to get to the body before he did.

"You might try slowing down," I told Mac as we barreled toward downtown in his bright red '59 Chevy. The only difference between that oversized vehicle and a fire engine is the tail fins and the lack of a ladder. "Noah isn't going anywhere."

Surprisingly compliant, Mac lightened up on the gas pedal without comment. But he lit a cigar, probably so I wouldn't get too cocky.

We saw the police cars when we pulled onto High Street. Mo's 911 call had brought a prompt response from the police station just a few blocks away.

"Look shocked when you see Oscar," I instructed.

"I do not think you will find my performance lacking, Jefferson."

Oscar, wearing his uniform hat as he always did on official business, greeted us at the door. Mo was nowhere in sight, and neither was her late employer.

"What took you so long?" Oscar demanded.

"What do you mean?" I wasn't acting. That was about the last thing I'd expected him to say.

"Don't play games with me, Jeff. I bet Popcorn told you about this as soon as I texted her. Hey, can that cigar, Mac. This is a crime scene."

Mac looked at me with a raised eyebrow—whether at the gift horse we'd just been handed or at Oscar's disrespect toward his cigar, I didn't know.

"You should talk," I muttered. Oscar always could be counted on to bum a cigarette from somebody when he was out of the office on a case and away from his octogenarian mother. After Lynda quit smoking and while she was still news editor at the *Erin Observer & News Ledger*, she used to carry a pack just to bribe Oscar.

But wait! That wasn't a cigarette in his hand.

"I'm not smoking," Oscar said, taking a drag. "I'm vaping."

Vaping?

"What looks like smoke is actually vapor," Mac said, "and the device in Oscar's mouth is a smokeless nicotine delivery system. I have seen photos."

So had I. I also knew that these e-cigarettes—unlike the tobacco kind—were legal to use everywhere. But I'd never actually encountered one of the little nicotine machines in real life. Oscar's was police blue.

The chief looked as sheepish as a man of his age and station could. "It was Popcorn's idea."

So that was it! Either concern for Oscar's health or distaste for smoker's breath, or both, had caused Popcorn to urge Oscar to give up tobacco. Clearly, Oscar had fallen hard for my assistant. When I had tried to do the same favor for Lynda years ago, my persistence about the subject had resulted in a break-up. (Well, there may have been a few other factors as well.) Fortunately, we didn't stay broken, and Lynda had quit smoking in the interim.

Mac looked around, as if searching for a place to put his cigar. "Not surprisingly, there is no ash tray in sight. I suppose I shall just have to make this excellent smoke *vanish.*" As he said the last word, in a typically theatrical manner, the cigar simply disappeared from his right hand. One second it was there and the next second Mac held up both hands to show that it was gone.

Oscar gaped. "How did you—"

"A magician never tells. Now, to the murder. Burglary?"

"The killer would like us to think so, Mac, but I ain't buying it. Come on, I'll show you."

"Where's Mo?" I asked.

"In the back with Gibbons."

Pages Gone By was such a warren of bookcases that one couldn't see the back from the front where we had come in. Oscar led us in that direction.

Lt. Col. L. Jack Gibbons, the chief's right-hand man as assistant chief, would have made a great recruiting poster for the U.S. Marines. He's so spit-and-polish that I thought his first name was "Lt. Col." until I saw the "L. Jack" on a theater program a few years ago. He had a softer side, though, judging by the way he was speaking to Mo in low, comforting tones in the office at the back of the store.

Mo's eyes were puffy and she held a shredded tissue in her hand. When she saw me, she turned on the waterworks all over again. "Oh, Jeff!" She threw her arms around me. Mo had never gotten that close to me the couple of times we went out together casually after her divorce and my temporary break-up from Lynda. But I guess I was a familiar, welcome presence in a surreal situation. Any old port in the storm.

"Did you call Jonathan?" I asked. *You know, your boyfriend?*

"I'm in charge of the invitations to this party," Oscar said, "and I'm not sending out any more." Apparently he had forgotten that he hadn't invited Mac and me. I didn't remind him.

"You indicated that this was not a burglary," Mac prompted.

"I'll show you."

The office had been built into a corner at the left back of the store. At the other corner was a small bathroom. Between the two rooms were a number of bins with magazines and paperback books. Behind them, at the unlighted far back wall, was a hard-to-see door that opened onto an alley. Oscar pointed to where the glass in that door had been smashed.

"But that didn't set off the burglar alarm because it wasn't on," Oscar said.

Mac stroked his beard. "You will notice, Jefferson, as Oscar undoubtedly did, that the glass is blocking the door on this side, which means—"

"It means," Oscar said, glaring at Mac, "that the killer didn't open the door to get in after breaking the glass. He either used a key or Noah let him in before store hours. Either way, Noah knew him. He kicked in the glass on his way out to make it look like some drug-crazed burglar did it." Oscar vaped.

Mac looked at Mo. "Then you must have come in the front door."

She nodded. "I was just explaining that to Officer Gibbons. Noah's usually here first and already has the store open before the official hours, so I come in the front way. Today that door was locked. That was unusual, but I didn't think anything of it. I just used my key. It opens both doors, but it didn't occur to me to go around to the back since I was already in front."

"And you found the body right away?"

"Within a few minutes. I walked around a little, calling Noah's name, thinking that he might be shelving some books or something. And then—"

She stopped. I patted her on the back, totally at a loss as to what I could say that wouldn't be a cliché.

But Mac knew what to say, and it had nothing to do with comforting Mo. "May we see the body, Oscar?"

"Sure. It's in the romance section."

Crumpled on the floor in front of a bookcase that ran parallel to his office, Noah seemed somehow smaller. And the back of his head was a bloody pulp. *"Who would have thought the old man had so much blood in him?"* Equally bloody was the black plaster Maltese Falcon, which I remembered being on display in the mystery section. It lay not far from the body.

"No fingerprints on the statue, of course," Mac observed.

Oscar smiled ruefully. "Of course not. *CSI.*" Oscar has this unreasonable—and unalterable—conviction that the world would be much safer if criminals didn't learn about fingerprints, DNA, and all manner of scientific crime detection by watching crime shows on television.

"Blood tends to splatter," I said. "Wouldn't the killer get some of it on him?"

Oscar nodded. "Looks like he washed his hands in that little bathroom over there. We'll dust the whole room for prints, but I'm not expecting anything."

"This wasn't planned," I said, "or else the murderer would have brought the weapon instead of picking up something that was here."

"Perhaps he did bring a weapon, but then saw a better opportunity," Mac said with maddening logic.

"Whatever." Oscar, ever the practical cop, waved all that away as if it were the vapor coming out of his e-cigarette. "The murder weapon came from there." He pointed unnecessarily across the room at the mystery section, identified with a silhouette of Sherlock Holmes. "And the victim was hit on the back of the head. Judging by the angle, the killer was right-handed, which narrows the suspect pool down to about ninety percent of the population or a little less. There was some premeditation—whether minutes or days, who knows. But I think the perpetrator was a pretty cool customer to fake a break-in."

"But why do that?" I said.

"To make it appear that the victim was a stranger." Mac rubbed his beard. "That suggests that he or she was not. So does the murder weapon. Anyone might have recognized the Maltese Falcon's potential as a blunt instrument, but a habitué of the store who had seen it often was more likely to do so."

Mac looked around. "The scenario seems clear. Noah was assaulted right here, at the end of the aisle. There is nothing to indicate that he was hit anywhere else and crawled here. Noah was walking along this bookcase, perhaps headed toward his office, when the killer came up behind him, having entered from the back door, and picked up the statue a few feet away. Perhaps Noah was talking to the killer, not sensing any danger.

"The killer struck him on the head repeatedly and then left him for dead. He was not yet dead, however. He lived long enough to pull a book off the shelf and he died clutching it in his hand."

I'd missed the book. I have to admit that. But it was a paperback, mostly concealed by the body. I bent down to look at the title—*Love's Dark Secret*. I blinked my eyes, but the title didn't change. I couldn't believe it. It was one of those sleazy Rosamund DeLacey romance novels featuring a lurid cover painting of a half-naked hunk. Popcorn seemed to read about one a month, but I think she re-reads her favorites. I can't be sure; the titles all seem alike to me.

"Maybe he needed something to pass the time before he died," Oscar said peevishly. "I think I know where you're going with this, and I just don't buy it. That doesn't happen in real life."

Mac regarded him. "It might when the victim is a dedicated mystery reader and sometime writer."

"What are you two talking about?" Mo asked. I'd almost forgotten that she was there. She hadn't spoken since we'd begun viewing the body.

"A dying clue, by thunder!" Mac said. "There can be little doubt that Noah grabbed that book to give us a clue to his murderer. As you know, the dying clue is a familiar gambit in mystery fiction, especially of the Golden Age. Ellery Queen specialized in it."

"Noah loved Ellery Queen," Mo said in a small voice. "He collected the Queen books and wouldn't sell one unless he had a duplicate. It depressed him that they're largely forgotten and mostly out of print these days except for a few available as e-books."

"The problem with Mac's theory," Oscar said heavily, "is that this isn't an Ellery Queen book. People who are dying don't think about things like that. Bartlett probably just yanked out that book by accident while he was trying to pull himself up."

My money was on Mac because I knew the victim. Noah was totally into mysteries, and probably would have operated an all-mystery bookstore—Mo's dream—if he thought Erin could support it. If anybody would have thought of a dying clue, it would have been him.

"Leaving that aside for the moment," Mac said, "it seems clear that the killer was someone who Noah knew—most likely someone he let in the back door this morning."

"Then you've already got a suspect," I said. It didn't take a Sebastian McCabe to figure that out. "We all heard Noah practically yelling into his cell phone the other night: 'You can't do that to me.' If that's not a threat, I never heard one. He was having a real blowout with somebody. That's your suspect. If that other guy were dead, *Noah* would be your suspect. All you have to do is find out who called him around nine-thirty on Monday night."

Oscar looked gloomy. "I already checked his cell and found the incoming call."

Never let it be said that Oscar Hummel doesn't learn from his mistakes. He'd failed to check the victim's cell phone while investigating the *1895* murder and missed an important clue.

Mo wrinkled her brow. "Is that even legal? I thought there was a Supreme Court case last year where they decided it's unconstitutional to get information from a cell phone."

"That only applies to suspects, not victims." In a lower voice Oscar added, "I hope."

"And have you had time to find out who the phone number belonged to?" Mac asked.

"I didn't need to," Oscar said glumly. "I recognized the number. I've had to call the mayor at home more than a few times."

Chapter Five
And the Mayor Cried

The mayor!

What had I said to Popcorn about this murder having nothing to do with St. Benignus? Her Honor was one of our most prominent faculty members.

Mac raised an eyebrow.

My response was not so muted. "You're saying that Lesley Saylor-Mackie is the person who had the heated argument on the phone with Noah—and you're just now getting around to mentioning it?"

In the news business, that's what's known as "burying the lead."

Oscar vaped, sucking on his e-cigarette as a baby would on a bottle. "I was hoping genius here"—he pointed at Mac, accusingly, I thought—"would wave his magic wand and come up with a better suspect."

"Even I would take some time to pull that particular rabbit out of my metaphorical hat, Oscar!"

I felt Oscar's pain (as well as mine). The mayor was a St. Benignus professor and department head, but she was also his boss. That wouldn't stop him from doing his job, but it would complicate it. The situation was particularly delicate because he and Saylor-Mackie were also allies in a major local issue. She had been pressing city council to build a new jail and police station, the answer to every small town police chief's prayer. Some subtlety was called for here, and Oscar was about as subtle as a Sumo wrestler.

He sighed deeply as he looked at his watch. "Ten-thirty Wednesday, so the mayor's holding office hours back at City Hall right now. This isn't even remotely kosher, but I want you two birds to go with me to talk to her."

A range of emotions flashed across Mac's broad face, none of them negative. But I wanted to see all of Oscar's cards.

"What's the deal?" I said.

"Just the obvious: You guys have known her a lot longer than I have and you don't report to her. You being there might reassure her, make the interview a little less awkward."

Oscar was a relative newcomer to town, having arrived as police chief about five years ago, while Mac and I had both worked at St. Benignus for many years—since I graduated from the college, in my case.

Hearing no objection to his game plan for facing Saylor-Mackie, Oscar turned to Gibbons. "Are you finished with Ms. Russert?"

"Yes, Chief."

"Then you're free to go home, Ms. Russert." One meeting of the Poisoned Pens together hadn't put them on a "Mo" and "Oscar" basis.

"Home?" She looked bewildered. "I thought I'd open the store." *The show must go on!* The enormity of how her life was about to change hadn't hit her yet.

Oscar shook his head. "Not today. This is a crime scene. My men will finish up as soon as they can, and then somebody will have to decide what happens to the store. Mr. Bartlett didn't have any close relatives, did he?"

"No. He wasn't married and his parents died years ago. He had a sister, but she passed away, too."

"Well, it'll all get sorted out."

Oscar chatted quietly for a few minutes with Gibbons while I offered Mo a few more comforting platitudes just in case I hadn't loaded her up with enough.

The chief, Mac, and I were just leaving when a familiar figure appeared on the other side of the door. "The press," Oscar muttered. "Just what I needed to make my day."

Johanna Rawls, a tall, Nordic type with straight blond hair and fair skin, wasn't the naïve young woman fresh out of college that she'd been when she had joined the *Erin Observer & News Ledger* three years earlier. Her blue eyes weren't quite so wide and she no longer gushed. But she still brakes for small animals and holds up my beloved Lynda as her role model.

Lynda! I felt a stab of guilt for not sending her a quick text about the murder so that she could pass on the news to the paper. Fortunately, Tall Rawls had other sources—maybe the police radio or a friend on Oscar's small force.

"Hi, Jeff, Mac, Chief." In her three-inch heels, she stood a couple of inches taller than me and towered over Oscar. Most of her long legs were visible below a short tan skirt. Not that I noticed. She pulled a narrow reporter's notebook out of her purse. "What's the story here, Chief? The radio said possible homicide."

"That was a half-hour ago. You're late."

"I was in the shower." Apparently sarcasm eludes her.

Oscar sucked on the ridiculous blue electronic gizmo. "Yeah, it's murder. Noah Bartlett, the owner. Mr. Bartlett's assistant, Ms. Maureen Russert, found the body this morning when she came to work. He was attacked from behind with a blunt instrument."

Johanna looked up. "What kind of blunt instrument."

"A heavy black plaster statue of a bird."

"The Maltese Falcon," I clarified. "As in the movie."

"What movie?"

I stared. "*The Maltese Falcon*! One of the greatest movies ever made!" What are they teaching in journalism school these days?

"Was it a foiled robbery attempt?" Johanna asked.

Mac's hirsute face did calisthenics. I could almost hear him sending Oscar a message by mental telepathy: *Don't say too much.*

"We really can't say at this time, Ms. Rawls. Our investigation has just begun. But I can assure you of this: My men *and women*"—*well played, Oscar!*—"will pursue every clue until we establish the perpetrator of this cowardly crime and see that justice is done."

Johanna scribbled. "Then you don't have any suspects? Just for the record."

"Just for the record, not at this time. Off the record, are you kidding? We've only been on the scene an hour and the perp forgot to leave his calling card."

She turned to Mac. "Are you consulting on this case, Professor?"

Mac paused, which he seldom did. "Let us say that I am confident that the matter is in good hands."

Yours, you mean.

Tall Rawls put away her notebook. That's when reporters are usually at their most dangerous, having put the interviewee off guard, but not this time. "I just have one more question, Chief. How do you like your e-cigarette?"

When I apply the adjective "distinguished" to Lesley Saylor-Mackie, I'm usually referring to her appearance. A handsome woman on the far side of fifty with never a strand of her gray-streaked sandy hair out of place, she looks dignified in business suits and elegant in a dress. But the word applies equally well to her career. Her award-winning 2011 biography, *William Howard Taft: Mr. Chief Justice*, had brought new respect to the patriarch of the Ohio political family that also produced two senators and a governor. She'd appeared on National Public Radio and a few highbrow TV shows and been quoted favorably by a couple of columnists, always identified as a professor at St. Benignus College in Erin, Ohio. Every small college would love to have that kind of publicity, and few of us ever get it. So Professor Saylor-Mackie, a native of Erin, is a well-known scholar as well as head of the St. Benignus history department. Unlike her principal subject, President Taft, she's also a heck of a politician. One of the hot topics in Herbert Hall, where she and Mac both have their campus offices, is whether she has her sights set on some higher elective office, or moving into Ralph Pendergast's digs as provost, or both. Nobody doubts her ambition. Her nails may be polished and painted a subtle shade of red, but they are sharp.

On Wednesday mornings, including this one, she hangs out at City Hall, where the nameplate says **MAYOR LESLEY SAYLOR-MACKIE.** I always appreciate the clarity of that, because other times I'm not always sure whether I'm dealing with the professor or the politician—not that the two are separable, really. And, just in case you wondered, I like them both. But then, we'd never been rivals for anything.

When Oscar, Mac, and I entered her mayoral office, she sat back and regarded us with a shrewd look in her hazel eyes. Then she smiled and said what she was obviously thinking:

"This can't be good. Who died?"

Well, that was possibly the most unintendedly ironic lame joke ever. At least, I hoped so.

Oscar cleared his throat. "Funny you should say that, Mayor. It was Noah Bartlett."

Color drained from her face. "What?"

"Noah Bartlett was found dead this morning in his store. I believe you knew him."

And the mayor cried. Her whole dignified, professional demeanor crumpled like a sand castle as she turned on the waterworks. It hurt to watch.

Mac handed her a handkerchief without saying a word.

"Thank you, Mac." Saylor-Mackie dabbed her eyes. "Yes, I knew Noah very well. We were old friends from high school days. That was a long time ago." I should have known then that her reaction was more than just that of an old classmate, but I didn't even suspect. "What happened?"

That was a natural enough question, given that Noah had been a hale and hearty fellow the mayor's own age with no signs that his expiration date was about to be reached.

Oscar squirmed in his seat. I bet he wanted to vape. "He was murdered."

"Murdered!" Her voice rose. "Noah?"

"Yes, ma'am. An unknown perpetrator bludgeoned him to death at his store, presumably early this morning."

"How awful!"

Oscar nodded solemnly. "That it is. I need to ask you a few questions."

Saylor-Mackie handed Mac his handkerchief back, all business now. I got the feeling she had just shoved her grief into a box until she could take it out and give it a better run when she was alone. "What kind of questions?"

But Oscar began with a statement. "You talked to the victim on Monday night."

She stared at Oscar as if he were a particularly dull student. "I most certainly did not, Chief Hummel. Where did you get that idea?"

This had to be Oscar's worst nightmare, part one. He shook off his boss's frosty tone and answered in a business-like way.

"Mr. Bartlett's cell phone shows that he received a phone call that night from your home phone, Mayor. Mac,

Jeff, and I, along with five other people, heard his end of the conversation—or at least part of it." *The loud part.*

"Oh! Well, that's easily explained." I was glad to hear that. "My husband must have called Noah on business. We only have one landline, and one of the phones is in Gulliver's home office."

Oscar looked relieved. "On business, you say. And you don't seem surprised at that."

"No. I'm aware that they'd had some ongoing discussions lately, and they weren't going well. I don't think Gulliver was very happy with Noah."

Somebody sure wasn't.

Chapter Six
Gulliver Unravels

Gulliver Mackie didn't have a big sign outside his small office on the outskirts of downtown Erin. His discreet business managing the investments of the Gambles and the Masons and some equally wealthy clients downriver in Cincinnati didn't need it. I'd heard that he wouldn't turn up his nose at a mere half-million-dollar portfolio, though.

I've never had a financial advisor, an accountant, or a travel agent, but I wouldn't have minded asking Mackie where he thought the stock market was heading. This didn't seem the time to ask, though. Oscar, Mac, and I arrived at his door just as he was opening it.

"On my way out to a business lunch, Chief," he announced with a smile. *In other words, come back later.*

Mackie, only slightly older than his wife, always gave me the impression that he must have been captain of the football team and student body president in his University of Cincinnati days. He had met his wife at Miami University of Ohio while they were both picking up their master's degrees, his being an M.B.A. They made a handsome couple, as I'd observed many times over the years at faculty and staff soirées. If he remembered me from those he didn't say so as he stood in the door. He probably dyed his hair, by the way.

"I'm sorry, Mr. Mackie, but this is official police business." Oscar tried to sound official.

"It's about Noah, isn't it? Don't look so surprised. Lesley called me. What a shock. Come on in. I'll just text my appointment and let him know I'm going to be late for lunch. Make yourself at home." His fingers flew over the virtual keys of his smartphone like those of a digital native while we stood awkwardly in the hallway of the well-appointed office.

How were we supposed to make ourselves at home at the Palace of Versailles? Though located in a 1950s Cape Cod house, Mackie's office was decorated to impress. A guy who could afford a mahogany desk the size of Rhode Island and plush chairs that looked like thrones must know how to turn a nickel into a buck, right?

We sat down. Mac gave a little sigh of contentment. It wasn't often that a chair accommodated his girth without a tight squeeze.

"Now then." Mackie sat down behind his massive desk—almost as big as Ralph Pendergast's—and put his smartphone in front of him. "If this is police business, what are Professor McCabe and Mr. Cody doing here?"

So he did know me. That he would know Mac, at least by sight and reputation, was never in question.

Oscar surprised me. "I guess you could say they're kind of unofficial deputies. They've helped me on several cases. But I can ask them to leave if that would make you more comfortable."

Mackie waved that away. "Not at all. We're all one big St. Benignus family, although I'm only an adjunct instructor. What can I do for you?"

Oscar sat forward. "On Monday night, Noah Bartlett took a call on his cell phone from your home landline. The conversation lasted three minutes and forty-two seconds. Toward the end, Mr. Bartlett was shouting. A number of people heard him, including us three. We happened to be in the store that night for a meeting. Mr.

Bartlett yelled, 'You can't do that to me! You'll find out.' And then he said something about it not being over."

"To be precise, he said, 'This isn't over, no matter what you think,'" Mac rumbled.

Oscar nodded. "Yeah, that was it. And I think eight people will testify to that, or most of us will." Mary Lou Springfield's hearing was questionable. "Mayor Saylor-Mackie said she wasn't home that night, and you must have placed the call. I'm sure she told you that she told us that. So I'm wondering if you can tell us what that was all about."

"Of course I can. The question is, do I want to? Of course I do. I have nothing to hide." Mackie couldn't have been friendlier. People who say they have nothing to hide always make me think they have something to hide, but that's not always the case. "Noah and I had what you might call a tenant-landlord dispute. I lost my head, came a bit unraveled, and raised my voice. So he raised his voice. We both said things we shouldn't have." He shook his head. "I'm sorry that was our last conversation."

"You own the Pages Gone By building?" Mac asked.

Mackie nodded. "Investing is more than just stocks and bonds, you know. Real estate should also be part of the mix." *Maybe I should have bought that duplex where Lynda used to live when I had the chance.* "I'm a strong believer in diversification, for myself as well as for my clients." Mackie made it sound like he dabbled in property. He actually owned a healthy chunk of downtown, which occasionally got him into the local news.

"Leaving your financial portfolio aside for just a minute," Oscar said archly, "what did you argue about?"

"It was very simple from my point of view, Chief." He spread out his hands. *I'm a perfectly reasonable millionaire landlord.* "Noah was behind on the rent. He hadn't made a payment in five months. If he didn't catch up by making all the back payments at the end of the month—next

Tuesday—he would be in violation of his very lenient lease. I made it clear that I intended to evict him if he didn't move out voluntarily. He told me I couldn't do that, but I could. It's in the lease."

"That would be very unfortunate," Mac said, "and not just for Noah. An empty storefront on High Street, in such a prominent location, would be a major negative for development downtown." *And that wouldn't be a talking point for Mayor Saylor-Mackie's re-election campaign.*

"That won't be a problem." Was that a note of smugness I detected in Mackie's voice? "I already have a tenant for the property—and it will be the best thing that's happened to downtown in years."

Mac raised an eyebrow. That's all it took to get Mackie to spill the rest.

"One of my clients, an executive at the Altiora Corporation named Charles Bexley, plans to open a brew pub here in Erin." Mac's eyes glowed. While not especially discriminating about what he consumes, as his corpulent figure attests, my brother-in-law has a particular fondness for malt and hop beverages. "He's eager to get that specific site because of its history—it was a speakeasy during Prohibition. The architect's renderings play on that."

Score one for Popcorn. She'd heard talk of a pub going into the Pages Gone By location, and passed the scuttlebutt on to me, but I'd neglected to tell Mac. My bad!

"A good brew pub should do well in our community," Mac said. "We have none, although craft beer has been flourishing in this country for several years now."

"That's very nice." Oscar sounded like a cat eying a mouse. "And now that Noah Bartlett's out of the way, I guess there's nothing to stop this brew pub from happening. I'd like to have the contact information for this Bexley guy. For some reason he was so confident about his project that he went ahead with architectural drawings for it even though you already had a tenant in the building."

"For some reason? He had every reason." Mackie didn't raise his frustrated voice, but I could easily imagine him doing so. He paused to write down a phone number and e-mail address on a piece of paper, which he handed to Oscar.

"Noah talked a good game when I told him on the phone the other night that I wanted him out by the first of May. He claimed he was coming into some money and could get caught up by the beginning of the month. You heard him—the last thing he said to me before he hung up was that it wasn't over." Mackie shook his head. "I think he was fooling himself. Ask around town. He didn't have any money or any way to get any. I did my own due diligence on that."

Mackie stopped. Maybe he'd heard himself talking and he didn't like it. "I'm sorry that Noah's dead. He was a nice guy who'd had a few tough breaks. But I have to admit I'm pretty excited about what comes next. It will be nice to get some income out of the building again, and the pub will be great for Erin."

He had reason to be upbeat, I guess—but not to kill somebody. When it came to motives, Gulliver Mackie seemed to be seriously lacking.

Chapter Seven
Love's Dark Secret

"Convincing," Mac said on our way to his car. "Everything the mayor's husband said was quite credible."

"Yeah, well, I think I can handle it from here, men," Oscar said. "After I grab a burger. Thanks for coming along."

I stared. "Handle what? Didn't we clear two suspects this morning? What's left?"

"Routine, Jeff. Boring, by-the-book police routine. I keep telling you guys, that's what solves cases." *Except when it doesn't.* "You don't think I'm going to take Mackie's story on faith, do you? I'll check it out with Bexley. That's why I got his contact info. Chances are, Mackie gave it to me straight and that blow-up on the phone had nothing to do with the murder, but you never know."

Mac dropped Oscar off at the stone fortress we call City Hall, where the police station and the jail are housed in the basement—but not for long if the Mayor and Oscar win the day.

"Now what?" I asked Mac as he aimed his oversized vehicle toward St. Benignus and our day jobs. "Where do we go from here?"

"The dying clue, old boy! Surely that is obvious. Although Oscar blithely dismissed the significance of *Love's Dark Secret*, I have not. What do you know about Noah Bartlett?"

"No more than you do."

"Who would know more?"

"I'm sure Mo does. She worked with the guy for four years."

Maureen Russert had been a high school English teacher before she'd taken time off to rear her two children. When her rich but boring husband, Arthur Bancroft Russert, had left her for a younger woman just at the time she was ready to re-enter the job market, teaching jobs were scarce. With comfortable monthly alimony payments making income a minor issue, she signed on part-time at Pages Gone By and set her sights on opening her own mystery-only bookstore.

Mac checked his watch. "I have a class in ten minutes." *How rare for a tenured professor.* "Since you know Ms. Russert better than I do—"

"I'll see if we can pick her brain later today."

Checking my smartphone while he drove, I found three phone calls and a couple of e-mails. At the top of the call-back list was a voice mail from Ralph, going ballistic over the *Higher Ed Insider* article on James Gregory Talton's YouTube performance on A. Lincoln. Scratch that—it was the nasty comments attached to this morning's article that had Ralph discombobulated. In Megaphone Nation, every Tom, Dick, and Harry thinks his opinion is important, and most of them have to share it. This is especially true of those negative types who run low on facts and high on venom. Such as: "Professor Talton should change his initials from JGT to KKK." And: "If that Oreo had his way, he'd be a slave today. And it would serve him right!" And: "Please kill yourself, Talton."

"We need to do something about this!" Ralph had directed my voice mail. Ralph has been somewhat nicer to Mac and me since we kept him from being charged with murder, but that's only in relative terms. And he still just doesn't get the Internet age. I've told him a million times there's nothing anyone can do about digital road rage. He should have been thankful for small favors. At least on the

Higher Ed Insider site most of the clichés were delivered with good grammar and correct spelling.

"Also," Ralph added in his message, "I need to brief you about an investigation the Athletic Department has undertaken. There have been allegations of steroid use by members of the wrestling team."

When it rains . . .

Hadley Reams, a new reporter for our student newspaper, the *Spectator*, and seventy-something Maggie Barton of the *Erin Observer & News-Ledger* both wanted to ask me "a few questions" about Professor Talton. *Who? Sounds vaguely familiar.*

By the time I'd finished listening to all those messages on the phone, I was walking into my office. Popcorn practically panted at the sight of me.

"Finally! What happened at the murder scene? I've been patiently waiting for the blow-by-blow, so don't leave anything out. And where have you been all this time?"

"I was with Oscar until about ten or twelve minutes ago. Didn't he tell you about it?"

She didn't look happy. "The last I heard from him was a text right after you left."

"He's probably saving the details for a dramatic retelling on your next date."

"Oscar isn't exactly the dramatic type. Besides, when we get together we don't usually talk about work."

To keep this revelation about the mating habits of two almost-senior citizens from quickly tail-spinning into Too Much Information, I said, "I'll debrief you as soon as I return some phone calls."

The conversation with Ralph was about par for the course, no worse than most. I let him vent for about five minutes before I gave him the hard truth. "There's no point in responding to idiotic comments, Ralph. You can't wrestle a pig without getting muddy. Besides, they're attacking Talton. We don't want to defend Talton—we want to defend academic freedom. We've already done that with our statement, which you and Professor Saylor-Mackie both approved. This thing might blow over if we don't give his detractors a new target to shoot at."

Blow over? Well, I did say *might*.

I took advantage of the heavy sigh on the other end of the line to change the subject.

"What's this about a steroid investigation?"

"It's in the early stages. Perhaps there's nothing to the report, Cody. But I wanted you to know in case *your friends* in the media get onto it."

Just because my wife's a journalist, he acts as though I'm in bed with . . . well, actually, I guess I am. But somehow I've managed to balance things so that I can keep both my job and my marriage, no thanks to Ralph.

After I got him off the phone, I popped a quick e-mail to Saylor-Mackie saying essentially what I'd just told Ralph. It doesn't hurt to put these things in writing.

Then I returned the calls from Hadley Reams and Maggie Barton, the budding reporter and the veteran. I read them both the prepared statement, trying not to sound like I was reading it.

"I've been looking at the student evaluations of Professor Talton's classes," Hadley said when I'd finished. Even a full professor had to teach a few classes. "They all rate him highly as a dynamic lecturer." *I bet!* "Does this negative publicity mean that one of the most popular professors at St. Benignus is in trouble with the Administration?"

That sounded like he'd already written the lead sentence on his story. Clearly the young man had a bright future in journalism.

"I think I already answered that," I said.

"How did you answer it?" If I'd said that, it would have been because I'm a wise guy. Hadley, by contrast, sounded genuinely puzzled.

"Review your notes." *The key phrase I uttered is "academic freedom." Maybe I should have worked in "tenured" to make it even clearer.*

Maggie didn't press. We'd been doing this dance for almost twenty years now, and she knew when I was trying not to say too much. She did ask me for some background on the professor, which I read from his C.V.

Talton, for his part, so far hadn't returned phone calls from Hadley or Maggie, or from J. Randolph Smith earlier. Whether that was a smart move on his part or not was a judgment call. Not talking to the media meant that he hadn't presented his side of the story. But maybe he didn't care what readers of *Higher Ed Insider*, the *Spectator*, and the *Observer & News-Ledger* thought about him. How would it change his life?

Some organizations, especially businesses, have tight protocols that require all requests for interviews to be bucked to the communications office. Not us. So if Talton did decide to talk, I might not know it until I picked up a newspaper. That's never fun. I made a mental note to talk to Ralph about developing a policy on that. If there's anything he loves more than budgets, it's policies.

"I'd better try to track down Talton and see what his game plan is," I told Popcorn.

She looked like a dog denied a treat. "Can't that wait? I want all the gory details. You promised!"

So I gave it to her from the top, everything that had happened since I'd left that morning, not neglecting to describe Oscar vaping at moments of high tension. Her mouth fell open when I described the book in Noah's dead hand.

"*Love's Dark Secret!* I can't believe it. That's one of my very favorite Rosamund DeLacey books. I've read it three times."

Please don't tell me the plot. But wait! Maybe the plot was the clue.

"What's it about?" I asked.

"It's about a woman who's in love with twin brothers who are total opposites and she can't decide which one to marry."

I've never read a romance novel, but that seemed conventional enough.

"What's the dark secret?"

"That's the cool part. They're really the same guy with dissociative identity disorder."

And I thought romance novels were light reading. "What's that?"

"They used to call it multiple personality disorder."

And before that they called it split personality.

"So does she marry the same guy twice?"

"Of course not! Who would believe that? In the second to last chapter, being a smart girl—she works for NASA—she realizes her two boyfriends are really only one guy because not even identical twins have exactly the same dental work. At the very end of the book she gets him professional help. From what I read on the Internet, that probably wouldn't cure him. But the heroine is hopeful on the last page as she takes him to his first appointment with the mature but attractive Dr. Allyson Macy."

Hopeful was not the word to describe me. Somehow it didn't seem likely that Noah was killed by somebody with a split personality, or whatever it's called these days. Maybe the chief was right about the book being meaningless.

"Oscar doesn't set any store by the dying clue," I told Popcorn. "He thinks Noah was just trying to pull himself off the floor and clutched the book in his death throes or something."

"Well, maybe. But you should read the book. There might be something else in there that's important."

"I'll put that on my to-do list." *At the very bottom.*

I moved on to recount our visit to Lesley Saylor-Mackie in her mayoral office.

"There was something between those two," Popcorn announced when I'd finished.

Huh? "What two?"

"Saylor-Mackie and Noah Bartlett."

"Yeah, they were old friends from high school."

Popcorn smirked. "Friends with privileges maybe. I saw those two standing a few feet apart at the opening of the Art in the Blood show at the Looney Ladies Gallery a while back[4] and believe me, Boss, they were more to each other than just old pals."

I remained unconvinced, silly me. "You've been reading too much Rosamund DeLacey. You should wash your mind out with soap for even thinking such a thing. The mayor is a married woman." *And quite attractive for her age.*

"Noah Bartlett was a man, and a darned handsome one. I wouldn't kick Gulliver Mackie out of bed, mind you, but maybe Noah had a better sense of humor." *No doubt.*

"Popcorn, I have to tell you that I find this speculation distasteful." She frowned. "More importantly, it's unhelpful and unnecessary. I bet Mo Russert knows all about Noah's love life, if any."

That reminded me: The pesky business of earning my salary this afternoon had made me forget my assignment from Mac to see if Mo could meet with us to answer a few questions. I texted her:

Can Mac and I see you around 5 pm? Have questions.

It couldn't be too much later than that. Mac and I, with our spouses, were going out to dinner at seven with Dunbar Yates. Mo responded almost immediately.

5:30 better. Come to Jonathans. Have big news!

---

[4] See "Art in the Blood" in *Rogues Gallery* (MX Publishing, 2014).

Chapter Eight
Noah, We Hardly Knew Ye

"She must have been really excited about this big news," I told Mac on the way to Jonathan Hawes's house later that afternoon. "I know that because she left the possessive apostrophe off of her boyfriend's name. That's not like her."

"Perhaps they have become betrothed, she and Jonathan."

"How romantic! You sound like Popcorn. I was kind of hoping her news was more in the line of a helpful development regarding Noah."

My efforts that afternoon to find James Gregory Talton had proved fruitless. He didn't have a class this quarter. Presumably he was doing whatever tenured professors did, researching his next book or something, but the history department's administrative assistant could shed no light on where he was doing it. He didn't answer his home phone and he didn't have a cell phone.

After smacking my head a few times against that particular brick wall, I'd worked with Popcorn for the rest of the afternoon on our new alumni magazine, *Ben*. (Ralph hates the casual nickname for St. Benignus, but Fr. Pirelli had overruled him on that one.) After a few hours of writing, editing, and choosing photos, I'd met Mac in the parking lot at five-twenty for the short drive to the Federal-style mini-mansion just a few blocks from campus.

Tall and thin Jonathan Hawes, Erin's leading undertaker, looks so much like Sherlock Holmes that he'd been a natural for playing the part in the play *1895*. It turned out that he could even act. I'm used to seeing him in a black suit (not a deerstalker), but he was casually dressed in dark slacks and a yellow polo shirt when he opened his front door. The shirt had *Hawes & Holder* monogrammed on the breast.

Jonathan was uttering a standard greeting when Mo appeared behind him. She was still dressed in the jeans and a plaid shirt she'd worn at the shop. "You won't believe it," she gushed. "I still can't believe it." Her pleasant face, which had been awash with tears beneath her dark bangs in the morning, was flushed with excitement.

"In the midst of tragedy, some good news," Jonathan said. "Have a seat."

We deposited ourselves on loveseats in a formal parlor to the left of the front door.

"Noah's attorney, Jim Bridges, called me right before I got your text," Mo said before we had sat fully down. "I'm Noah's heir. The store and his private collection of mysteries are mine. It looks like I'm not out of a job."

I hadn't thought of that minor consideration—that Noah's death presumably would mean that Mo had lost her employment as well as her employer. With the lease payments in arrears and Gulliver Mackie eager to rent the property for a trendy new tenant, chances looked good that would still happen. She would get a lot of books, but no place to sell them. I looked at Mac. *Should we tell her?* He didn't move a muscle. No, she'd find out soon enough. Let her enjoy the euphoric feeling of being an heiress for however long it lasted until reality smacked her in the face.

"This legacy came as a surprise to you?" Mac asked.

Mo nodded. "Totally out of the blue!"

"Why do you suppose he did it?"

"I guess because he knew I want to open a mystery bookstore." She smiled. "Everybody knows that, if they know me, but especially Noah."

"That is understandable, to a point," Mac allowed. "However, I have any number of friends with admirable dreams. I do not plan to fund any of them in my will." He paused. This was going to be delicate with her boyfriend sitting so close to her that I understood why they called it a loveseat. "He must have been especially fond of you."

Was it just my imagination or did Jonathan press his lips together?

"I think he was, Mac. He was only about fifteen years or so older than me, but I think he took a fatherly interest, you might call it. He disliked my ex-husband even more than I do, and he never even met the jerk."

"He had no one else?"

"I guess not." She appeared to think about that a moment. "Noah was a bachelor, of course. He didn't talk about himself much, but I knew that his parents and sister were dead. He dated from time to time, but his romantic relationships never seemed to last long."

This seemed like promising territory to me. A whack on the back of the head with a blunt instrument was a dandy way to spurn a lover with extreme prejudice—or to eliminate a rival.

"Anybody we know?" I asked, keeping it light.

"Noah never named names, at least not to me. He was very private about that. Just yesterday as we were leaving the store he mentioned that he was meeting someone for dinner, but he didn't say who."

I'm no super-sleuth, but I didn't have to be hit in the head with a big red sign saying *CLUE!* to realize that this piece of intel wasn't a throwaway.

"Did Noah say anything at all about this dinner?" Mac asked. "For example, did he indicate whether it was actually a date, whether he knew the other person well, where they were eating—anything at all?"

She shook her head. "If he did, I don't remember it."

"Can you remember anything at all that he ever said about a woman in his life?"

Jonathan Hawes seemed to take offense at Mac's browbeating of his girlfriend. He frowned, making his narrow face seem even longer. "I think she's already—"

"No, wait!" But we didn't have time to wait, because Mo rushed on: "I'm sure this doesn't mean anything but he did mention to me once that he'd been married."

"Married!" I exclaimed. Noah had always seemed like a male spinster to me.

"I was surprised, too. He said he was married for a short time many years ago and it had been a big mistake. He was trying to console me about my own marriage, speaking of mistakes."

"What did he say about his ex-wife?"

"All I can remember is that he said she made fun of his low tastes in literature because he liked mysteries. And then he laughed and said, 'How ironic!' You don't think that can mean anything, do you?"

Mac shrugged. "Who can know? It meant something to Noah."

"Very coy," I said as soon as I'd buckled up my seatbelt in the Macmobile. "You know better than anybody that whether it's a mystery novel or real life the only suspect better than a wife or a girlfriend is an ex. This was a good afternoon's work."

Mac looked thoughtful. "That is undeniably true, as I am sure Oscar would have to acknowledge. Unfortunately, it is equally true that our friend Mo's 'big news' has given her a big motive as well."

Chapter Nine
Motives

While we changed for dinner with the McCabes and the departing Dunbar Yates, Lynda and I spent a few minutes catching up. She told me that she'd contacted the Grier TV station news directors to appeal for sweeps month series ideas and I told her about everything I'd left out of my texts throughout the day, mostly regarding the murder.

"Wow," she said. "You did all that since I saw you this morning? How do you keep your real job?"

"I have good help."

"She should get another raise."

The Roundhouse, one of Erin's two fine-dining restaurants, isn't as formal as Ricoletti's Ristorante. How could it be, set down in the center of an old railroad roundhouse repurposed as a mall? But it was nice enough for Lynda to wear her newest dress, a black and white striped number with gold fringes on the bottom, and her honey-blond curls up in a chignon. My sister, Kate, wore the Sherlock Holmes necktie she'd bought in London three years earlier, along with a white blouse and black slacks, no jacket. (Did the women plan the color coordination? I wouldn't put it past them.) Mac and I also wore ties—his a bow tie, as usual—but I doubt if Dunbar Yates owned one. He was decked out in a gray mock turtleneck shirt and blue jeans, topped with a blue blazer.

"Well, Dunbar," Mac said after we'd put in our drink orders, "what is your take on the murder of the unfortunate Noah Bartlett?"

Yates had heard about my wife's profession. "This is all off the record, okay?"

"I'm no longer a member of the working press," Lynda protested.

Oh, really? If it's not work that you do for Grier Ohio NewsGroup, what is it?

She meant, no doubt, that the tensions between our respective jobs weren't as strong as when she'd been news editor of the *Erin Observer & News-Ledger*. But she still kept her office there. And she still had a nose for news—an adorable one, although a bit crooked.

"Still," Yates said. "Off the record. For everybody."

We all murmured meaningless agreement.

"Okay, then, off the record . . . I don't have a take. I don't know anything about real-life murder, except what I've read. I'm a writer, not a detective."

"The two are not mutually exclusive," Kate said, with a glance at her husband. She is thirteen months older than me, almost as tall, and with the same shade of red hair.

Mac seemed to regard his wife's comment as an invitation to pontificate on his own view of Noah's death. "As hackneyed as it may seem, that classic trio of motive, means, and opportunity remain invaluable leads in matters of murder. In this case, the murder weapon was available to anyone in the store. Noah afforded the opportunity when he opened the door that morning to his killer—presumably someone he knew, but that does not narrow the field much. Consequently, our efforts have been directed at learning who might have a motive."

He halted as our server—a fresh-faced St. Benignus grad student named Chuck—distributed the beverages, handing Lynda her Manhattan first. *Good call, Chuck.*

"*Your* efforts?" Yates grabbed his scotch. "I don't see a badge on you, Mac."

"Chief Hummel asked for our assistance." *And then he told us to get lost, but we're ignoring that part.* "You may recall that I have had some minor success in previous cases." That was Sebastian McCabe trying to be modest, and it almost hurt to watch.

"Yeah, I recall. You're a regular—what's his name? The mystery writer who solves mysteries."

"Ellery Queen," Mac supplied.

Yates shook his head. "No, no. Not Queen. Haven't thought of Queen in years. Castle! That's the guy. On a TV show my wife watches. So, anyway—motive. How did that work out for you?"

Mac took a first sip of his draft beer, the same Moerlein OTR ale that he has on tap in his study. "Noah was well liked and inoffensive, but at least three people profit by his death: the owner of the building on which Noah stopped paying rent months ago, an entrepreneur who wants to put a brew pub in that building, and Maureen Russert, to whom Noah left his business."

"Isn't that the girl in the writers' group with the black bangs?" Yates said.

"That's Mo," I said.

"But Mo wouldn't hurt anybody," Lynda said, "not even her ex-husband."

Mac nodded. "I share that sentiment. However, it is only a sentiment, a feeling. The fact remains that Mo and the other two individuals mentioned have all benefited from Noah's death. None of them appears to have gained all that much, I grant you. The brew pub project would have gone ahead even if Noah had lived, unless he was able to come up with the rent that had eluded him for five months. And the value of Pages Gone By is highly questionable, given that it did not provide Noah with enough income to pay his rent."

"Okay, where does that leave you?" Kate asked. As an artist, she tends to look at the big picture. This one was fuzzy.

"It leaves me remembering our discussion of motives the other night at the Poisoned Pens meeting," Mac said. "Dunbar, you mentioned then that you pay a lot of attention to motive. 'If the motive doesn't work, nothing works,' I believe you said. You also made the fascinating revelation that the motives in your books all come from the traditional seven deadly sins of greed, pride, lust, envy, sloth, gluttony—"

"And wrath," I finished, raising my voice a bit. "Noah added that. He'd just finished his phone call when Dunbar was naming the deadly sins. Noah interrupted to say, 'wrath, otherwise known as extreme anger or rage.' And then he said, 'I'd say that's a damned good reason to kill somebody.'"

"Yeah, I remember." Yates cuddled his second glass of scotch protectively, as if he were afraid somebody would take it away from him. "*He* sounded like he wanted to kill somebody."

"His landlord," I said. "That's who he'd been talking to on the phone."

Mac filled him in on what we'd learned about the lease, finishing just as our server brought us our meals.

"All three of your prospective suspects would be motivated by greed," Yates noted. "There we are back to the seven deadly sins."

"Surely those aren't the only motives in the world!" Lynda said.

"No, no, of course not. That's just something I play with in my writing. Like I said, I don't know anything about real-life murders. Most of them are drug-related or domestic violence, aren't they? That's the impression I get from watching the news." He paused. "But years ago I read a great article about motives by Harold Q. Masur. I've never forgotten it. Masur was a good mystery writer, mostly in the '40s and '50s, but not well remembered today. In this article he divided motives into two categories, gain and fear. Gain included not only money and power, but also psychological satisfaction—such as settling the score for a past wrong. The past is a rich vein for motives, I've always thought."

"Revenge was a favorite motive in the Sherlock Holmes stories," Mac pointed out, "starting with the very first, *A Study in Scarlet*."

"Whatever." Apparently the creator of Gumm & Beauregard had little time for Holmes and Watson. "Fear was a smaller category, and the big item there was fear of exposure, like from a blackmailer or from a conscientious citizen who could be counted on to report something to the authorities. In novels, this is usually the motive for the second murder."

"Retribution and fear of exposure are both motives that hearken back to the past," Mac observed. "I have used them often in my own work." He put down his fork, which clued me in that whatever was on his mind was even more important than steak. For Sebastian McCabe, that was saying a lot. "You knew Noah in New York. What can you tell us about his time there?"

Yates laughed, which seemed a little forced to me. "We didn't eat at each other's houses. I only saw him at Crimes & Punishments Bookshop when I was buying books or signing my own. I don't think I even noticed when he wasn't there anymore. I guess I'm not very observant. I wouldn't make a good sleuth, would I?"

Nobody answered that. We all know a rhetorical question when we hear one.

"When I met him here in Erin, I couldn't believe it was the same guy at first," Yates continued. "He was so out of context."

"Well, one thing was the same," Lynda said. "Noah Bartlett's life revolved around books, even his life in the big city. And he died with a book in his hand. That must have some significance, don't you think?"

This was news to Yates. "I didn't hear about a book. What was it, some mystery? Don't tell me it was one of mine. That would be too creepy."

"*Au contraire*," Mac said. "It was a romance novel by one Rosamund DeLacey called *Love's Dark Secret*. I secured a copy this afternoon and began reading it. The process is a painful one, I assure you."

"The two brothers that the main character is in love with are really just one guy who thinks he's two," I said. *Oops—spoiler!*

"Ah, you saw that, too, Jefferson? I suppose it was rather obvious to an aficionado of mystery fiction." Sometimes Sebastian McCabe is insufferable. *Sometimes?* "One has to wonder whether the clue that Noah meant to give us is to be found in the plot of the book or in the title."

"It's not likely that he would have actually read the book, is it?" Kate said. "I'm sure he didn't come close to reading all the books he sold, and men don't usually read romance novels. And if he didn't read it, he wouldn't know the plot, so that's probably not what the clue is about."

Nobody could argue with that logic. The sound of murmured agreement went around the table.

"Ms. DeLacey's style is rather too, er, graphic for my taste and the plot is implausible, but she is not without writing talent," Mac reported.

Lynda's gold-flecked brown eyes widened. "Maybe that's the clue—the author!"

"She's local?" Yates asked.

I chuckled. "Hardly."

Mac looked thoughtful. "The back cover blurb gives no significant biographical information about the author, not even where she lives. It is possible that Noah could have known her from New York."

"Don't most romance writers churn out about a book a month under a handful of different names?" Lynda said. "Maybe Rosamund DeLacey is really somebody else and she——or even *he*—does live in Erin."

This was getting out of hand, piling one speculation on top of another with nothing but sand for a foundation. How could I bring this discussion back to earth diplomatically?

"Brilliant!" I looked at Lynda. That was no chore. "We should try to find out who Rosamund DeLacey is, if she isn't Rosamund DeLacey, and whether Noah might have known her. But there's a closer-to-home woman in his life—his ex-wife. We ought to find her first. Maybe she was Noah's dark secret."

Without intending to, I had staked out a tentative position in favor of the "title is the clue" school of thought.

"Admirable, Jefferson!" Mac boomed. "I believe you are on to something." Did he have to sound so surprised?

"The mayor might know, since she knew Noah back in the day." I was on a roll.

"Indeed she might. However, it could be to our advantage to keep the search for Mrs. Bartlett below the radar screen. For that reason, I checked the marriage records on the county website late this afternoon. Unfortunately, the older records are not yet online. I shall have to look them up in person at the courthouse first thing in the morning."

If only w'd known how much heartburn that was going to cause us.

Chapter Ten
A Rousing Failure

"So you don't think Rosamund DeLacey is the clue?" Lynda set a box of shredded wheat in front of me on the breakfast table with a bit of a thump. *Uh-oh.* She must have been chewing over that all night.

"I didn't say that, Lyn. I just thought we shouldn't lose sight of the ex-wife. Obviously Mac had the same idea before I did."

"Hmph."

She picked up the *Erin Observer & News-Ledger* and hid behind it as she read the front page. The story down the side was about an investment advisor in Cincinnati being sentenced to fifteen years in prison for defrauding his investors in a Ponzi scheme, making me glad I stick to index mutual funds. Johanna Rawls's story about Noah's murder got the full treatment across the top: **BOOK DEALER SLAIN IN STORE.**

I grabbed the local page and indulged my masochistic tendencies by reading Maggie Barton's story about Professor Talton:

A YouTube video by a St. Benignus College history professor has gone viral—and so has the controversy generated by his remarks about President Abraham Lincoln.

James Gregory Talton, a tenured professor
of history whose courses are popular with
students, is seen in the video calling Lincoln a
"tyrant" and suggesting that the Civil War was
his fault.

The story went on for another thirteen paragraphs,
including the quote from me and, predictably, one from the
Honest Abe Association. It could have been worse. At least
it wasn't on the front page. I was sure I was going to have
the chance to point that out to Ralph.

Thinking of Ralph reminded me of the steroids
investigation he'd mentioned. I knew there was something I
should be worrying about, and that was it. If there really was
a steroids problem in the wrestling program at St. Benignus,
the news wouldn't be confined to the local page of the
Observer when it broke.

Lynda put down the paper. "Johanna did a nice job
on Noah's murder."

"I'm not surprised."

"I mean she did well with what she had. But she had
no idea of what you and Mac were up to." Her tone wasn't
quite accusatory. Was it?

"Our day's work amounted to dead ends and
speculation." I didn't sound defensive. Did I?

"Don't be so modest. You accumulated quite a few
facts." She counted them out on her fingers, starting with
her right thumb. Her nails were seasonally painted green
and pink to look like watermelons. "Noah had a loud
argument with Gulliver Mackie two days before he died.
Mackie has a tenant lined up for the building, one that
presumably can actually pay the rent. Said tenant is eager to
get that particular property so that he can play on its
Prohibition history for his brew pub. Mo inherited the
bookstore." That accounted for a thumb and three fingers.

"The bookstore might not be worth much. It apparently wasn't worth much to Noah."

Lynda held up her little finger. "Noah had once been married."

That made a whole handful of facts that hadn't seen the light of day in the *Erin Observer & News-Ledger*. Put like that, it did seem like there was a lot more to report than what Tall Rawls had learned from Oscar. And I could hardly dismiss the importance of the ex-wife, since I'd ridden that horse pretty hard last night. Mac would resume looking for her name in a few hours, as soon as the courthouse opened at ten o'clock.

"Well, today's just the first-day story. Johanna can come back tomorrow with—"

The Indiana Jones theme song erupted from my smartphone, halting me in mid-sentence. *Saved by the bell.* I looked at it. "It's Mo."

As soon as I said hello, she announced herself and told me that she was at Pages Gone By. "I think you and Mac should come over here."

My grip on the phone involuntarily tightened. "What's up?"

"I've been looking at Noah's financial records. What I found might interest you."

This time I didn't tell her to call the police. Not knowing anything about inheritance law, I wasn't sure she should be there—much less poking into her benefactor's financial records. Even though the provisions of the will were known, it hadn't been probated yet.

"All right," I told Mo. "We'll be over."

"You're going to skip the gym and be late for work, aren't you?" Lynda said.

"Possibly. I'll text Popcorn. Right after I call Mac."

Mo met us at the front door of Pages Gone By.

"I got into QuickBooks," she said without preamble.

"Wasn't it password protected?" I asked.

"Sure. But I found the password in his address book, which was in his office." She held out a square yellow Post 'Em note, on which had been written in ink:

<u>Password</u>
RoHaMy1929?

It took me a few seconds to realize that the question mark didn't indicate uncertainty.

"Very secure password," I noted. "Eleven digits, capital and lower case letters, and a punctuation mark."

Mac's bearded face clouded for only a moment before he smiled in obvious satisfaction. "It is also a password that Noah Bartlett could never forget, even if he had not written it down. The first Ellery Queen novel, *The Roman Hat Mystery*, was published in 1929. The early Queen books all followed that title formula—a national adjective followed by a noun and the word 'mystery.'"

Of course. Who didn't know that?

"Do either of you know QuickBooks?" Mo asked.

We did not.

"Oh. Well, Noah had me learn it because he said I would need it when I had my own business. Here, let me show you."

Mo led us back to Noah's office, where a laptop computer lay open on his desk. I like numbers when they have dollar signs in front of them, but business accounting is something I know zilch about.

"Bottom-line me on this, Mo," I said. "What's going on here?"

"I never thought that Pages Gone By was much of a money-maker, but it's worse than that. The store has been bleeding red ink for some time. I inherited a rousing failure. And worst of all, there are no rent payments recorded and no pot of money to pay the rent. Noah probably broke the lease. If I don't get a call from the landlord today demanding payment, I'll be surprised."

That was no news to Mac and me, of course, but Mo looked crestfallen.

"Noah left me all the assets of the business, according to the attorney, but it looks like there aren't any except the inventory—all these books and a little furniture and equipment."

"Maybe he didn't record everything in the business bank account," I said.

She shook her head. "No, QuickBooks is linked to the account. What you see is what he had, at least as far as the bookstore goes."

"I am sorry that your bequest was without value," Mac said. "You must be deeply disappointed. Why did you want us to know?"

She shrugged. "I just felt I had to tell somebody."

I'm glad it wasn't Oscar. He might have to arrest you for breaking into the books.

Mac's train of thought must have been running along the same tracks because he said: "Perhaps we should keep your enterprise among ourselves for the time being."

"Why? Do you think all that red ink means something in connection with Noah's death?"

"I am certain of it," Mac said. "However, what it means is not yet clear. Noah told Gulliver Mackie that he intended to get current on the rent payment within days. These records indicate that he had no funds with which to do that—at least not in his business accounts. Either he had the money elsewhere in some illiquid form that had to be converted into cash, which seems highly doubtful, or he had somehow developed a future money stream, or he was expecting a windfall shortly, which I find most likely."

Mo frowned. "That's something, I guess, but I wish you had more. Did you see Dr. Bloomie on TV4 last night?"

Mac raised an eyebrow.

Dr. Sydney Bloomingdale was something of a regional celebrity even before she auditioned for and landed a role on that syndicated medical show, *The Shrinks*. She's a psychotherapist, not a shrink, but that's close enough for TV. Her first television gig was at TV4 in Cincinnati, doing a segment for the local morning gabfest. That led to spots on *Oprah*, and then a regular turn as part of the panel on *The Shrinks*. She still lived and practiced in Erin, although I'd read in the *Observer* that she was mulling a move to Chicago, where her show was recorded. She was divorced, no children, so that wouldn't be too much of a wrench in her life.

The woman had to be coining money. Why did she stick with that ridiculous nickname? "Dr. Bloomie" reminds me of bloomers, not Bloomingdale's. But she'd been called that ever since her TV4 days, if not before.

"She said the murder weapon, the fact that it was the Maltese Falcon and not just any blunt object, is highly significant because it says something about the murderer."

"What specifically?" Mac asked.

"She didn't specify."

"How politic of Dr. Bloomingdale!"

This was the first time that I could recall Dr. Bloomie holding forth about the psychology of a murderer. The cynical side of me—the only side I have when it comes to television personalities—suspected that speaking out in this case was her agent's idea.

"I think maybe she was being circumspect because she knows more than she can say," Mo added.

"From what source?" Mac said.

"She was Noah's therapist when he first came back to Erin from New York."

"Therapist?" I repeated. I couldn't let Mac ask *all* the brilliant questions.

"Yeah. He had some kind of breakdown when he was in New York. That's why he came home. His sister was still alive at the time. He talked about it once or twice, and he said that Sydney helped him a lot. I didn't pry into the details. Is that important?"

Mac stroked his beard. "Perhaps. It is certainly a reminder that Noah Bartlett had a past—and that perhaps it was an interesting one. What was it, Jefferson, that Dunbar said about the past?"

"He called it a 'rich vein' for motives."

While Mac went off to mine that vein at the courthouse, looking for a record of Noah's marriage, I went back to the salt mines.

You know it's going to be a challenging day when a reporter gets to your office before you do, even when he's just a sophomore working on the campus paper. Hadley Reams sat in the chair next to Popcorn, his fingers flying over his smartphone. I gave myself ten to one odds that he was playing Angry Birds, but he could have been texting his girlfriend.

He stood up when I entered. "Good morning, Mr. Cody." Hadley was a skinny kid dressed in jeans, a white shirt hanging out, and a trilby hat. "I was hoping I could talk to you for a few minutes about Professor Talton."

Oh, *him*.

"Sure. Come on into my office. Ms. Pokorny, hold my calls."

That last part was a joke.

Inside my office, Hadley pulled out a reporter's notebook (not a tablet!) and made himself at home.

"I guess you have a few more questions since we talked on the phone," I observed.

"Just a few. My editor wants me to ask you more about the increasingly negative pushback against Professor Talton's comments. Have you been reading the comments on YouTube, *Higher Ed Insider*, and the *Erin Observer & News-Ledger?*"

I'd read enough to know that Talton ought to have somebody start his car in the morning and taste his food for him.

"We're certainly aware that Professor Talton's somewhat unconventional view of President Lincoln has generated some vigorous exchanges of opinions," I said. *I especially liked the comment that began "Please kill yourself."* "That's not a cause for concern. On the contrary, it's part of our mission as an institution of higher learning. Would you like a Coke?"

Hadley looked up from his notebook. "Uh, sure."

Sylvester Link, the lead reporter at the *Spectator* at the time of the Peter Gerard case,[5] would have turned me down, suspecting a bribe. I missed Serious Sylvester, now a general assignment reporter at the *St. Louis Post-Dispatch*. Hadley not only accepted the gift horse that I pulled out of my small office refrigerator, he looked it in the mouth. "Caffeine-Free Diet Coke?"

"That's how I roll."

I gave Hadley a can and opened one for myself. Could caffeine really be good for you? I pushed the thought aside as the nascent newshound read from his notebook: "How do you react to the comments of Luther Martin, president of the Honest Abe Association?"

"What did he say?" I already knew that from Maggie's story, but I was teaching young Hadley how to work for what he wanted.

He flipped back a few pages in his notebook. "He said, 'This scurrilous attack on a great man by an unknown man will be little noted nor long remembered. The thought that this lightweight is teaching impressionable young

---

[5] See *Holmes Sweet Holmes*, MX Publishing, 2012.

college undergraduates is frightening.' What do you say to that, Mr. Cody?"

I say the man scares easily.

"As you are well aware"—actually, I couldn't count on that—"Professor Talton is truly a distinguished, if low profile, scholar. He holds degrees in economics and history from eminent universities and he's published many books. Do you have his C.V.?"

He looked up from scribbling. "Yes, sir."

"Good."

"But a C.V. doesn't tell everything, does it? I was wondering whether there have been any other complaints or controversies surrounding Professor Talton in his time at St. Benignus."

I shook my head. "As you noted yesterday, he's one of the more popular profs on campus."

Hadley went back to the notebook. "Do you think that Professor Talton's comments will hurt St. Benignus?"

There's no such thing as bad publicity. Wait, that's not true. In fact, it's stupid. There is such a thing as bad publicity, and sometimes it makes alumni hold on to their wallets.

"On the contrary. Thousands of people across the country have been exposed to the name of St. Benignus College for the first time. If they start looking into us, I think they'll be pleased with what they see." *Holy moley! I'd better get Popcorn to update the "About Us" section of the website.*

Hadley closed the notebook. "I guess that's all I wanted to ask you about Professor Talton."

"No, no, no." *Sylvester Link would never stop there.* If I didn't help this kid, my conscience would bother me.

"No?" He looked so young with a Coke in his hand and a trilby hat on his head.

"You should ask me whether the college is standing by Professor Talton."

Hadley opened the notebook again. "Are you?"

"We aren't just standing behind one accomplished professor, Hadley. There's something much bigger at stake here. We're standing behind the concept of academic freedom." *Not to mention the even more sacred principle of tenure.* "I think President Lincoln would understand that. In all of our country's history, nobody stands for freedom more than he does." *Never mind that habeas corpus stuff that has Talton's shorts in a bunch.*

"Thanks, Mr. Cody. Oh, I almost forgot. Have you heard anythingg about an investigation of steroid use on campus, maybe on the wrestling team?"

I almost spit out my Coke. "Where did you hear that?"

He got a canny look on his fresh face. "I can't reveal my sources."

"Well, I couldn't reveal an investigation if there were one. And that means I also couldn't reveal if there weren't one, because if I did it would answer your question every time I didn't answer your question. Do you understand?"

He shook his head. "Not at all."

"Good."

I thought that went well.

Hadley left with a puzzled expression on his face, and I spent a half-hour or so catching up on e-mail and essential social media sites before Mac called me.

"I found the record of Noah Bartlett's marriage, Jefferson." Why did he not sound like his usual buoyant self?

"Excellent!"

"*Au contraire*, old boy. I believe I can predict with confidence that you will not be pleased about what I have learned. Far from it, in fact."

Chapter Eleven
The Ex-Mrs. Noah Bartlett

Popcorn looked up from her computer as I rushed out of my office. "Maggie's story about Talton has been linked on *Drudge*. I'm afraid this thing's going to spiral out of control."

"Least of our worries right now," I called behind me as I hustled out the door. "Fill you in later."

I didn't even stop to tell her that she'd been right about Lesley Saylor-Mackie and Noah Bartlett.

I met Mac at Herbert Hall outside of Saylor-Mackie's department-head office. We barged in together without a lot of preliminary chit-chat. Saylor-Mackie looked up from some paperwork, peering at us over half-moon glasses that I'd seldom seen her wear.

"What now? You two look like the hangman. Is it Jim Talton again?"

"Would that it were!" Mac exclaimed. *Easy for you to say.* At the back of my mind I knew that exposure on the high-traffic *Drudge Report* blog had just made our formerly obscure history professor a national issue. But the back of my mind was just where it belonged right now.

"Why didn't you tell us that you were once married to your old 'friend' Noah Bartlett?" I didn't even try to not sound angry.

"You didn't ask."

I silently counted to one. "Excuse me for being blunt, but that is really lame. Maybe an academic wouldn't get that, but a politician should. Do yourself and me a favor: If anybody else asks you about your relationship with Noah—the police, for instance—just tell the truth, the whole truth, and nothing but the truth." I was too peeved to pre-edit the cliché in my head before it came out of my mouth.

"It took me approximately ten minutes to find the record at the Sussex County Court House," Mac said.

What a train wreck! If Mac and I thought that the ex-Mrs. Bartlett would make a dandy murder suspect, so would somebody else—like Oscar Hummel or my gym buddy Marvin Slade, the county prosecutor. And Slade did double duty as the county chairman of the political party opposite the mayor's. Maybe we could figure out the murderer before they had a chance. Unless—

"This is kind of a delicate question," I said, "but by any chance did you happen to visit Noah early yesterday morning, maybe get into an argument, get carried away by your anger of the moment, and hit him in the back of the head?"

"Very subtle, Jefferson," Mac mumbled.

Saylor-Mackie's elegant face sagged. She seemed to age ten years right before my eyes. "Of course not! What a horrible idea! Will people really think that?"

"They might if they knew you had the perfect opportunity to tell us—who are on your side, by the way— that you had once been married to the man and you didn't do it." I wasn't losing steam—not even close.

"That was a stupid mistake the two of us made a long time ago, Noah and I. I don't enjoy reliving the experience by talking about it." She sighed. "Obviously we were more than friends in high school. We were sweethearts. That's an old-fashioned term, but it fits. Our relationship in those days was very sweet, very romantic. Puppy love always is. But it doesn't trump biology."

She looked past us, maybe all the way to the 1970s. "We got married right after high school graduation because I thought I was pregnant. People still did that in those days—got married because they were pregnant. A good priest might have told us that was a terrible idea, but we didn't go to a priest. We went to a judge.

"When it turned out that I wasn't pregnant after all, or maybe I had a miscarriage so early I didn't even know it, I tried to make the best of the situation. But by a year after the wedding, our married-student dorm room at the University of Kentucky wasn't big enough for the two of us. Noah felt trapped. Once he even accused me of lying about being pregnant to get him to marry me. The marriage was over by the time we were juniors. It was later annulled."

Saylor-Mackie stopped and favored us with some eye contact. "Father Pirelli knows all this, by the way. I told him years ago. I'm sure there are a number of people around town who would remember the whole sad story with a little prodding. Many of them have sad stories of their own, I'm sure.

"You know, or can assume, the rest: A few years later, after grad school, I met Gulliver and I found out what real love is like. So for me there was a happy ending. For Noah, things didn't work out so well. I never asked him exactly what happened to him in New York; that didn't seem important. I just know that he came back home to Erin like a wounded animal. So that's the Noah and Lesley story. Satisfied?"

"Almost," Mac said mildly. "You told us yesterday that you had become friends again. That cannot have been easy, in the light of your shared history."

She nodded. "When I heard that he'd come back to town, as I had years earlier, my feelings were very mixed. You always have a soft spot in your heart for your first love,

I suppose, but our parting had not been a good one. So I went out of my way to avoid him. Then one day I ran into him at Daniel's Apothecary. To my surprise, he couldn't have been nicer. I stopped avoiding him. We even went to lunch together once in a while."

Was that what Popcorn had seen flashing between Noah and Saylor-Mackie that night at the Art in the Blood opening—an adolescent love that had mellowed into a nostalgia-nourished friendship? For a bizarre moment I wondered if Madame Mayor was acquainted with the works of Rosamund DeLacey.

Mac fingered his beard. "Did your husband know about all of this, including the occasional lunches with his predecessor?"

"Certainly. Keeping my first marriage a secret from Gulliver would have been a recipe for disaster." She smiled and added dryly: "Gulliver was equally candid, and he had a considerably longer list of romantic entanglements before we met than I did. And as for telling him about my lunches with Noah, that was only natural. We always discuss our day with each other while he's cooking dinner."

"And how did he react?"

Saylor-Mackie stared, and then emitted a sound that coming from anyone else might have been called a giggle. "You mean was he jealous? Don't be silly, Mac. Gulliver and I have total trust in each other. We've been finishing each others' sentences for close to thirty years."

Was it possible for a marriage to be so idyllic after nearly three decades? I hoped so. I was counting on it, in fact. And so far so good at the Cody ranch.

If Lesley Saylor-Mackie was telling the truth and she was right, that was good news for St. Benignus (and me). For a high-profile faculty member's husband to be seriously suspected of murder would be almost as bad as for the faculty member herself to be under the magnifying glass— especially if the motive was a romantic triangle.

I must have been thinking too loud, because Saylor-Mackie seemed to hear me.

"From what I read in the *Observer*, I gather that Noah was killed yesterday morning, a few hours before the body was found, not the night before," she said. "Is that correct?"

"Yes," Mac affirmed. The coroner's report had confirmed the initial assumption. Noah's last meal had been cereal, obviously breakfast, undigested at the time of death, which had been caused by blunt-force head trauma.

"Then you might be interested to know that Gulliver was with me all morning until I went to City Hall at nine-thirty. We always have breakfast together at Beans & Books on Wednesdays."

"A spouse isn't the greatest alibi," I told Mac as soon we closed the door of his office, two floors below Saylor-Mackie's. "But she would hardly lie to protect a husband who killed a man he was jealous of—would she?"

"Oh, I don't know, old boy." Mac lit a cigar off of the "Thank You for Not Breathing While I Smoke" sign on his desk. "Stranger things have happened. Surely it would not be to the advantage of either of the Mackies to break up their romantic and political alliance."

Polymath though he is, Sebastian McCabe is almost clueless when it comes to politics. Gulliver Mackie wasn't the unalloyed blessing to his politician-spouse that Mac seemed to believe.

"Mackie contributes a lot of his money and raises even more for his wife and other candidates of her party," I conceded. "But on the other hand, it's kind of embarrassing when his investment properties run afoul of city codes or when the mayor has to remove herself from a city development issue because he stands to profit."

Mac grunted.

"You don't think there's a chance in Hades that Saylor-Mackie did in her ex, do you?" I asked. "After all, we only have her word that they were on good terms. Reading between the lines, it sounded like he was the one who wanted out of the marriage. I suspect she could be very good at holding a grudge."

Mac shrugged. "It is not beyond the bounds of possibility. One can easily envision Oscar constructing a scenario out of passion and wounded pride. It would be the stuff of grand opera! For that reason I hope that our friend does not find out, at least not soon, that Lesley Saylor-Mackie was once Mrs. Saylor-Bartlett."

She might not have used that name. But I knew what Mac meant.

"As she said, there must be a lot of people in town who would remember that those two were once married," I pointed out.

"Fortunately, Jefferson, Oscar is not one of them."

People tend to think of small towns as insular burgs, populated by a cast of characters who are born, live, and die there. But college towns get new arrivals every semester, and some of them stay. Oscar, Mac, Kate, Lynda, and I all came from somewhere else. None of us had known much about Noah Bartlett when he showed up to open Pages Gone By, and none of the locals had filled us in. We weren't unique in our ignorance; Erin had gained a lot of new residents since the Altiora Corp. had established operations here several years back.

"Actually I was hoping you would pooh-pooh Saylor-Mackie's credentials as a suspect and suggest a better one," I said. How had he missed that?

Mac drummed his fingers on the desk, a rare gesture of impatience. He stopped. "Dr. Bloomingdale!"

"Dr. Bloomie did it?"

"Blast it, Jefferson!" He was in no mood for jokes. "Dr. Bloomingdale gave a television interview that impressed Mo. Since we are running seriously low on ideas of our own, I think it would behoove us to watch that interview."

Within a few minutes, he had found the video clip on the TV4 website. Brian Rose, the veteran co-anchor of the 6 P.M. news, had hauled himself from behind the anchor desk to interview Dr. Bloomie in what appeared to be her tastefully decorated office. When the camera pulled back for what they call a "two-shot," the interviewer and the interviewee in one frame, it became clear that they faced each other on a couch. Apparently psychologists have them as well as psychiatrists.

That image was the lead-in, a few seconds of video (what's called "B-roll"), accompanied by a voice-over from Rose's perky female co-anchor: "Tonight, TV4's own Dr. Bloomie talks to Brian about a vicious murder in a quiet Ohio River town."

Then the camera went live with Brian, his middle-aged face framed by horn-rim glasses, looking seriously at the camera. A logo projected behind him said, *Murder in a Tiny Town*. (FYI, Erin is small, but hardly tiny.) "Good evening. The Ohio River community of Erin is still reeling tonight from the mysterious bludgeoning death of well-liked bookstore owner Noah Bartlett. I discussed the case today with renowned psychologist and TV4 commentator Dr. Sydney Bloomingdale."

The next shot was a close-up of the celebrity in question. The good doctor was an attractive, athletic woman, pushing sixty-five but handling it well. My father, who was of her generation, had once proclaimed her "a fine-looking woman." She had blond hair (possibly with a little help from Clairol or something similar) worn shoulder-length so that it spilled over a simple but expensive dress of some soft camel-colored material. Her gold necklace would have looked fabulous on Lynda, its design vaguely Egyptian by way of Art Deco. That was complimented by a gold cuff bracelet on her right wrist in the shape of flat knots with artistic embellishments. The jewelry was expensive without being flashy.

"I don't think it's accidental that the murderer employed the Maltese Falcon statue as his instrument of death," she informed Brian. "I've never been to Pages Gone By, but I suspect there were a number of heavy items that would have served the purpose. It seems to me that the murderer was making a statement by choosing to use that statue to kill."

"What kind of statement?" Brian's question came from off-camera.

"We can't even surmise at this point, Brian." She paused. "Perhaps the killer had some connection with mystery stories," she surmised. "*The Maltese Falcon* is a famous book and film, but it's also an icon for the mysterious, particularly in the hard-boiled genre."

Who would have guessed that Dr. Bloomie was so well versed in matters *noir?*

The camera switched to Brian. "That's a little bizarre, Dr. Bloomie. Does this indicate to you that the killer was insane?"

"Insane is not a medical term, Brian. I would certainly say he had issues with Mr. Bartlett."

That's like saying the Incredible Hulk has an anger management problem. Why the reserve? Maybe she was less cautious on *The Shrinks,* when she wasn't dealing with a hometown homicide. Although I'd seen Dr. Bloomie on TV4 from time to time, I'd never caught her appearance on the syndicated show.

"The victim was clutching a book in his hand, a romance novel called *Love's Dark Secret,*" Brian observed. "What do you make of that? Some have speculated that Mr. Bartlett was trying to name his killer."

Cody's Law: Beware when a reporter says "some" or "many." Such vague pronouns usually refer to the chattering classes or to the reporter himself or herself. In this case, of course, the anchor could have been talking about Mac, but he probably didn't know it.

Back went the camera to Dr. Bloomie. "It would be highly inappropriate for me to speculate about Mr. Bartlett's mindset as he lay dying."

The video ended there and Brian Rose was back live (when it was recorded), looking straight at the camera through his horn-rims. "And that's the view from Dr. Bloomie. We'll continue to give you breaking news on this shocking murder in a tiny town as it happens."

This is where Brian's bouncy brunette co-anchor, Tammie Tucker, would have interjected either, "What a puzzling case, Brian," or "On a much lighter note . . ." But since we were watching a snippet on the computer, the report ended there.

"Well?" Nobody can say I don't ask insightful questions.

Mac smoked in silence. I was about to start hacking, just to make a point, when he said, "Mo could well be right that Dr. Bloomingdale knows something revealing based on her knowledge of Noah Bartlett."

"She didn't seem to."

"Perhaps the good doctor was being circumspect for ethical reasons, the therapist-patient relationship. Her use of the words 'highly inappropriate' would seem to indicate that. However, if we were to speak to her privately—"

My phone cut him off. The Indiana Jones ring tone tends to do that. It was Mo.

"What's up?" I asked, skipping the niceties. "What is it now?"

"Mary Lou Springfield. She's insisting on a special meeting of the Poisoned Pens tonight. She has this crazy idea that the Pens can solve the murder."

Chapter Twelve
Grilling

"What can the Poisoned Pens do together that Mac can't do alone?" Lynda asked, quite sensibly.

"Argue with each other," I said.

"Just because an elderly librarian who writes hard-boiled mysteries"—I'd read some of Mary Lou's more purple passages to Lynda—"forces a meeting of the writing group, that doesn't mean that you have to go, does it?"

"I think I'd better. Mac's going, and you know how he is without adult supervision."

The late afternoon was warm for early spring, as several days had been lately. We sat on the back deck, next to our newly purchased grill. I had changed into shorts and Lynda wore a bright yellow tennis dress with a white blouse that nicely accented her dark complexion. She sipped her Manhattan and I my urologist-pleasing lemonade.

"How is it that you make such good Manhattans when you never drink them?" she asked.

"Cause and effect: Not drinking them makes me more objective, and therefore I can do a better job."

I'm not a total teetotaler, but pretty close. I know my limits when it comes to alcohol, and they are low. A glass of wine or a couple of beers and I shed my inhibitions like a snake shedding his old skin. Results: Nine of the ten stupidest things I ever did or said were fueled by alcohol. You could say my temperance is a stupidity-avoidance tactic. It's mostly successful.

We moved on to the "how was work" part of cocktail hour.

"You were right on the money with the idea of asking the TV stations to come up with their own ideas for sweeps month investigations," Lynda said. "They really came through with some great stuff. Everybody had multiple ideas."

"Such as?" I loved seeing her look so excited.

"Human trafficking, gun violence after concealed carry came to Ohio, steroids in college sports, and who's already given how much for next year's U.S. senate race. Those were my top four."

Does anybody else have such cocktail hour conversations?

At the end of the list, I was still back on "steroids in college sports." *Holy crap! If there's anything to that accusation about the St. Benignus wrestling team . . .*

"Steroid stories have been kind of done to death," I said with a yawn. "But you can't over-report human trafficking. It's real, it's here in Ohio, and it's mostly ignored because it sounds too awful and too exotic to be true."

Lynda smiled. "That's just what I was thinking. We can do some of the other stories later."

But not the steroids one!

"Why did Mo call this morning?" Lynda said. "I kind of expected you to text me with the details."

"Oh, sorry. I hardly had time to pull my phone out of my pocket all day."

I prepared dinner on the grill—pork chops with an herb and spice rub complemented by potatoes, carrots and onions wrapped in tin foil. Lynda is an amazing Italian cook, especially when using her *nonna*'s recipes. Cannoli? *Mamma mia!* But I am master of the grill. As my beloved nursed her Manhattan, I told her about my day from the top. Her jaw dropped when I got to the part about Lesley Saylor-Mackie's teenage marriage to Noah Bartlett.

"I wonder if Johanna—" she began.

"That's ncient history, Lyn. It probably has nothing to do with the murder. Bringing it up would serve no good purpose and could do some real harm. It would drag the mayor into a business where she doesn't belong."

"And that would be bad for St. Benignus."

"That would be unfair to Saylor-Mackie."

Good thing I wasn't imbibing an adult beverage. I might have gotten testy at that point if I'd been under the influence.

Lynda chewed her lip thoughtfully. "You're probably right. I've been thinking. Yates was right about gain being the most common motive in real life, you know. Who gains by Noah's death? The most obvious answer is Mo."

I hadn't liked that idea when Mac floated it, and I didn't like it any better now. I opened my mouth to object, but Lynda leaned over and put a silencing finger on my lips.

"You told me a long time ago that she had a big dream to own her own mystery bookstore. She just inherited a ton of inventory. She can gradually dump the romance novels and all the other non-mysteries and presto, dream come true."

I pulled the pork chops off the grill.

"This is Maureen Russert you're talking about. I know Mo, and I can't believe she would kill her friend and employer to get control of his business—which by the way is a loser. A 'rousing failure,' she called it."

"Maybe she didn't know it was a loser until she got a look at the books."

"Mo is smart. She knew it." At least, she knew it wasn't a very successful business even before breaking into Noah's QuickBooks. That's what she'd told Mac and me, anyway.

"I thought you liked Mo," I said.

"I do, darling. She's very sweet. But we can't go by that. Sherlock Holmes once said the most winning woman he ever knew poisoned three children for the insurance money. No matter how much you like her, she could have killed her boss. She had means and opportunity—and maybe a motive we don't know about, on top of the obvious one. For instance, suppose she found out some book in the shop is worth a million dollars. Okay, that's far-fetched but not impossible. 'When you have eliminated the impossible . . .'"

I tuned out while she quoted Sherlock Holmes. Could she be right? Was I letting my fondness for Mo close my mind to a real possibility?

Before I could answer those questions, I gave myself another one: What really motivated this Mo-as-suspect scenario that Lynda was force-feeding me?

I'd never told her that I'd taken Mo out during what I thought of as the Great Hiatus, that painful month when I thought that Lynda Teal and I were through. But I'd long suspected that Lynda somehow knew. I couldn't put my finger on it, but there was something about the knowing way she looked whenever Mo's name came up. Was that why Lynda was determined to promote her as Suspect Number One? I pushed the thought aside as unworthy of me. My beloved would never be so petty. *Would she?*

We took our dinner to the screened-in porch off the kitchen, one of my favorite parts of the house. All the while I was trying to find the right words for what I wanted to tell her.

After we said the blessing and took our first bites, I launched into it.

"I actually know Mo better than you might think." *Or maybe not.*

Lynda put down her fork and gave me the full attention of her gold-flecked brown eyes. "Do tell."

The pork began to feel dry in my mouth. My palms felt sweaty. *How about if I get a couple of glasses of wine? And one for you, too?*

"You may recall that four years ago things weren't going so well between us." Lynda rolled her eyes. "Okay, that's an understatement, but we've agreed not to rehash the past. Let's just say we were no longer a couple—by your choice, I might add."

"I even considered joining Polly's religious community," Lynda recalled, a bemused look on her face.

"I'm sure you would have made a wonderful nun, but I'm glad you didn't. Meanwhile, I got lonely a week or so after we split."

"That soon?"

"I missed you so much it hurt, but I thought I was just lonely in general. So I took Mo to a movie. It wasn't long after her divorce and she was lonely, too. And then I took her out to dinner the following week. So I guess you could say we went out together twice. That's why I feel so sure about Mo. I dated her."

She smiled. "Oh, Jeff, darling, I know that. I've always known that."

Just as I deduced! Then why had I been so nervous about telling her what she already knew, and I knew that she knew? Just being me, I guess.

"How?"

"When you asked Mo out the first time, she called me for a reference."

Good thing I was sitting down.

"She called the ex-girlfriend for a reference?"

Lynda shrugged. "Who would know Jeff Cody's foibles and eccentricities better than me?"

Eccentricities? *Me?*

I forced a chuckle. "Well, obviously you gave me a good report or she wouldn't have gone out with me."

"Absolutely. I rated you a solid four-point-five out of five."

Wait a minute here. You're saying I'm not a five?

But on the other hand, four and half isn't so bad—is it? Not at all! I'm thrilled with that many stars in an Amazon review. So why did Lynda give me the old heave-ho to begin with if she thought I was a four and a half?

"You look perplexed, Jeff."

"Never mind."

Lynda got up slowly and moved around the table until she was standing behind me. "I just don't know how Mo let you go." She leaned over and I bent my head back. Kissing upside down always makes me lightheaded. Not that I'm complaining. After several moments of silent communication, Lynda broke away and added: "Of course, you are younger than Mo. Maybe she didn't like being a cougar."

Why are you still thinking about that? I'm not still thinking about that.

She slid onto my lap and put her arms around me in one fluid, graceful motion. "I had my cougar moment once."

"Eh?" This was totally news to me, and I didn't think it was good news.

"Right about the time you were test-driving a relationship with Mo, I went out on a date with Connor O'Quinn."

"Connor?" I felt myself frown. "I thought you were trying to be a nun."

"Not the whole time—a weekend retreat and some good advice from Polly settled that. I spent quite a few nights by myself at Bobbie McGee's. When you do that you get to know the bartender. He asked me out and I said yes. Why not? He's good looking, muscular, and he makes excellent Manhattans. And I didn't think you and I were going to work out."

She tried to distract me with a kiss. I let her think it worked, for a while.

"But you only went out with him once," I observed when we came up for air.

"Why do you think I learned taekwondo? He was a little too handy for me, if you know what I mean. I do like his unshaven look, though." She ran a hand down my cheek. "You ought to try that."

Suddenly, I hated Connor O'Quinn. Maybe he killed Noah Bartlett!

"I'm just glad we're together for good now," Lynda added. She snuggled closer. "I didn't bring any work home tonight. Are you sure you have to go to that meeting?"

"I'm afraid so."

Her response was non-verbal.

"But not right this second," I added.

A few minutes later, Lynda said, "My college roommate posted on Facebook today that she's pregnant." *Uh-oh. Not again!* Pregnancy seemed to be approximately a weekly occurrence in Lynda's circle. Not always involving the roommate, of course. "Why doesn't that happen to me, Jeff? We've been married three years."

This was not a new question.

"It's not my fault," I said. "That you haven't gotten pregnant, I mean. I think I'm doing everything right." *And I know you are.*

"No doubt about that. Maybe it's the radiation from the smartphone in your pocket."

Lynda was starting to think like me. Even I found that scary.

"I don't think so," I said. "I've got that covered. I move the phone around so no one body part gets too much electromagnetic radiation. As I've said before, maybe you're just under too much stress at work, what with job cuts and sweeps month and all that."

"So, should I quit?"

Money has always been of interest to me. Collecting it is one of my hobbies, and Lynda makes a lot more of it than I do. The loss of income if she left Grier would be dramatic. But we wouldn't lose the house. "If that's what you think you need to do, you know I'll support you."

She squeezed me. "You're the best, Jeff."

"No, you are. But I'd better get to that Poisoned Pens meeting."

I have to admit that I made no attempt to move, however.

"You can be late for the meeting, *tesoro mio*."

I love it when she talks Italian, especially when she lowers her Lauren Bacall voice like that.

"Well, if you really—"

"Shhh."

Chapter Thirteen
The Erin Bookseller Mystery

"You look happy, Jeff," Mo said.

You have no idea.

"Sorry I'm late." *But not too sorry.* "I see that I'm not the last one, though. Oscar's not here."

"He wasn't invited," Mary Lou Springfield snapped. "We don't need the cops."

"The chief isn't really an official member," Ashley said. "He's only come to one meeting." She looked happy to point that out. Maybe she was remembering the time Oscar interrogated her as a suspect in her husband's murder, cheered on by the prosecutor, Marvin Slade.

It was hard for me to see what constituted an "official member" of the Poisoned Pens. The group was fluid, with no dues paid and no membership cards issued. But I let that pass. Oscar's absence didn't bother me a whit.

Connor O'Quinn, Ashley's current squeeze—and Lynda's one-time date, I couldn't help thinking—sat next to her on the loveseat in Jonathan Hawes's spacious living room. Jonathan was nowhere in sight, proving that he was smarter than me. Or maybe he had a funeral that evening. Roscoe Feldman hovered over Mary Lou, as if he were too nervous to sit.

"As I understand it," Mac rumbled, "the purpose of this meeting is to brainstorm a solution to Noah's murder on the theory that multiple heads are better than one. I suppose the early Ellery Queen might have called this *The Erin Bookseller Mystery*."

"Ellery Queen isn't here," Mary Lou pointed out. Have I mentioned that Mac's mystique is somewhat lost on her? "But we have a bunch of other mystery writers."

"It does look like Chief Hummel could use some help, doesn't it?" Roscoe said.

"Gosh, yes," I said. "The body was found yesterday morning and he hasn't arrested anybody yet."

"That's not such a bad thing," Ashley said, apparently oblivious to the old Cody sarcasm. "It's more important to get it right."

"I'm sure that's true," Mo said, "but I agree with Mary Lou that a whole room full of mystery writers ought to be able to figure out who killed one of our own. I suggest we start by each saying whom we suspect. This is all off the record and it doesn't leave the room, so say what you think. Mary Lou, since this was your idea, you go first."

Mary Lou didn't hesitate a second. "I don't know who yet, but I think it's one of us. Don't look so shocked, people. Didn't you hear what Dr. Bloomie said?" She must have seen some blank faces—not everybody is plugged into TV and the newspaper, although they certainly all knew the good doctor's name. "She said the murder weapon is a highly significant psychological clue. If that's so, who but one of us would pick the Maltese Falcon to kill Noah? We're all mystery fans as well as writers. It would be a natural. Does anybody want to confess?"

At first, the only response was a few nervous titters.

"Since when is Dr. Bloomie some kind of amateur detective?" Mo asked.

"Since when is Oscar Hummel a professional detective?" Mary Lou shot back. *Ouch.* "I think she's on to something."

"But we were all Noah's friends," Roscoe said finally, to my surprise. "None of us would kill him." I didn't think he had it in him to argue with Mary Lou.

"Most murder victims aren't killed by strangers," she volleyed back. "They're killed by people who know them and therefore have reason to want them dead."

"I am not at all certain of that," Mac said mildly. "Surely the killer and the victim are unknown to each other in a significant percentage of homicides, if one discounts domestic violence and drug deals gone bad. However, in this case, with robbery and random carnage out, I agree it is highly likely that Noah knew his slayer. He apparently opened the door for him or her. I am unconvinced of the significance of the murder weapon as a clue to the killer, however. That seems too obvious."

By all means, let's not consider the obvious.

"He met somebody for dinner the night before he died," Mo said. "I don't know who, though."

"That sounds like a suspect to me," O'Quinn said.

Me, too. I gave myself a metaphorical slap in the head, and I could see by the expression on his face that Mac was doing the same—to my head *and* his. Mo had mentioned this to us the day before and we hadn't followed up on it. Both of us had lost track of what seemed like a potentially important line of inquiry.

But Ashley didn't think so. "If whoever he had dinner with on Tuesday night wanted to kill him, why come to the store the next morning to do it?"

"Who is your preferred candidate?" Mac asked.

"I don't know—maybe Dunbar Yates. Yeah, Yates. He's a mystery writer. And he knew Noah in New York." Pushed to come up with a suspect, Ashley had dropped her aversion to naming one with remarkable speed.

"What possible reason would Yates have for killing Noah?" Mary Lou asked.

Ashley shrugged. "I don't know. Something that goes back to New York, maybe. The motive could be in the past. Why would any of us want to kill him under your theory?"

"Well, which one of us gains by Noah's death?" Mary Lou didn't even try to avoid looking at Mo.

"I lost more than I gained—a boss and a friend," Mo said. "I don't know about anybody else. Maybe the motive isn't obvious."

"So who do you think did it?" Roscoe Feldman asked Mo. "Was it the person Noah told you he was having dinner with the night before he died or somebody else?"

Please don't say it was his ex-wife.

As heads turned to Mo, I mentally ran through everybody's position on the most likely killer: Mary Lou had her knives out for Mo, but probably would settle for any other member of the Poisoned Pens, with the possible exception of her non-committing boyfriend; Roscoe, hesitant as always, even in the face of his amour's firmness, was dubious about the whole killer-among-us trope; Ashley offered Dunbar Yates, with an unknown motive connected to the past; and Connor O'Quinn was ready to finger somebody we couldn't even put a name to—Noah's dinner companion the night before.

"I'll put my money on Mac and Jeff," Mo said.

Mac raised an eyebrow. I almost fell out of my chair.

"I mean," she clarified, "I'm sure they'll figure it out."

Mac nodded slightly. "We appreciate your confidence, Mo. I trust it has not been misplaced. As a matter of fact, Jefferson and I have not been idle. We have quite vigorously pursued Noah's assailant over the past two days."

"And just what did you come up with?" Mary Lou demanded in a tone that strongly suggested Mac had failed to return a library book due in 1972.

A poker hand full of blank cards, thanks for asking.

Mac demurred. "I would rather not be specific at this point. I can assure you, however, that we have a number of promising leads."

"That sounds like a whole lot of nothing," Mary Lou said. "Well, this hasn't accomplished what I'd hoped. If we can't come to an agreement, and if nobody's going to confess, maybe we should call in Dr. Bloomie to sort it out."

Earlier, Mac himself had been on the verge of suggesting a conversation with the good doctor to find out if she'd been holding back something from TV4. But he reacted coolly to Mary Lou's suggestion.

"I hardly think that shall be necessary," he said. I could almost hear him thinking "*I shall do the amateur sleuthing around here!*"

Chapter Fourteen
Dying Clue or Red Herring?

After that, the meeting fizzled out, the only result being mutual suspicion and a lot of bad tempers.

I went to sleep later than usual because of the confab, but Friday morning's issue of the *Erin Observer & News-Ledger* brought me full awake. The right-hand column featured a story by Johanna Rawls that hadn't been in the online edition I'd scanned before going to bed. The headline screamed:

**Did victim
Leave clue
To killer?**

I read on with fascinating puzzlement, ignoring Lynda and barely tasting the whole-grain cereal I was shoveling into my mouth.

A book clutched in the hand of murder victim Noah Bartlett may have been intended as a clue to his killer, according to Police Chief Oscar Hummel.

"I think he was trying to tell us something," Hummel said. "Why else would he go to the trouble to pull that book off the shelves?"

The book was a romance novel, *Love's Dark Secret*, by the prolific and popular author Rosamund DeLacey.

Bartlett, the owner of the Pages Gone By used-book store on High Street in Erin, was found dead . . .

"What's the matter?" Lynda asked.

"I can't believe this story," I said. "Oscar totally dismissed the dying clue idea as being mystery story stuff. But listen to this." I read it out loud. Although Lynda occasionally gets a whiff of *Observer* stories in the making because of her office there, she'd been busy dealing with her TV project on Thursday and had no advance notice on this one. When I got to the part where Tall Rawls noted the substantial number of Rosamund DeLacey books on the shelves, Lynda said, "I still think maybe that's the clue—the author, not the book."

"Dr. Bloomie doesn't agree." I read her the next paragraph:

Erin psychologist Dr. Sydney Bloomingdale, TV's "Dr. Bloomie," expressed skepticism that Bartlett's dying act will be of any help in solving his murder.

"If this book was meant to identify the murderer, it's hard to say in what way," she said.

"She's being very cagey," I said. "On TV the other day she refused to speculate on Bartlett's mindset. I think she's afraid to go on record saying something that might be disproved in a few days when somebody gets arrested. That makes sense, from her point of view. Oscar suddenly embracing the dying clue theory doesn't. You know how stubborn he is."

"Yeah, but he's not stupid."

"Sometimes I forget that. Mac will be happy to see that Oscar has come around, but he won't like seeing Dr. Bloomie quoted. I think he feels threatened by her."

Her eyebrows flew up. "Why?"

"Because he's Sebastian McCabe, Erin's famous amateur sleuth, and he doesn't like claimants to the throne."

"Wow. If that's the way you talk about your best friend, I'm glad I'm just your wife. He's not really that bad. He just forgets sometimes that he's only the star of the show and not the whole cast."

"Oh, crap!" My exclamation didn't indicate a disagreement with Lynda. Paging through the paper, I had reached the op-ed page. About a third of it was taken up with responses to James Gregory Talton's controversial comments about the Great Emancipator. They came both from Republicans ("How does this absent-minded professor think the slaves got freed?") and from liberals ("If Lincoln were alive today, he'd be ashamed of his party") and all were in strong disagreement with Talton.

Ralph was going to hate this.

I held up the page, showing it to Lynda without another word.

"You're going to have a bad day, aren't you?" she said.

"I already am." I pulled out my smartphone. "But this kerfuffle is just one of those things we have to ride out. Professor Talton didn't say anything that's racist, sexist, or homophobic—he just gave his scholarly opinion about a man and a moment." *Not bad; I should write that down for my talking points.*

"Then who are you calling?"

"The big guy."

He answered on the third ring. My three nieces and nephews were waging World War III around him at the breakfast table, judging by the background noise—a typical weekday morning at the McCabe household.

"Did you see Oscar's quotes in the morning paper?" I asked without preamble.

"Yes, and I am still in shock."

"What do you think happened, Mac?"

"Why engage in idle speculation when we can ask him?"

So at 9 A.M., after making a brief guest appearance in my office to pick up a travel mug of decaf and tell Popcorn to hold down the fort, I walked with Mac into Oscar's office.

The chief was hunched over his desktop computer with his hands still, a scowl on his face. Deeply engrossed, he didn't seem to notice our entrance.

"Writer's block?" Mac inquired.

Oscar started. "Oh, it's just you two. What now?" He took a drag on the e-cigarette that had been reposing in an ashtray next to the computer. *Why does an ash-less cigarette need an ashtray?* I chalked it up to habit.

"What finally convinced you that Noah was using that book to tell us who killed him?" I asked Oscar.

He shook his head. "Nothing. I'm still not convinced. Just the opposite."

"But Johanna Rawls quotes you as saying—"

I stopped myself when I saw the grin spreading across Oscar's broad face.

Mac caught on before I did. "You planted that story with malice aforethought," he declared. "It was no more than a ploy. And to what end?"

Oscar reached behind him to the credenza and started pouring high-test coffee. "I got to thinking. Maybe I was wrong about Bartlett just pulling any old book off a shelf in his death throes. Because maybe the murderer put the book there as what you call a red herring—something to throw suspicion the wrong way." He chuckled. "Rosamund DeLacey! Popcorn loves her crap."

"So you let Johanna think you bought into it," I said.

"Uh-huh." Oscar handed Mac the java he had poured into a McCabe-size mug he keeps on hand for him, the one that says **I SEE NO REASON TO ACT MY AGE.** I had my travel mug of decaf. "I want the killer to think I'm going down that rabbit hole. The idea is to make him feel overconfident. That's when the bad guys make mistakes."

"An interesting gambit," Mac said. "You realize there is a danger."

Oscar's eyes narrowed and he set down his coffee after a healthy swig. "Danger? How's that?"

"You have gone on record as believing that Noah attempted to identify his killer. Dr. Bloomingdale has dismissed that theory, both on television and in a newspaper interview. It would be rather embarrassing to you if she proved to be correct while you were in error."

"Dr. Bloomie!" Oscar spat out the name. "What does she know about it? She should stick to shrinking heads that are still alive."

That image didn't work for me.

"Fortunately," Mac said, "I believe that your stated belief—although it is not your real one—is the truth. In the end you will be vindicated for espousing a theory in which you do not believe. The irony is delicious."

Oscar looked as if he didn't know quite what to make of that. "Yeah, well, the hell with theories. What have you two been up to? I know you too well to think that you've just been sitting on your duffs."

What should we tell him, what should we not tell him? That wasn't as tricky as it sounds: Tell him what he's going to find out anyway as long as it doesn't look bad for Lesley Saylor-Mackie.

"Noah's financial straights were desperate," Mac said. "He was about to lose the lease on his store. Mo inherited the business, but it appears to consist of inventory of uncertain value and perhaps some debts as well."

"Where did you get that?"

"We have our sources," I said, just to keep my hand in. Plus, I've always wanted to say that.

"Yeah, well, so do I. I got the same dope from Amy Quong at Gamble Bank. I also talked to Charles Bexley, by the way. He confirmed everything that Mackie told us. You got anything else?"

I thought about last night's meeting of the Poisoned Pens. Mary Lou Springfield seemed convinced that one of us bashed our friend Noah's head in. I sure wasn't going to tell Oscar that. "Mo said that Noah had dinner with someone the night before he died."

"Who?"

"Mo didn't know."

"She didn't tell me that."

I shrugged. "I'm sure she wasn't hiding it from you. She just happened to remember it while we were chatting. It probably has nothing to do with the murder."

"Maybe, maybe not. I think I'll ponder that in the john. Be back in a few. If you get tired of waiting, I'll see you later."

As soon as Oscar disappeared down the hallway, Mac said, "I wonder what he was so diligently doing at his computer? He had a guilty look on his face when we interrupted his concentration."

"Why wonder?" As I talked I went around the desk and sat in Oscar's well-warmed chair. A Word document was on the screen. At the top were the words *Murder Up a Tree*.

"It's his mystery novel!" I speed-read a few paragraphs. "It's just in the early pages. Oh, this is lovely. Listen to this: '"It is precipitating felines and canines," said D'Artagnan Grey. Looking out the window at the storm, the rotund professor stroked his beard and considered this latest clue.' That's you, Mac!" I chuckled as I read ahead. "Oscar really gave the thesaurus feature on Word a workout. Grey sounds just like you—or a parody of you. I mean, he's you on steroids." *Steroids? Don't remind me. That's another shoe waiting to drop.*

"A roman à clef about me? That is rather surprising, given the sometimes-competitive nature of my relationship with the chief. Well, he has on occasion acknowledged my—"

"Um, Mac, I don't think you're the hero."

"Oh?"

I'd gotten to the part that introduced "Holden Justice, the handsome and brilliant police chief."

I stood up and moved back to the side of the desk I'd been on when Oscar had left to go to the men's room. "I don't think we need to read any more of this. Besides, how long can Oscar be gone? He didn't take any reading material with him."

"Oscar's creativity with names surprises," Mac said. "I would even go so far as to say I am impressed. I rather like the moniker 'D'Artagnan Grey.' It has a certain ring to it. What did he call you?"

"I'm not in the book."

"Of course you are! Where would D'Artagnan Grey be without his loyal friend and brother-in-law?"

"Oh, Grey has a sidekick—Benjamin 'Straight' Arrow. But he's not me. That character is nothing like me; he's a bundle of neurotic ticks." There was no need to get into the quickly-glimpsed details, such as Arrow's unhealthy obsession with his health. (*"Hamburger! That stuff will kill you! It's red meat!"*) "Lynda would never marry somebody like that, Mac."

"She almost did not, old boy."

I'm sure I would have come up with a clever riposte to that if Oscar hadn't come back just then.

"Still here?"

"Just leaving," I said.

If we'd stayed any longer there might have been another murder in Erin.

Chapter Fifteen
The Confession

A couple of hours later, as I went through the doors of Hawes & Holder's Market Street funeral home for Noah's visitation, I was still steaming about Oscar's stupid book.

"Now I'm afraid to say anything to Oscar because it might wind up as dialogue in his book," I told Mac, speaking in a funeral parlor voice. "What if it gets published?"

"That possibility seems remote in the extreme, Jefferson." Mac wrinkled his eyebrows and looked like he wanted to puff on a cigar. "However, if he has a good story to tell and a willing editor—"

I tuned out and looked around the spacious viewing room. Is there anything sadder than a small crowd at a funeral? When I was just out of college, my semi-girlfriend at the time and I gave a New Year's Eve party where only one other couple showed up—and they left early to go to another party. Noah's visitation, held two hours before the funeral service, felt like that. Noah was the guest of honor at a party where almost nobody had showed up.

Mo was there, of course, sniffing into a handkerchief. Mary Lou Springfield, with Roscoe Feldman in tow, saw her and looked skeptical of her grief. Ashley Crutcher appeared sans Connor O'Quinn. I also spotted Fred Gaffe, the octogenarian author of "The Old Gaffer" column in the *Erin Observer & News-Ledger*.

Mo's boyfriend, Jonathan Hawes, bustled around looking busy, as funeral directors always do. I probably wouldn't even have noticed him if I hadn't been making a point of seeing who was there.

"Jonathan is like the invisible man in Chesterton's Father Brown story," Mac said. "He is around so much that you fail to notice him."

I stared at Mac, impressed despite myself at the Sherlock Holmes gimmick of reading my thoughts.

"I followed the line of your sight. It was obvious that you were looking at Jonathan. Had you begun to think of him as a suspect?"

No.

"Of course I did. He's an obvious one." *Now that you mention it.* "He might have been jealous of Mo and Noah, even though he had no reason to be." We only had Mo's word for that, but I believed her. I'd seen the two together dozens of times, and I'd never noticed any goo-goo eyes being exchanged. Jonathan, on the other hand, might have reached a different conclusion. "Maybe if you hang around death as much as he does, it just naturally occurs to you as a solution to a problem."

Mac seemed startled by this perfectly sensible observation. "If that were the case, old boy, the annals of crime would be replete with homicidal morticians, not to mention physicians, coroners, EMT personnel, clergy—"

"Okay, okay. Right church, wrong pew. He still has a motive. Don't cross him off your list. And I know you have a list."

To my satisfaction, Mac clammed up. That meant I was right on both points.

Or maybe he just didn't want to be overheard by Lesley Saylor-Mackie. She was coming from the direction of the open casket, strolling our way in a manner so casual it immediately set off my Spidey sense. Elegant as always, she wore a simple black dress accented by a sheer gray scarf and white earrings. Her clear hazel eyes were dry.

"Hello, Lesley," Mac said. "This is a sad day."

I murmured something that I hope was sympathetic. I've never been able to figure out how to deal with a former spouse at a funeral.

"Thank you." She hit us both with a wan smile. "As a historian, most of the people I 'work with,' in a sense, are dead." *Just like a mortician!* "But there's always something poignant about death, and never more so than the death of someone who shared one's youth. Enough of that! I don't have time to be maudlin. There's something I need to tell you. Can we talk?"

Mac didn't bother to answer; he just started walking out the front double-doors and toward the far end of the driveway, with the mayor and me following like a couple of ducklings.

"I'm very disturbed by this morning's paper," Saylor-Mackie said as soon as we were safe from prying ears.

I'd expected to hear something like that from Ralph.

"There's not much you can do about letters to the editor," I said. "This whole business will blow itself out in a couple of days unless it gets some more oxygen."

"What?" For a moment her face was a study in puzzlement. Then she understood. "Oh, Talton, you mean. Never mind him. I was referring to the front-page story about Noah's murder. The focus on that poppycock in his hand, the romance novel, is most unfortunate. I'm afraid that eventually someone may wonder who Rosamund DeLacey is. And if they find out, that could be very damaging to St. Benignus and to me."

Mac raised an eyebrow. "I take it that you already know?"

Lesley Saylor-Mackie, mayor of Erin and head of the History Department at St. Benignus College, the most dignified of women, looked like she would rather be anywhere else on earth—even on a TV game show.

"I'm afraid so," she said miserably. "*I* am Rosamund DeLacey."

Chapter Sixteen
Nom de Plume

"I know I should have told you earlier," Saylor-Mackie said later in her office at St. Benignus, "but I never dreamed that anyone would think my little secret had anything to do with Noah's murder. Besides, I had this silly idea that I could *keep* it a secret."

Our confab in the parking lot had ended prematurely when Mo approached our trio. That was just a couple of minutes before the start of the funeral.

"Thank you for coming, Mayor," Mo had said. With Noah Bartlett having no close relatives, she seemed to have assumed the role of funeral hostess. "Noah always seemed to enjoy talking to you. You're a good customer."

Saylor-Mackie had smiled wanly. "Call it quid pro quo. Noah carried a lot of my books."

Who would have guessed that she meant titles like *Love's Sweet Sting* and *Love's Forbidden Embrace* as well as *William Howard Taft: Mr. Chief Justice*?

Popcorn had been addicted to Rosamund DeLacey's bodice-rippers for years, little suspecting that behind that romantic nom de plume lay the gracious Lesley Saylor-Mackie. I had tried to wrap my head around that all during the funeral, but my head wasn't buying it. And now, post-funeral, Mac and I were huddled with the historian for an explanation.

"Silly doesn't begin to say it, Professor." I was in no mood to hold her hand. "Your ex-husband, who very few people know was your ex-husband, was found dead clutching a book that you wrote while hiding behind a pseudonym. Yeah, I think you should have told us earlier. A communications director likes to know these things."

"I'm sorry, Jeff. I can only say that I've been deeply upset and wasn't thinking clearly."

I'll say! It would have been impolite to bang my head against her wall, but don't think I wasn't tempted. How could somebody so book-smart be so dumb, no matter how discombobulated by the murder of an old lover? She should have told Oscar about her relationship with Noah and her secret life as Rosamund DeLacey right away. Her not doing that was going to look suspicious as hell if Oscar found out now.

Mac cleared his throat. "I have to confess, Lesley, that I am astonished to learn of your, er, non-scholarly literary endeavors."

She sighed. "You're being kind. I know you must be shocked and appalled that I would write such drivel."

The thought had occurred to me, but I kept my mouth shut. That was my professional training coming through.

Mac squirmed in his chair, which was no easy task because the thing was only slightly bigger than his rump. "I suspect that the story of your alter ego is an interesting one."

"Not really. Sorry to disappoint you. There wasn't much to it. Like a lot of intelligent, educated women, I began to read romance novels for relaxation when I was doing a lot of heavy research for the Taft book. After the first dozen or so, which I read in a couple of weeks, I thought, 'I could write better than that.' So I quit reading the romance and started writing it in my off-hours from scholarship. I regarded it as an innocent pleasure. It was fun and it helped me de-stress. Don't look at me like that, Jeff."

I can't help it if I have an expressive face.

"I finished my first romance novel about the same time I started the actual writing of *Mr. Chief Justice*. I didn't think anything more about it for a couple of years while I worked like a demon on my historical magnum opus. But when I finished, there was a kind of emptiness. The biggest project of my life was over and I had nothing to replace it. Then one day I found the manuscript of *Love's Dying Ember*, which I had completely forgotten about. On a lark, I sent it to the biggest publisher of paperback romances. But I couldn't use my own name. Who took Erich Segal seriously as a classics scholar after he wrote *Love Story*?"

She lost me there. *Love Story* was an old movie that I'd never seen and didn't want to. Was it also a book?

"Besides," Saylor-Mackie added, "my work was somewhat graphic, shall we say."

Mac nodded. "Yes, we shall."

"As I said, it helped me de-stress. But I didn't think Father Pirelli would approve of my prose. So I invented the name Rosamund DeLacey. That sounded to me like someone who would write *Love's Dying Ember*. The book was accepted by the publisher faster than I thought possible, and then it sold more copies than I dared dream."

"So you had to write more," I said.

"I never even thought of *not* doing so. The extra income was welcome—we had two children in college at the time, not at St. Benignus, and Gulliver hadn't yet made his pile. But there was more to it than that. The thought of living this secret life as a romance writer was exhilarating. So I wrote more—one every nine or ten months. It was actually kind of addictive after a while."

"You enjoyed your success, and yet you dare not trumpet it because it conflicted with your academic persona," Mac said.

She nodded. "Exactly. This may not hurt my political career—it might even help—but it would ruin my chances of ever advancing in college administration."

There—she'd almost said it. While she hadn't confirmed in so many words that she would like to succeed Ralph as provost, as widely speculated in our little groves of academe, she didn't have to draw me a map.

"So what this comes down to is that you have a dark secret," I said. I hope I didn't emphasize the last two words, like Dr. Evil in the Austin Powers flicks, but I may have. "Did Noah know that?" Maybe Lynda's conviction that Noah Bartlett's dying clue pointed to the author of *Love's Dark Secret* was on the money.

"He knew that I'm Rosamund DeLacey, yes." Saylor-Mackie's tone verged on the defiant. It wasn't a tone of voice that I would have used in her position, but I cut her slack for being under tension. "That's why he had a lot of my books. We'd become friends again. I told you that. I certainly had no fear that he was going to tell anyone about it, if that's what you're thinking."

That's just what I was thinking.

"Did the plot of *Love's Dark Secret* have anything to do with Noah?" Mac asked.

She looked horror-stricken. "No, not at all. What could it possibly have to do with him?"

"I have no idea." If Mac had added "old girl," it would have sounded perfectly natural. "I am simply trying to find some connection between this book and someone Noah knew."

"The obvious connection is that I wrote the book and Noah knew that I wrote the book, but I have no idea why he had it in his hand. Perhaps it means nothing."

"That is conceivable," Mac acknowledged. But I could tell he didn't believe that. Deep in his romantic, mystery-loving heart, he didn't *want* to believe it. He longed for the dying clue.

Mac shifted uncomfortably in his seat once again. "Mo said that you were a good customer at Pages Gone By. You mentioned in our conversation yesterday that you lunched with Noah occasionally. It appears that you two were in frequent contact."

"We had a lot of lost time to make up."

"You assured me yesterday that your husband was not jealous. Are you totally confident of that?"

She didn't hesitate for a nanosecond. "Totally. I made it a point to tell him in advance every time I saw Noah so that some gossip didn't mention it to him first. If he had any problem with that, I would have been the first to know. We are very frank with each other, Mac."

All of a sudden, I had a scary idea. "You didn't happen to meet Noah for dinner the night before he died, did you?"

Mac beamed. "Excellent question, Jefferson!"

Saylor-Mackie shook her head. "No. We never did dinner. Why do you ask?"

"Because Mo said he had a date, or at least an appointment, with somebody for dinner that night, presumably a woman. I'm glad it wasn't you."

Despite her assurances, an objective observer would have been casting Gulliver Mackie for the role of jealous husband—and Jonathan Hawes for jealous boyfriend. Which of them would I prefer? Jonathan, of course—he had no connection to St. Benignus. But I liked him.

Suddenly, I had a brainstorm. Saylor-Mackie may have been sure that Noah wouldn't spill the beans about her embarrassing alter ego, but that didn't mean he couldn't have threatened his landlord—Mackie—with it in the effort to save his bookstore.

"You realize that Gulliver's innocence may be beside the point," Mac said, ignoring my unspoken thought. "The wheels of justice sometimes grind slowly. There is a lot of smoke here even if there is no fire."

She nodded like a bobble-head. "And, needless to say, the prosecutor won't be inclined to cut me or Gulliver any slack. In Marvin Slade's new position as chairman of the other party, it's his side job to help his mayoral candidate beat me in November. Mac, you've got to help us."

Mac raised an eyebrow. "We would be happy to do so. How might we be of service?"

"You've got to solve Noah's murder, of course—and do it as soon as possible."

Now, why didn't we think of that?

Chapter Seventeen
Roman à Clef?

Back at Mac's office some minutes later, I was still trying to picture the stately Lesley Saylor-Mackie as a prolific romance writer. That didn't work for me, but it explained one thing: "Do you remember Mo telling us that Noah said something about how it was ironic that his ex-wife used to dis his low-brow taste in literature because he read mystery novels?"

Mac pulled a cigar out of his breast pocket. "Indeed I do. That makes eminent sense now that we know that his critical former spouse is guilty of somewhat less-than-edifying literature herself. Mo knew more than she thought." He paused from firing up his smoke. "I cannot escape a nebulous feeling I have had—a sense that she told us something else worth paying attention to, something that struck me as somehow out of place. Oh, well, it will come to me."

Not waiting for that, I hit him with my notion about Gulliver Mackie.

"Maybe Noah tried to blackmail him over his wife's secret life," I said. "Even if it's true that he would never tell, as the mayor insists, Mackie couldn't know that for sure."

My brother-in-law regarded me with respect. "Ingenious! Perhaps you should return to fiction writing, Jefferson. However, I believe you have forgotten something."

"Which, of course, you are going to remind me about."

He nodded and puffed. "Gulliver has an alibi—the mayor."

And we presumed that she was telling the truth—because if she weren't, that would be bad for St. Benignus.

"Oh. Yeah, I see what you mean. Well, I hope you have another idea to replace that one."

It would be unfair to describe Sebastian McCabe as smirking, but "self-satisfied" would be a good label for the look on his face. "As a matter of fact, I believe I do. Oscar's roman à clef has inspired me. Perhaps Noah wrote his own novel based on a secret, a dark secret that someone would kill to keep from seeing the light of day even in a fictionalized account. This book could have been where he expected to get the windfall to pay his back rent."

My face must have registered the skepticism I was feeling. I have seven unpublished mystery novels tucked away in a trunk in my garage.

"Instant success in any literary genre is hardly something to bank on, I grant you, Jefferson. However, we have all heard the siren song of the e-book sensation, the unknown writer who makes a hundred thousand dollars self-publishing on Kindle. Perhaps Noah had unrealistic expectations, particularly in light of the damage e-books were doing to his business."

E-books, e-cigarettes—what next, e-food?

"I guess it's possible," I allowed. "But he never talked about a current writing project at the Poisoned Pens meetings."

"That is inconclusive. Some writers prefer to keep their work to themselves until they are ready to spring it fully formed, like Athena coming out of the head of Zeus."

Whatever.

I could see that Mac wasn't dropping this idea easily, but I wasn't out of objections to it. "Why be coy about this book, which I am pretty sure is about as mythical as Athena and her daddy? The whole point of the Poisoned Pens is to share and critique our work. But if Noah really did write such a book, and that's why he was killed, then the killer would have deleted it from the computer."

"My understanding, admittedly limited, is that nothing is ever truly deleted from a hard drive."

He had me there. "But you'd need an expert to find it."

"Meanwhile, I suggest that we ask Mo. If anyone would know whether Noah was writing a book, it would be his daily work companion."

Or maybe the woman he had dinner with the night before he died. I'm not sure why I didn't say that out loud. Maybe it was because I didn't have the time. Right then the Indiana Jones ring tone on my smartphone told me I had a call. Popcorn's face filled the screen, which reminded me I should get a special ring tone for her—maybe something jazzy by Sinatra.

"Cody here," I answered. "How may I disappoint you today?"

"It's not me you have to worry about, Boss. Talton is heading your way, and he's not in a good mood. Sorry. He made me tell him where you are."

"Thanks for the warning, Traitor."

Mac raised an eyebrow at the histrionics.

"It's Talton," I told him. "He's coming here to talk to me. I don't think he's bringing flowers."

"Well, you did want to speak to him, old boy."

That was true enough; I was just having trouble shifting gears to get my head back into the job I was getting paid to do.

"Jeff Cody!" I would have recognized that raspy voice from the YouTube video even if I hadn't met him once before.

I stood up. "Professor Talton! We've been trying to reach you."

Although he was a head shorter than me, the full Karl Marx beard and the impressive scowl on his face telegraphed the message that he was a force to be reckoned with.

He ignored my outstretched hand. "I've been away. That's no excuse for you throwing me to the jackals of the PC patrol."

"I did no such thing!"

He snorted. "The hell you didn't. I read your quotes—a lot of bullshit about academic freedom. I'm the victim of a high-tech lynching and you're covering the college's collective ass."

Stay cool, Cody. "What would you have me do, Professor?"

He arched his back, reminding me of a bantam rooster. "Defend me! Support my scholarship!"

Unconsciously, I found myself backing up. "I offered your department chair a chance to say something more specific if she wished, but she liked my approach." *Hey, I just work here!*

Talton snorted. "Saylor-Mackie!"

"She *is* your boss. I think you need to be talking to her about your concerns, and I think she might have a few that she wants to discuss with you."

Somehow this wasn't going right. Talton was causing St. Benignus a major PR headache, but he had me on the defensive. My words came out all right in the end, but it was all I could do to keep myself from apologizing.

"I am curious," Mac announced, his first words since Talton had barged into his messy office.

"You're McCabe," Talton retorted. *Amazing deduction, Holmes!* "Curious about what?"

"A high-tech lynching, you said."

"That's right—YouTube, Twitter, Facebook, all that!"

"Who is holding the rope?"

"Eh? Don't talk in riddles, man."

"Your metaphor of a lynching presumes a hangman. Who do you believe is out to get you?"

"The people who are calling for my head, of course! That's a remarkably stupid question."

Stupid is not a word that has ever been used to describe Sebastian McCabe, whose IQ is higher than my bowling score. "What I really meant was, who do you think posted the video?" he said.

"I'm not worried about that, McCabe. The problem isn't what I said in the video. I've been saying that for years and I'll keep saying it. Maybe whoever put it on YouTube was a right-thinking undergrad who wanted to share my wisdom with the broader world."

Mac didn't look like he bought that. "I wonder about that. When was the recording made?"

"I didn't even know there *was* a recording. It was made without my knowledge. From looking at it, I'd say it was done last semester."

"Did you have any disgruntled students?"

"Of course not. They all love me."

"All of them?" I said with the appropriate measure of skepticism.

"Why shouldn't they? I'm the best teacher they've ever had."

We met Mo after work over coffee at Beans & Books. She had closed Pages Gone By for a day of mourning, but would be back in business on Saturday—at least until Gulliver Mackie kicked her out. As the employee, she would be allowed to continue operating the business with the proceeds going to the estate that she would eventually inherit.

She'd changed her clothes from the funeral, into a blue-striped blouse and tan slacks, but she still had a funereal air. After a few preliminaries about how the funeral went and who showed up and all that, Mac asked if Noah had said anything to her about a work in progress.

"Yeah, as a matter of fact, he was writing a novel," she said. "He called it 'high-concept.'"

"Why didn't he share it with the group?" I asked.

"I don't know if he had anything to share yet. He only mentioned this to me maybe a week ago. Maybe he was just in the plotting stage."

"Did he hint at what the book was about?" Mac asked.

Mo shrugged. "Just that it was a mystery. No surprise there."

"Did he indicate, perchance, that it was based on something that actually happened?"

She wrinkled the brow beneath her bangs in thought. "I don't think so. But I can't really remember one way or the other."

Mac fiddled with his beard and then drummed his fingers on the table. I don't know whether he was driving me nuts on purpose or that was just a side benefit for him.

"Mo," he said finally, "would you be willing to look in Noah's computer at the office and see whether he had begun writing a mystery novel on it? The chances that you will find anything are quite remote. He may have another computer at home or the killer may have deleted the novel from the computer or Noah may have never written a word. Still, it is a possibility worth exploring."

That was all he had? I could have come up with that.

"Sure," Mo said. "I'll do it when I get in the store tomorrow morning. But why would the killer bother to wipe out a novel?"

"Just a notion I have about the motive. Perhaps it will come to nothing."

Mo leaned forward, looking fresh and eager and younger than her forty-something years. "I have a notion of my own."

"Spill," I said.

"I think we should invite Dr. Bloomie to come to the store."

Mac raised an eyebrow. I give him credit for not exploding. "To what end?"

"To see the scene of the crime. I know you pooh-poohed the idea that she could help solve the murder, Mac, but maybe if she actually saw where it happened she'd spot something significant that we missed. Maybe we're all too close to the subject."

"On the surface, that sounds plausible. However, the record shows that acquaintance, even friendship, with victims, killers, and crime scenes has not impaired my efforts in the past."

Except for local pride, I was no big fan of Dr. Bloomie. Like all TV doctors, she was more TV than doctor. But I was enjoying Mac's ego-induced unease.

"What have we got to lose?" I said. "You aren't actually afraid that she might crack the case, are you?"

If looks could kill, I would have been at least severely wounded.

"Of course not, Jefferson. Do not be absurd. Very well, then. Never let it be said that Sebastian McCabe left a stone unturned. However, I do not know Dr. Bloomingdale and I have no special pull to get her here."

Mo smiled. "I'm sure she knows you and that would be pull enough. But I'll see if I can reach her. I read once that she tapes *The Shrinks* in Chicago once a week, so that could be a problem. But I bet telling the receptionist that I found Noah's body will get me through to her wherever she is. She'll probably think I need counseling."

"Maybe that's not a bad idea, some counseling." I put a brotherly hand on her shoulder. "That experience may have affected you in ways you haven't fully processed yet."

She shook her head. "No, I'm fine, Jeff. Thanks for caring. Jonathan's helping me get through this. He's been just wonderful."

Jonathan—the potentially jealous boyfriend!

"That reminds me," I said. "You and Noah were obviously good friends or he wouldn't have left you the store. You said he took a fatherly interest in you, but he was a handsome man only about fifteen years or so older than you." I paused. There was no delicate way to say this. "Did Jonathan ever appear to take Noah's interest amiss?"

She paused long enough to make it clear she was thinking about it, but not so long that it seemed to be a hard question. "Never. Don't tell me you two suspect *Jonathan?*"

"Only one of us does," Mac rumbled.

"I don't suspect him," I said defensively. "I was just, uh, exploring a possibility."

"Well, explore no more," she fired with some heat, but not enough to burn. "First of all, it's a stupid idea and you should know better because you know Jonathan. And besides . . . well, he was with me that morning."

"That early?" On the job, I usually know when to keep my mouth shut. After hours, it's hit and miss.

"Yes, that early and the night before, too," she snapped. "We had a lot to talk about."

Is that what they call it?

"I see," said Mac.

"No you don't. When all the talking was finished, we got engaged that morning. We drank champagne for breakfast and woke up my girls and told them."

When I could finally talk, I said, "That's great, Mo! Congratulations!"

"Felicitations, indeed!" my brother-in-law added.

Mo smiled. "We haven't told anybody but the kids. It just doesn't seem right to be so happy with Noah dead. I'll start spreading the word next week."

It wasn't until later that I realized that Mo and Jonathan each provided the other's alibi for the time of Noah's murder—which meant that, as with the Mackies, neither alibi was worth very much.

Chapter Eighteen
Playing with Oscar

"If Mo is marrying Jonathan Hawes, she doesn't have much of a motive for doing away with Noah," Lynda observed the next morning. "Hawes must have gobs of money. It was a harebrained idea anyway."

This was one time I thought it better not to agree with my beloved spouse. Love means never having to say, "I told you so." But I was gratified that her suspicion of Mo was dead and buried.

Getting ready to leave for the first Saturday morning practice of her all-girl softball team this season, Lynda filled out her Cincinnati Reds T-shirt better than any player who ever lived. And I loved the way her honey-colored locks were gathered in a ponytail that spilled out the back of her ball cap.

A car horn honked. "That's Polly. See you later." Lynda gave me an all-too-quick smooch and bounded out the door and into an aging blue Civic driven by Triple M, who made a very short shortstop. On the way out she grabbed a banana for breakfast, which I had to approve as being healthful if not substantial. I had other plans for breakfast.

Daniel's Apothecary has been frozen in time since about 1959, judging by the jukebox, the Route 66 clock and the posters of Elvis Presley, Marilyn Monroe, and James Dean on the walls. Why change what works? The Daniel family has been serving up prescriptions on one side of the building and food on the other since 1904. Since it's located on Main Street, next to the offices of the *Erin Observer and News-Ledger*, Lynda and I meet there a lot. But this time I was meeting somebody else. Two of them.

Sebastian McCabe was already waiting for me at one of the black and chrome tables, drinking coffee.

"What, no milkshake?" I said. At Daniel's they're made with Hershey ice cream.

"Sometimes my self-control amazes even me, old boy."

Vern, a round woman who has been cheerfully taking orders at Daniel's since before I came to Erin, poured me a decaf without asking. She had a glass carafe in each hand, and mine came out of the one with an orange handle. "The usual, hon?" She meant the food.

"Why not?" I said.

"I will also have my customary breakfast," Mac said. "But please hold our orders for—oh, here he comes."

And Oscar made three. Before even sitting down he ordered a Buddy Holly, which is steak and eggs with Texas toast.

"How goes the case, Chief?" I asked. I'd opted for the neutral approach, as opposed to saying something provocative like, "Arrested anybody yet?"

He scowled. "I got a visit from Marvin Slade. He wanted to discuss the investigation. That's never fun. He's a good prosecutor, but he's also a political animal. I don't want to get caught in the crossfire between him and the mayor and wind up collateral damage."

"That's tricky," I said sympathetically. *Just stay away from Saylor-Mackie and her husband. That will make it easier.*

Oscar nodded gloomily.

"What is it that Slade wants of you?" Mac asked.

"He's pushing me to take a hard look at Gulliver Mackie."

"On what grounds?" *I can think of several.*

"The guy is a little dodgy. There's never been any implication that his investment business isn't strictly on the up and up. It's not a Ponzi scheme or anything like that. But he spreads so much money around in political campaigns you have to think he expects a little something in return."

"Oh, come on!" I threw up my hands and almost hit Vern as she brought Mac's sausage and gravy (the Fats Domino) and my stack of buttermilk pancakes (the Beaver Cleaver). Hey, don't judge me. It was Saturday, and they were whole wheat.

"Slade and all of his candidates have contributors, too," I went on. "You know the old saying, 'money is the mother's milk of politics.'" My companions looked at me with blank faces. "Well, you should know it. And there's nothing nefarious about Mackie parting with some of his cash—I mean, nothing more than usual. I'm sure his largesse helped his wife's career."

"And that's another thing," Oscar said with his mouth full. "His wife."

"The mayor," Mac said.

"Your boss," I added, just to underline his point.

"Yeah, yeah, her." Oscar looked around and lowered his voice. "I could never see those two together. He's big money and all, but he doesn't have her class. They make an odd couple."

"Love is irrational," I pointed out.

Mac begged to differ. "Love is intentional. Passion is irrational. Are you implying some marital discord in the Mackie household that could have a bearing on the case, Oscar?"

Like maybe, for example, some fallout from the teenage marriage and current friendship between Saylor-Mackie and Noah Bartlett?

Oscar sighed heavily. "I dunno. Just grasping at straws, I guess." He shoveled food into his mouth in consolation. "So far routine police work isn't cutting it on this case and my plan to make the killer overconfident hasn't paid off yet. That leaves me approximately nowhere."

At least you're not alone. Mac and I had possibilities, scenarios, and outright guesses, but nothing more substantial than cotton candy. That is, of course, unless Mac wasn't telling me something. It wouldn't be the first time.

Sebastian McCabe, not one to kick a man when he's down—at least, not Oscar—was all empathy. "Come, come, surely you exaggerate. You and the estimable Gibbons must have made some progress. What have you learned?"

"Okay, let's lay it all out. Pages Gone By was a failing business. Mo Russert seems like a smart gal, so she probably knew that. Not much of a money motive there for her, even though she inherits the business and it's widely known that she did want to own her own bookstore.

"Noah Bartlett wasn't making lease payments and his landlord, the First Gentleman of our fair city, was about to kick him out. That would benefit Mr. Mackie, who probably prefers tenants who actually pay, and a dude named Charles Bexley who wants to open a hoity-toity brew pub there. Bartlett's death would have helped them if he was about come up with his back rent, which Bartlett claimed he was. Have I left anything out?"

"*Love's Dark Secret,*" Mac said immediately.

Oscar snorted. "So what am I supposed to do, arrest Rosamund DeLacey?"

Let's change the subject. "Dr. Bloomie, Erin's own Sigmunda Freud, thinks the murder weapon is significant," I pointed out. "If Mary Lou Springfield had her way, you'd arrest the entire membership of the Poisoned Pens, except for her."

"In that case, I guess I'd have to arrest myself since I guess I'm kind of a member now." His chuckle was short-lived. "Okay. What do you guys have? You gotta have something, and I want it."

Mac and I looked at each other. We had to give him something. He'd never believe that Mac had come up completely empty-handed. But we couldn't throw the mayor under the bus by telling him what she should have told him herself on Day One.

"We already told you that Mo recalled that Noah mentioned having a dinner date the night he died."

Oscar nodded. "And she doesn't know with who." I almost said "with whom," a knee-jerk correction, but I know a lost cause when it's eating steak and eggs right in front of me.

"Indeed," Mac acknowledged. "That is an angle for you to pursue."

Pursue it as far away from St. Benignus as you can get.

"I put Gibbons on it," Oscar said. "Nothing yet."

Mac spread his hands. "We can but try—the motto of the firm."

Oscar concentrated on cleaning his plate.

"How's the novel going?" I asked him.

"So-so."

"Just taking a wild guess, I bet the police chief is the hero."

"Hey, good guess! In my book, the crime is solved by dogged police work. See, I'm making it realistic."

"You mean like, for instance, taking real people—people who are your friends—and putting them in your book under other names and then making them look ridiculous?"

Oscar almost spit out his coffee. I don't know if it was my question or the accusatory tone of my voice. He eyed me suspiciously. "What are you implying?"

"Ahem," Mac said. "I am sure Jefferson is not implying anything."

Right. I'm saying it flat-out.

"Hey, none of the characters in my book are based on real people, living or dead, and any resemblance to you guys is purely coincidental."

Instead of reacting to that big fat fib, I said, "What's Popcorn's name in the book?"

"Mela—" He shut up in mid-name and ostentatiously looked at the Timex on his wrist. "Hey, look at the time. I'd better haul ass." *That will take two trips, Oscar.* "Speaking of Popcorn, I'm supposed to meet her at the Farmer's Market."

"Before you take your leave," Mac said, "tell us more about your novel. I am most intrigued by this literary endeavor."

I thought Oscar would take another theatrical gander at his watch, but he didn't; this was a question he was happy to answer.

"It's kind of a locked room mystery, but with a twist. This guy, what you call an eccentric, is killed in a fancy treehouse. The only way in or out is through one of those little glass elevators. There are no windows—it's one big room with books on three sides and a desk with a big painting on the fourth. The victim actually *liked* closed-in spaces. When his administrative assistant shows up in the morning, the elevator is at the top. She figures he's up there, nothing unusual about that. She brings it down, rides it back up, and finds the body. Get it? The only way for the killer to get out was through the elevator—only he didn't, because the elevator was still at the treehouse level."

"What would prevent the killer from taking the elevator down, then on the way out pressing the button for the upper floor to send it back up?" Mac asked.

Oscar looked smug. "This elevator needs a key to operate for security purposes. I told you the victim was eccentric."

"How do we know the administrative assistant didn't do it?" I asked.

"Because she's the police chief's girlfriend!"

"Excellent!" Mac beamed. "You have created a nice little problem. However, what about the housing code? A second exit is mandatory, is it not?"

The chief law enforcement officer of Erin, Ohio, shrugged off the legal issue. "The guy who built it didn't sleep there. It was his office. Maybe it's still covered by the housing code and maybe it's not, but this guy's above that. And if the city had a different idea, he would fight it in court for years if he had to. I told you he was eccentric, which means he was both wacko and rich."

"Gosh, Oscar, that sounds a lot like Jonah Wittle," I said. "What an amazing coincidence that Erin's most prominent architect has announced plans to build a three-hundred-thousand-dollar treehouse and use it as an office."

"Oh, has he?" Oscar's innocent tone wouldn't have fooled my Aunt Tilly, if I had one.

"Oscar, you amaze me."

"Thanks."

That wasn't a compliment.

"So what's the gimmick? How does the killer get out of the treehouse without taking the elevator down to the ground level?"

"Beats me," Oscar said. "That's why it's such a great mystery."

Oscar was clearly a pantser, a seat-of-the pants writer. But he'd gotten his pants caught in a treehouse.

Chapter Nineteen
Return to the Scene of the Crime

"It's a puzzler, you have to admit that," I told Mac as we walked from Daniel's over to Pages Gone By. Mo had called to say she had something to show us, and that Dr. Bloomie had agreed to meet us at the bookstore.

"Indeed." Mac puffed meditatively on an after-breakfast cigar. "Oscar has conceived a situation worthy of John Dickson Carr, the undisputed master of the locked room mystery. I can only think of three solutions. It will be interesting to see what Oscar comes up with, if anything."

"I predict a severe case of writer's block, followed by Oscar adopting a new hobby."

Only two people were in the bookstore when we got there—Mo Russert and Gulliver Mackie. I don't claim to be as adept at reading male-female body language as Popcorn, but even I could tell the tension between them was thicker than a London fog.

Mo turned toward the door and gave us a tired smile as we walked in "Hey, Jeff, Mac."

Mackie, dressed in a sports shirt and chinos for a Saturday morning, offered a perfunctory "Good morning." I felt about as welcome as an ant at a picnic.

"Mr. Mackie was just evicting me," Mo said with a sad counterfeit of her usual cheerfulness.

Mackie frowned. He knew bad PR when he heard it. "Hardly that. I was making sure that she understood the status of her lease. It wouldn't be fair for her to be surprised when I take the building back."

You're all heart.

"I admire your restraint," I said acidly. "You waited until the day after Noah was buried."

He looked hurt, I'll give him that. "I wouldn't be here if Ms. Russert weren't open for business. I'm sincerely sorry about Noah, and I'm sure Ms. Russert is devastated, but obviously she has recognized that business is business and life has to go on."

What really steamed me about that self-serving sermon is that I couldn't think of a comeback. I still can't, which really worries me because it might mean that Mackie had a point. But Mac knew what to say.

"I look forward to Mr. Bexley's new enterprise," he proclaimed. "I am quite fond of lager, ale, stout, and porter, especially when locally brewed in small batches." He gave his large head a slow, sad shake. "However, this store is a treasure, and Erin will be poorer without it."

So there!

"If there's a market for it, I'm sure that somebody will start another used-book store. Or if you can come up with a better business plan than your boss had, Ms. Russert, maybe an investor will help you move to another location."

"I doubt it," Mo said.

"Well, I wish you the best." The landlord offered his hand all around. I took it, but I wasn't happy about it. Gulliver Mackie was no comic book or musical comedy villain, just a guy trying to make a few (million) bucks. I totally got it that he didn't invest in buildings so that they could be occupied rent-free. But I couldn't help but think what the end of Pages Gone By would mean to my friend Mo, and to a lesser extent the Poisoned Pens, Triple M's science-fiction book club, and the other groups that gathered here.

As the door closed behind Mackie, Mo let out a heavy sigh. "Have a great day, Mr. Scrooge," she muttered.

"Do not despair," Mac said. "He may be right that there is a way to salvage your dream. Erin is a very literate community. At this moment, however, I confess to being more concerned about justice for Noah, by which I mean finding his murderer."

Mo set her jaw. "So am I."

"Did you find a novel on his computer?"

She shook her head, sending her bangs flying. "No, but I did find this." She held up a handsome red leather notebook, about five inches by seven. "I was just starting to look at it when Mackie showed up."

"I should have expected that," Mac said. "Every writer keeps a journal of some sort. Noah even alluded to having 'a whole notebook full' of ideas, I believe he said."

Noah's certainly had class, being leather and all. My journal says "Hogwarts" on the outside. I bought it on sale at Walgreen's.

"May I look inside?" Mac asked. If he were any more eager he would have had to wipe the drool out of his beard.

"Sure." Mo handed it over. I stood behind Mac as he opened it to the first page. The word *"Titles"* was written across the top.

I channeled Sherlock Holmes. "Noah wrote with a fountain pen, I see."

Mac nodded. "It was a Waterman Edson."

Gravity did a number on my jaw because skepticism asserted itself. "You made that up."

"By no means, old boy! Noah always carried a pen in his shirt pocket, and always an Edson."

Only later did it occur to me that, all writers having various eccentric practices, he might have kept a special pen just for writing in his journal. Not that it mattered.

"Silly me," Mo said sweetly. "I thought you'd want to see what he wrote, not what he wrote it with."

Point taken. Sebastian McCabe has no shame, but my face must have turned as red as my hair.

"It is rather sad to contemplate the unfulfilled promise behind these prospective book titles Noah wrote down," Mac said. "*Bookmarked for Murder,* for example. Why, that could refer to—"

A loud knocking came from the back of the shop.

"Maybe that's Dr. Bloomie," Mo said as she rushed toward the sound.

She let the TV psychologist in the back door.

"So this is Pages Gone By," I heard the psychologist say as she stepped over the threshold. "I've only walked by, I'm ashamed to say."

Why do people seem shorter in person than in the movies or on television? I'm sure they aren't always, but every big screen or small screen personality that I've seen close up turned out to be shorter than I expected. Not that Dr. Bloomie was vertically challenged. She stood about five-seven, half a foot below my eye level.

Even in a plaid shirt and tan slacks she looked like she could take up modeling if the supply of people needing counseling dried up. Her make-up was faultless. She wore a gold strand around her neck and her matching gold cuff bracelet, proving that her fashion sense hadn't taken the weekend off.

"You must be Ms. Russert," she said.

"Yes, I'm Mo."

"Please call me 'Bloomie.' Almost everybody does, even my patients. How awful all of this must be for you. I hope I can be of some help." All of her attention was focused on Mo as she spoke to her. But then she pivoted, turning our way and there was nobody else in the universe but us. "Sebastian McCabe, I've wanted to meet you for a long time. And Mr. Cody, I've so enjoyed your books of Professor McCabe's cases."

Aw shucks.

She was good, oozing professionalism and empathy in equal measure. As she stood next to the much taller Mac, with her blond hair cascading over one shoulder in a very feminine way, it suddenly struck me again that the two were rivals of a sort—competitors in solving Noah Bartlett's murder. But if she had any sense of that, she didn't show it.

"Now," Dr. Bloomie said, "explain to me again how you think I can help."

She said that to Mo, but Mac answered before Mo had a chance. "We understand that you had a relationship with Noah Bartlett."

Her response was quick and clear. "A relationship? No, of course not. That would have been completely inappropriate." There was that word again— "inappropriate."

Mac raised an eyebrow. "I apologize for my lack of clarity. I meant to say that you had a *professional* relationship with Noah. I am not certain whether the ethics of your profession will allow you to acknowledge that, but if we did not already know it for a fact, your reaction just now confirmed it. Your professional relationship with him is undoubtedly what made a personal one 'completely inappropriate'—it would have been a breach of ethics."

You can see why my brother-in-law always beats me at chess, but the look of satisfaction on his face would have been a major "tell" for anybody facing him across a poker table.

"I think that's beside the point," Mo said hurriedly. "My idea was that coming here might give Dr. Bloomie some additional insights into the mind of the killer."

"Understood," Mac granted with a slight bow. "Our idea was somewhat different." *It was?* "We thought that perhaps Dr. Bloomingdale's professional relationship with

Noah would provide a window into his thoughts, an explanation of his dying clue."

Dr. Bloomie shook her head. "I don't believe he intended to leave one."

Ignoring her, Mac walked the few feet to the romance section with the rest of us following. "Noah died right here with a copy of this book in his hand." He picked up a paperback, one of several of the same title. "*Love's Dark Secret.* Perhaps Noah was pointing to a secret that he had or that someone else had that was the key to his murder. You may be the only person who can shed light on that, Dr. Bloomingdale."

She was a better poker player than Sebastian McCabe, but not so good that I couldn't see that the question jarred her. The "tell" was in the nervous way she fiddled with her shirt collar.

"Whatever I might know about Mr. Bartlett, I couldn't even tell my husband, if I were still married." *Been there! In fact, I seem to live a lot of my life there.* I gave Dr. Bloomie points for alluding to Sam Kincaid, who had left her for a younger woman about four years earlier to general snickers. "The only person who can release me from patient confidentiality is the patient. In this case, that seems highly unlikely to happen."

"Your dedication to the ethical principles established by the American Psychological Association is quite admirable," Mac said. He never used a crowbar when butter was handy. "I knew a lawyer who went to jail rather than break the confidence of a deceased client."

"I hardly think that will be necessary for me, but I have to be a stickler. In my position of public prominence, one lapse would ruin me and damage the profession."

"Do you get anything at all from being here where the murder happened?" Mo asked.

Dr. Bloomie shook her head. "I can't say that I— Where was the murder weapon?"

Three index fingers pointed to where the Maltese Falcon had stood guard over the mystery section. "One would walk past it on the way to where Noah was found," Mac pointed out.

"Yes, I see that," Dr. Bloomie allowed. "One also would walk by those heavy brass bookends shaped like elephants in the religion section and the bust of Shakespeare on that case with the rare books. I stand by my earlier comments that the choice of the Maltese Falcon as the murder weapon was fraught with significance for the killer." She smiled. "But I'm no detective, just a TV psychologist." She took the copy of *Love's Dark Secret* from Mac and held it up to Mo. "I'd like to buy this book."

"That was kind of painful, that 'poor little me' ploy there at the end," I told Mac as soon as our feet hit the sidewalk. "I think she was trying to make us think she doesn't really know anything, which means she really knows something. What do you think?"

Mac paused to light one of his dirigibles, which isn't illegal yet on sidewalks but ought to be. "I would be the last to disagree that she is not a detective! However, her reaction to *Love's Dark Secret* was unmistakable. She knows something. I only hope the killer does not know that she knows."

Chapter Twenty
Dead Man's Journal

That afternoon in Mac's study, Mac paged through Noah Bartlett's journal while I looked over his shoulder. In a neat, unhurried handwriting that made me imagine the author lovingly at work, Noah had written down the raw material of fiction under various categories: *Titles, First Names, Last Names, Full Names, Clothing, Characters,* and *Storylines.*

I could give you examples, but I won't. They belong to Mo now, and she's working on turning some of them into stories under the shared byline of Noah Bartlett and Maureen Russert. Only one paragraph in the journal matters for the purposes of this adventure anyway. It was the second most recent entry under the *Storylines* category, and this is what it said:

> *A famous mystery writer with writer's block calls in another writer, skilled but far less successful, as a ghost writer on a book for which he has a contract. The ghost begins to identify with the writer and his protagonist. This becomes obvious to the writer, who feels threatened—and all the more so when the book is a big seller. The ghost begins to think that the more famous writer wants to get rid of him.*

"What do you make of that, Jefferson?"

"It's a departure from the rest of his notes—a suspense novel, not a whodunit. I don't see any influence of Ellery Queen here."

Mac smiled. "This plot is not in the typical Ellery Queen mold of the traditional detective story, but there may be an EQ influence nonetheless. Anyone with the slightest interest in twentieth-century detective fiction knows that Ellery Queen was the pseudonym of two cousins, Frederic Dannay and Manfred B. Lee. For many years they tried to be coy about how they collaborated, but it eventually became known that Danny was the plotter and Manny was the writer—except when he was not. For Manny suffered periodic attacks of writer's block. A number of the books that appeared under the name of Ellery Queen were written by Theodore Sturgeon or Avram Davidson, both science-fiction writers, from outlines by Fred Dannay."

"And you think that's what gave Noah the idea?"

"I think it is a possibility."

I suddenly felt a chill up my spine.

"I can think of another possibility," I said. Mac cocked an eyebrow. "Noah was a good writer. Suppose he was the ghost writer in this plot he wrote down. I don't mean that he actually thought the writer he was ghosting for wanted to kill him. That was just the creative writer taking a situation and building on it. But what he didn't know is that the writer really *was* willing to kill him."

"You mean because Noah was, in some sense, trying to take over this other writer's career, a sort of literary body snatcher?"

Nice image.

"Maybe. That's what it sounds like Noah had in mind for the character in his book. And if Noah had some kind of mental problem, whatever drove him to Dr. Bloomie a few years ago, maybe he *did* have trouble separating himself in his mind from this other writer. But the motive could be a lot simpler than that. Maybe the writer just didn't want anyone to know that Noah wrote a book under his name."

"What book, old boy? Noah had none on his computer."

"The killer erased it. We always knew that was a possibility." I was on such a roll I was starting to believe myself. "Of course he had a copy of the book in his own computer, which he sent to his agent under his name."

Mac wasn't far behind me. He stroked his beard. "We once encountered a similar motive in a previous case—the concealing of true authorship."

"Exactly. Look, maybe Dr. Bloomie was right about the significance of the murder weapon and Oscar was right about that romance novel in Noah's hand being a false clue. Both point to the mind of a mystery writer."

"By thunder, Jefferson, it does all hang together, I must confess. It is an intriguing and plausible theory. However, I wonder if you have stopped to consider that the only published mystery novelist in Erin is your very obedient servant."

Actually, no I hadn't.

Fortunately, I didn't have to yell *j'accuse!* at my best friend or abandon my beautiful theory. I saw a third possibility.

"The killer doesn't have to live in Erin," I said. "He just had to be here when Noah died. I think we need to talk to Dunbar Yates."

Chapter Twenty-One
New York, New York

So, Monday morning found Jeff Cody and Sebastian McCabe on a plane bound for New York.

Lynda sat next to me.

She squeezed my hand. "I still can't believe we're going to New York."

"I can't either," I mumbled. *This is costing an arm and two legs.*

Don't get the idea that this trip was an easy sell to Sebastian McCabe. I had the feeling that he didn't want to admit that Dr. Bloomie might be on to something about the significance of the murder weapon. Eventually, though, he went along—whether to humor me or to have an excuse to visit Crimes & Punishments Bookshop, I was unsure at the time. But I didn't for one minute think that he really bought into the possibility that his friend Yates had done in Noah Bartlett.

When I'd told Lynda that "we" were going to the Big Apple for a discussion with Dunbar Yates best handled in person, she and I were not the "we" I had in mind. But she was so excited at the prospect that I didn't have the heart to disillusion her. Besides, she deserved a few days off.

The concept of "days off" is an illusion, of course. All three of us had our smartphones with us. I'd barely arrived at the airport when my Google alert for the name "James Gregory Talton" told me that another video of the professor had hit YouTube. He was wearing a different tie this time, so it wasn't from the same lecture. But the subject matter was the same. He looked into the camera as he said:

"All empires have gotten an economic boost from slavery, whether they called it that or not," he declared. "That's how they became empires. I'm talking about Greece, Rome, Great Britain, Brazil, the United States of America—all of them. But that's just in the short run. In the long run, slavery is too expensive to be economically sustainable. It's cheaper to pay people measly wages than it is to feed, clothe, and house them. Who had the stronger economy before the War Between the States—the North or the South? Anybody who says the South is just whistling 'Dixie.'

"So don't give Abraham Lincoln so much credit for his Emancipation Proclamation, which only freed the slaves in the rebel states. Slave owners would have done it themselves eventually! And if Lincoln hadn't blocked secession, the two countries—North and South—would have learned they needed each other. They would have eventually gotten back together or become very close trading partners. There would have been no half a million brave soldiers killed, and no subjugation of the South under Reconstruction."

Lynda, leaning over to watch from the seat next to me in the airport, looked thoughtful. "Does what he's saying make sense, or is Talton a whack job?"

She thinks I know something about economics.

"Probably both. It's not an improbable thesis, and I'm not sure it's unique. But I can't figure out why Talton is so passionate about it. We're a couple of weeks from the hundred and fiftieth anniversary of Abe Lincoln's last trip to the theater. He's been a long time dead."

"And yet, Jefferson," Mac chimed in from the other side, "as you yourself have noted, the memory of our first murdered president still stirs affection in the hearts of his people. Professor Talton's first video evoked strong reactions and I suspect this one will as well. I cannot help but wonder who posted it to YouTube and why."

"What, you don't believe 'TrueAmerican' was the person's real name?"

While Mac's mystery-solving genes had him consumed with the question of who posted the video, I was more concerned with how to deal with the consequences. That is my job, after all. While Lynda flipped through magazines on her tablet and Mac wrote on his laptop during the two-hour flight, I pondered how to react to what I was sure was going to be a second tsunami of attention to Talton. There's nothing the media like more than a "mounting controversy" story.

By the time we landed, I had my three talking points firm in my mind. I try not to have any more than three. They could be turned into a statement if needed.

1. *Slavery, the Civil War, and Abraham Lincoln are all topics that evoke strong emotions and passionate opinions—especially in this sesquicentennial year of President Lincoln's assassination.*

2. *Professor Talton is an expert on those topics and his opinions, while controversial, are not out of the mainstream of academic thought.*

3. *Just as we respect his academic freedom, we also respect the ability of our students to form their own opinions as mature partners in the learning process.*

The first point put the situation into context—emotions are running high here, folks.

I hoped the second part of the second point was true. Was I overly influenced by the pugnacious professor's grievance that the college had insufficiently supportive of him? Possibly. But I also didn't like the idea that somebody was using YouTube to take him down. I'd rather he did that on his own.

The third point was a two-fer, combining the old academic-freedom trope with a reminder that he was teaching grown-ups, not high school kids.

As soon as we landed, I checked my smartphone. Popcorn had sent me a text message. After asking, *"Having fun yet?"* she informed me that a petition drive on change.org was demanding that Talton be fired "for his support of the Confederate States of America, slavery, and slave wages."

I called Ralph even before I picked up my luggage. I wanted to make sure he wasn't going to blow away my finely crafted talking points by giving in to the mob (which at last count numbered 4,000 signatures, none of them local).

"Fired?" he repeated. "Don't be ridiculous. Professor Talton is a scholar." *Unlike Sebastian McCabe, you mean.* So, we were on the same side on this one. That left me a little disoriented. When I regained my equilibrium, I said, "Have there been any complaints from his students, anything that would require a hearing?"

"There's been nothing of the kind." The impatience in Ralph's voice was impossible to miss. He wanted to get back to cutting somebody's budget. "I reviewed the record a couple of hours ago. The only negative in his evaluations is the usual grumbles from C students who think they should have gotten an A. Professor Talton won't bend his standards to accommodate mediocrity. Nevertheless, his classrooms are usually at capacity."

That tracked with what Hadley Reams, the fledgling reporter for the *Spectator*, had told me: Talton was a rock star with his students. I made a mental note to work that into my talking points.

"Okay," I said in a wrapping-up-this-conversation tone. "I'm officially on vacation today, and out of town, but I'm available by cell and I can deal with anything that comes up."

"Very well, Cody. Enjoy your day off."

I strained to hear a hint of sarcasm there, but there wasn't any. I decided that Ralph and I had rubbed each other the wrong way for so long that the rough edges of our relationship were getting smoothed over.

Baggage collected, we took a cab from LaGuardia to the Dumont NYC hotel, where we'd be spending the night. While Lynda freshened up, I put in a couple of calls. The first was to Maggie Barton.

"Consider this an off-the-record tip," I told the veteran reporter. I was sure that Lynda couldn't hear me in the shower. "You ought to find a few students from James Gregory Talton's classes and see what they think of him. His student evaluations are sky-high. I understand his classes are usually closed out, even though his grading standards are high."

"That's a good idea, Jeff. Say, have you heard the latest on Talton?"

"That depends. What's the latest?"

I loved bantering with the old gal.

"There's a new video. In this one he says the, quote, 'American empire' was based on slavery, and he refers to Reconstruction as 'subjugation of the South.' Would you care to comment on that?"

"Sure. Slavery, the American Civil War, and Abraham Lincoln are all topics that evoke strong emotions and passionate opinions . . ."

And so forth.

My next call went to Hadley. He seemed taken aback to hear from me.

"Oh, hi, Mr. Cody."

"I'm in New York and I haven't got long to talk." *Lynda will be out of the shower any minute.* "I just wanted to make a suggestion. You ought to talk to some of Professor Talton's students and see if anybody is planning on starting a petition of support for him."

"Oh! That's a good idea." *Yes, it is. And I'm hoping one of Talton's acolytes will run with it once you ask the question.* "Thanks, Mr. Cody."

"I'm here to help, Hadley."

Just as I was disconnecting, Lynda came out of the bathroom, dressed in a bright green frock with yellow accents.

"How's work?" she said.

"Exhausting."

While Lynda went exploring the canyons of the city, Mac and I called on Dunbar Yates at his Art Deco apartment building on Central Park West.

"Apparently Yates has done well for himself," I observed.

"Indeed," Mac said. "Dunbar married Juliet Axe, who inherited one fortune and got divorced from another."

So he wasn't dependent on book sales to keep him in cigarettes and beer.

We barely made it over the threshold before Yates lit into us.

"What in the *hell* is with that professor of yours?" If he hadn't been so dark skinned, he would have turned red. For the first time, I could actually picture an enraged Dunbar Yates as the murderer of Noah Bartlett. Up to now that had just been a theory.

"Could you be more specific?" I asked, although I was at least ninety-nine percent sure I knew who he meant.

"This Talton lunatic. I've been seeing his ugly face all morning on CNN. There's a story in the HuffPost, too."

Mac shrugged. "If the academic environment did not suffer eccentrics, where would I be?"

"Writing even more books, probably. Okay, the hell with Talton. You said on the phone you wanted to talk about the murder of Noah Bartlett. We already did that. I can't believe you came all the way to New York just to resume that conversation."

Yates sat down in one ornate loveseat and Mac and I sat in another, facing him over a glass-topped coffee table. "We had a reason," I said. His in-your-face attitude made it easier for me to be blunt. "Dr. Sydney Bloomingdale is convinced that the murder weapon is a psychological clue, that it had a meaning for the killer other than being the first heavy object at hand. I couldn't help but remember that when you talked to the Poisoned Pens you said that Hammett, was your mystery writing hero. And he wrote *The Maltese Falcon*."

If you didn't see that coming, neither did I—it just snuck up on me on the way to Yates's apartment.

I stopped there. The man had written this scene himself over and over again. Surely I didn't have to connect the dots for him.

Surprisingly, it took Yates a few seconds.

And then he threw back his bald head and burst out laughing. After careful study, I decided there was about a fifty-fifty chance that he was acting, but I've never been good at calculating odds. Looking at Mac, I didn't think he was any more certain than I was.

When Yates finally stopped hooting, he put a look of astonishment on his broad features. "Hey, you're serious."

Mac nodded. "I am afraid that he is."

"And what about you?"

"Let us say, rather, that I am curious. I wondered how you would respond."

"Put me down as somewhere between pissed and puzzled. Why would I want to kill Noah Bartlett? I barely knew the man."

"So you say," I said. "I'm sure Hector Gumm wouldn't settle for that." *Even Beauregard wouldn't settle for that.* "Maybe you knew him better than you've let on. Maybe you knew him so well you had him write a book that writer's block kept you from delivering to your publisher. Let's say that new series you talked about wasn't working out for you. The big payoff that Noah was expecting to bail him out could have been a check from you for secret services rendered. But that might be a secret you would kill to keep from being revealed—more to preserve your reputation than your wallet."

Yates stared. "What? *What?* Okay, now I am *totally* pissed. That plot has more holes than a sieve. It wouldn't even work on television. First of all, I *didn't* know Bartlett very well and I hadn't seen him in years. I didn't even know he had a couple of published short stories to his credit until Mac told me after that night at the bookstore. Secondly, I don't need anybody to write my books for me, and I can show you the manuscripts in my computer if you want. But if I needed a ghost, why would I hire an unknown writer? I can afford a lot better. And thirdly, what kind of a secret is that to kill for? Writers seem almost proud of not writing their books these days. They put both names on the book and call the other guy the co-author."

He was good, I have to admit that. And he'd hardly taken a breath.

Mac raised an eyebrow. "You seem to have covered all the bases."

"Not yet." He got a funny smile on his face. "There's one more thing. I have an alibi."

"Alibi?" I said weakly.

Yates looked at Mac. "Bartlett was killed on that Wednesday morning, right? I was staying at your house. I was with you all morning."

At that moment, Sebastian McCabe was lucky that I wasn't armed with a lethal weapon. Never had I been so angry at him. He must have realized all along that Yates had an iron-clad alibi, and yet he'd let me invest the time and money—*lots of money!*—to come to New York just to humiliate me. Or so I thought, until Mac said in a dangerously mild tone of voice:

"Not quite, Dunbar. You stayed in Jefferson's former apartment above my garage. Noah opened the store for his killer some hours before the normal opening time, presumably to assure secrecy. You could have easily slipped out of the apartment at some early hour of the morning and returned in time for breakfast in our home, leaving Kate and me none the wiser."

The logic wiped the smile off of Yates's face. "Yes, but . . ." At first he had no "but." It took him a while to work out a comeback. "How would I get there? It's miles from your house to downtown Erin. I didn't have a car— you picked me up at the airport—and it was too far to walk. If I'd called a cab there would be a record of that. Check and you'll see that there isn't. This whole idea is ridiculous. I don't need an alibi. But I have one."

"Yes, I realized that Dunbar could make a convincing argument that he had an alibi," Mac said distractedly as we looked for a cab. "However, I wanted to see if he realized that."

"How's that again?" I was still glum.

"Dunbar did not immediately pose the objection that he had no convenient way to get to Pages Gone By early on Wednesday morning. He had to think about it. A guilty man would have been better prepared."

I sighed, defeated and dispirited. "So I guess that's that."

"By no means, old boy!" Mac's cheerfulness was the polar opposite of what I was feeling. "Never let it be said that I failed to fully explore what we might call the Bloomingdale-Cody theory about Noah's dying message. Let us make one more attempt to find some support for it."

He'd lost me.

"Where?"

"At Crimes & Punishments Bookshop."

Crimes & Punishments, located just around the corner from St. Patrick's Cathedral, is like a multi-story shrine for mystery readers. The first floor alone reminds me of Professor Higgins's library in the film version of *My Fair Lady*. And the contents of new and used books are catholic with a small "c." If what you're looking for falls within the broadest possible definition of mystery, whether it's a Hildegarde Withers detective story from the 1930s or the latest Harry Dresden wizard/vampire/werewolf romp, chances are good you will find it at Crimes & Punishments. There are sections devoted to cozies, romantic suspense, hard-boiled, horror, Golden Age, police procedurals, espionage, true crime (where you may have found this book), Sherlockiana, historical mysteries, short stories, and I don't know what all. There's even a section of "how-to" books on magic, reflecting another interest of Alexian Rowe shared by Mac.

Rowe, not yet fifty and already celebrating twenty-five years as the founder and owner of the world's largest mystery bookstore, hurried over to greet us as soon as he got word that Sebastian McCabe was in the house.

"Mac! I wish I'd known that you were coming! I'd have arranged a book-signing!"

The vigor of his hand-pumping matched the enthusiasm of the exclamatory greetings. At six-foot-five or so and lean, Rowe towered over me. And I'm six-one. He wore a three-piece gray suit with a white and purple orchid in his lapel. With his long brown hair combed straight back to just below his collar and a neat goatee decorating his narrow chin, I thought he would have looked perfectly at home in a top hat, like the wonderful Mr. Mysterious in the Sid Fleischman book I'd read as a kid.

"Our visit was not long-planned," Mac rumbled. "Have you heard about the death of your former employee, Noah Bartlett?"

The tall mystery maven turned solemn. "Yes, I have. Dunbar Yates was in on Saturday. He told me Noah was murdered." He shook his head. "I've never known anybody who was murdered."

I wish I could say that.

"As you might imagine, Jefferson and I have taken a particular interest in helping the local authorities untangle this skein. Was Dunbar a particular friend of Noah when the latter worked here?"

Rowe's face was one big question mark. "Not that I know of. I certainly never got that sense. Why do you ask?"

"I was just leaving no stone unturned. In this same vein, do you know why Noah left New York? Apparently he entered treatment with a therapist shortly after returning to Erin."

"As a matter of act, I do. He was in a serious relationship with a woman and she died. It tore him up. He got depressed, went into a downward spiral. I finally had to let him go. He understood."

"Died, you said." I was still stuck back on that.

Rowe nodded mournfully. "Yes, very sad. I met her a few times. She was a nice woman named Jane who lost a three-year battle with breast cancer. There was nothing mysterious about her death, nothing dubious."

"So no brother or father who might have blamed Noah for her demise," Mac muttered.

In other words, we'd hit a dead end.

Chapter Twenty-Two
Speaking Out

When I got back to the hotel room, the little hallway was thronged with shopping bags. Lynda had been busy. Seeing the look of horror on my face, she said, "It's mostly Christmas gifts."

Oh, well, okay then.

"This is March, Lynda."

"But I found so many cute things for the McCabe kids."

"We'll need another piece of luggage to haul all this stuff home!"

"No worries. We can get that at the airport."

After dinner with Mac at a hideously expensive restaurant, highlighted by Lynda spotting some famous actor I'd never heard of, we returned to our room in a New York mood. The window shades were up, and the lights of the city were a thousand points of light.

Lynda pointed. "Look at the shiny building over there, the one with the needle at the top."

"That's the Chrysler Building, and it's my favorite in the whole world. You know how much I love Art Deco."

She put her arm around me and rested her head on my shoulder. "It's beautiful out there, Jeff, with all those lights."

I turned to her. "Yep—the second most beautiful thing I've ever seen." I continued on that theme non-verbally for a while. We had just turned back to the light show when my phone made that pinging noise that let me know I had a text message. Not wanting to break the romantic mood, I ignored it.

But Lynda sighed. "Go ahead and see what it is. I'll still be here when you're finished."

She looked over my shoulder as I pulled out the smartphone. The text was from Popcorn.

Turn on PNN right away. Talton!

Prime News Network is not watched much in the Cody household. I seldom view TV except for sports, and Lynda prefers WSTV and the other gastronomically inclined stations. But if James Gregory Talton was going to be holding forth, this was must-see TV. And even I knew that PNN's niche was controversy, even if they had to create it themselves. *Joseph Pulitzer, call your office.*

"Call Mac and let him know, please," I told Lynda as I picked up the remote. When I finally found PNN through rapid channel surfing, the caption in the upper right corner informed me that we were watching *Speaking Out with Barry Winslow.*

Barry Winslow had been an anchor on one of the Big Three legacy networks for decades until he'd been put out to pasture. Not taking this forced retirement well, he immediately signed on with the cable station as host of a nightly interview program created for him. At PNN, he was determined to prove that he still had the chops to play hardball. He was past seventy years old, distinguished-looking if not handsome, with silver hair and lots of it. We joined the program right at the end of a question to Talton, who was seated across a studio desk from Winslow, wearing his customary pinstriped suit and overgrown hair. The line at the bottom of the screen read PROF. JAMES GREGORY TALTON: CALLED LINCOLN 'TYRANT.'

". . . slavery was wrong?" Winslow finished.

Maybe it's unfair to call Talton's smile condescending, but that's the way it looked to me. "Wrong?

Of course it's wrong, whether you call it slavery, serfdom, indentured servitude, or communism. I believe in human freedom and self-determination. Taking away a man or woman's freedom is one of the greatest immoralities there is. But I don't teach moral theology. We have other professors who do that at St. Benignus. I teach history."

Now it was Winslow's turn to smile, and there was no doubt at all about the nature of it: It was a classic "gotcha" grin.

"Professor, you gave an interview in today's *New York Times*"—*What? What interview? Holy crap, why didn't somebody tell me?*—"in which you said, quote, 'At least slavery got us here. As a black man I'd rather live in the United States of America than in any country in Africa.'" The words went up on the screen as he talked. "Is that an accurate quote?"

"You're damned right it is."

Winslow popped his eyebrows dramatically, like a caricature of Groucho Marx. "So, aren't you saying that slavery is a good thing?"

"No, I'm saying that sometimes God writes straight with crooked lines."

Winslow looked taken aback. Maybe none of his previous guests had ever mentioned God, not even in a cliché.

Talton went on:

"But Lincoln didn't wage that terrible bloody war to free the slaves. He was perfectly clear about that in his famous letter to Horace Greeley in 1862, in which Honest Abe wrote, 'My paramount object in this struggle *is* to save the Union, and is *not* either to save or to destroy slavery.' That's what he said. If you don't believe me, Google it."

"So, are you saying that Abraham Lincoln was a racist?" Winslow had that gotcha look again.

"I never use that word because it's totally subjective, always a pejorative, and usually used to induce white guilt as a way to further some social engineering project. The great Henry Clay—"

That's where Talton lost me. He managed to mention his book, *Henry Clay: American Icon,* at least twice before Winslow shut him down. But don't ask me what point he was making. I don't think Winslow was paying much attention, either, because he didn't ask a single question about the Great Compromiser. Instead, he went for the closing lines that he must have had in mind all along.

"We only have a few more minutes, Professor," he began. "I'm sure you know that you offended many Americans with your comments about President Abraham Lincoln. Many prominent politicians have criticized you and a petition drive has called for your resignation. I'm giving you a chance right now to look at our audience across America and apologize."

Talton's face filled the TV set in a close-up. The director would have been ready for the dramatic moment and planned the shot. "Apologize?" Talton looked aghast. "Isn't that what football players do when they get caught beating up their girlfriends? Isn't that what Congressmen do when they get caught cheating on their wives? I have nothing to apologize for. As Henry Clay once said—"

Enough of Henry, already!

"Thank you, Professor." The camera went back to Winslow. "This has been Professor James Gregory Talton speaking out with Barry Winslow tonight on why he believes that Abraham Lincoln was a tyrant. No apologies, either! Join us again tomorrow night for another headline-making interview with a controversial figure in the news. Now stay tuned for—"

I didn't, choosing instead to hit the "off" button on the remote. Within a minute after I'd done so there was a knock at our door. It was Mac, full of insincere apologies "for intruding upon your domestic bliss." *What bliss? The text from Popcorn ended that.*

"What did you think of Talton's performance?" I asked him.

"I think James has just demonstrated a surprising capacity to turn adversity into economic opportunity," he said. "I predict a substantial uptick in sales of his book. The publisher should be quite delighted."

"I guess Talton should be grateful to whomever posted those YouTube videos."

"Perhaps he should." Mac looked thoughtful.

"Myself, I'm not so pleased."

Before I could expound on that, Mac's phone rang. It actually rings, just like a telephone, of all things.

"McCabe here. Oh, hello, Oscar. What! When? How is she? Thank you for letting me know. No, that is quite impossible. At the moment I am in New York City with Jefferson and Lynda. We will be back in Erin tomorrow. I will see you then."

"What is it?" my favorite journalist demanded. "What happened?"

"Dr. Sydney Bloomingdale was attacked by a knife-wielding miscreant earlier this evening at her office."

Chapter Twenty-Three
A Not-So-Close Call

The injuries weren't life-threatening. We learned some of the details from Johanna Rawls's **DR. BLOOMIE STABBED** story in the *Erin Observer & News-Ledger* on our smartphones the next morning during breakfast at the hotel.

"The headline is a bit overstated," I commented.

"You can't fit 'glancing wound' in type that big," Lynda said, somewhat defensively.

You can on a website, but never mind.

Johanna reported that Dr. Bloomingdale had been attacked as she walked out the back door of her office. It was seven-thirty at night and she was alone, her receptionist having left an hour earlier. Her assailant was described as a man, taller than her, but she apparently was too busy saving her life to note anything helpful about his body type or possible age. He wore a handkerchief over his face. Dr. Bloomie had fended him off with a combination of kung fu kicks, spray from the can of mace on her keychain, and a police whistle—but not before he had inflicted a few minor cuts on her arms and legs. The emergency room doctor at St. Hildegard Health had bandaged her up and sent her home, shaken but not stirred.

"Another case of martial arts saving the day," said Lynda, who for years took taekwondo classes with Triple M.

"I wonder why a knife instead of another blunt instrument," Mac mused. "Killers are usually creatures of habit. And I wonder why he covered his face if he intended to kill her."

"In case anybody besides Dr. Bloomie saw him," Lynda speculated.

"Perhaps."

"And perhaps you think too much," I told Mac. "The important thing is that Dr. Bloomie knows something and the killer knows that she knows it. The attack proves it."

"Ah, but does she know that she knows it?" Mac countered. "Jason Bird didn't."

Jason Bird, a once-troubled young man that Triple M had taken under her wing after he wound up in Oscar's jail, had almost been run over because of something that he saw on the night of a murder. Ironically, he didn't even remember that he'd seen it until Mac pulled it out of him under hypnosis.[6] That seemed to be a completely different situation than this one, given that Dr. Bloomie had been very vocal with her view of the murder without any hocus-pocus. So I ignored Mac's comeback.

"How did Oscar sound when you talked to him this morning?" I asked. Murders and attempted murders tend to make him cranky.

"I believe I detected the same note of triumphalism in his voice as when he called last evening with the news about Dr. Bloomington. You will recall that he was not pleased that she shared with the news media a theory about the murderer contrary to his own."

"Oh, yeah?" Lynda said. "How did he act when you pointed out that the attempt on her life is a pretty good indication that she was barking up the right tree?"

Mac smiled. "He merely grunted, of course."

---

[6] See *The 1895 Murder* (MX Publishing, 2012).

We were at the airport, waiting for our flight to be called, when it hit me: "There's something wrong here. Dr. Bloomie is the most famous resident of Erin. Half the town must be talking about her theory that the murder weapon is the most significant clue in Noah's murder. So wouldn't the killer know that taking her out would draw even more attention to that idea?"

"Indeed. That is why I wonder what else she knows, and whether she knows that she knows it."

"At least you can rule out Yates on this one," Lynda said. "I don't think he had time to hop a plane to Cincinnati and then drive to Erin right after he talked to you guys, but if he did he would have left a paper trail a mile long."

"He could have subcontracted the work," I said. Don't get the idea that I was hanging on to Yates as a suspect out of pride of authorship, or maybe because I preferred him to a homegrown alternative from Erin. That's not it; I was just pointing out a possibility that I didn't think should be overlooked.

Lynda chewed her lip. "Murder-for-hire guys don't advertise on Craigslist. It's a lot more likely that it was the killer himself who tried to get rid of Dr. Bloomie. And that means we now know one thing about him—he was a he and not a she. That cuts the suspect list in half."

"More than that," I said. "I think we can rule out Roscoe Feldman because he can't move that fast. And if the assailant was, uh, corpulent, Dr. Bloomie would have mentioned it, so that leaves you out, Mac."

He raised an eyebrow. "I had not realized that I was a suspect."

"Of course not," Lynda assured him, "even though you do match Dr. Bloomie's psychological profile of the killer as somebody strongly connected with mystery stories. You have an iron-clad alibi—unless you've added bi-location to your other talents."

Don't give him any ideas.

As Lynda said "Dr. Bloomie," I practically heard the name in stereo. Right above her, on one of those flat-screen TVs that can't be turned off in any airport I know, a talking head had just mentioned the psychologist's name. I held up my hand in an appeal for silence so we could hear the rest of it.

Actually, we didn't need to hear it to get the most important part. The image on the screen went from the talking head to video of Dr. Bloomie's TV4 interview about Noah's murder. The caption below informed us that she'd suffered minor wounds in a knife attack. "The motive for the stabbing is unclear and no suspect has been arrested," the talking head said. "Dr. Bloomie was treated at a local hospital and released."

And that was it.

"If she'd been killed or seriously injured there would have been a media feeding frenzy," I said. TV4 was probably giving a pretty good imitation of one all by itself.

One of the nice things about having a distinctive ring tone on my smartphone is that I was pretty sure the Indiana Jones theme song was coming out of my pocket and not from one of the other two hundred or so people immediately around me.

It was Popcorn.

"I thought you'd want to know that there's going to be a student demonstration tomorrow regarding Professor Talton. I heard it from a friend of mine who works in History."

Speaking of a media feeding frenzy . . .

"Is this a demonstration for him or against him?" Either way hurt St. Benignus because it kept the controversy fresh by providing a new angle for news coverage, but a "pro" rally would be a nice change of pace.

"Sally didn't know. She heard it from somebody who heard it from somebody."

"Okay. Thanks for calling. Work your sources and see if you can find out anything more. Our plane is boarding. I'll call you when we land."

"What is it?" Lynda asked.

I shrugged. "Oh, you know. Same old, same old."

Chapter Twenty-Four
Dr. Bloomie Demurs

Mac drove us in his Florida-sized car from the Cincinnati/Northern Kentucky International Airport directly to Oscar's office, dropping Lynda off at the nearby *Observer & News-Ledger* building on the way.

The long drive gave me plenty of time to talk to Popcorn on the phone and get the lay of the land regarding the planned demonstration on campus.

"The students are going to rally tomorrow in the Quadrangle in favor of Professor Talton," she reported. "But we haven't had any media calls about it yet. Maybe they're too busy covering the attack on Dr. Bloomie."

"Maybe."

And if so, was that good or bad? A little of both, I guess. No school, or any other institution, ever wants a controversy to hang around like an unwanted guest at a party. On the other hand, the show of student support was a nice counter-balance to calls for the St. Benignus administration to "do something" about Talton. And it wasn't protesting anything the administration had done yet. If a reporter or three called, I could say something like, "St. Benignus appreciates the passion of our students who are exercising their free speech in support of . . ."

"Why the furrowed brow, Jeff?" Lynda interrupted from her seat in the back of the car.

"Just thinking."

"Cut that out."

We parted a few minutes later with a quick kiss and mutual wishes for a good day. Mac and I went on to Oscar's. We didn't have an appointment, but he was used to us dropping in. What were the odds a small town police chief would be busy?

He was busy. I never even got the chance to ask him how his book was going.

Dr. Sydney Bloomingdale, her arms covered and her legs decorated with a number of small bandages, sat in one of the chairs Mac and I usually occupied during our visits. She was dressed in a more professional fashion than she'd been at Pages Gone By, wearing a gray skirt and a cream-colored blouse that accented her gold jewelry. Her blond hair was tucked up in a knot.

"We have come at an inconvenient time, I see," Mac said. "We can return later."

"You might as well stay," Oscar growled, as I'm sure Mac had hoped that he would. "You've met Dr. Bloomingdale?"

"We recently had that pleasure."

"I didn't expect to see you again so soon," Dr. Bloomie said with a quirky little smile.

Storm clouds gathered over Oscar's broad face. "What are you talking about that I'm probably not going to like?"

Mac cleared his throat. "At the urging of Mo Russert, Jefferson and I talked with Dr. Bloomingdale on Saturday at Pages Gone By. Mo thought perhaps that being at the scene of the crime would inspire a new insight from Dr. Bloomingdale."

Oscar opened his mouth, but Mac cut him off. "Rest assured, Oscar, that it did not. If it had, we would have alerted you."

Mac never lies; that would be a sin. So that must have been a slight prevarication. We'd been not alerting Oscar to key information since Day One of this case for fear that he would put the long arm of the law on the wrong person. *But what if Saylor-Mackie or her husband was the* right *person?* I repressed the thought.

"I'm a psychologist, not a detective," Dr. Bloomie protested.

I had a flashback to Bones McCoy in the original *Star Trek.* "Damn it, Jim, I'm a doctor, not a . . ." So why was she spouting off on TV and in the *Observer* with her theory about the killer if she had no pretensions to amateur sleuthdom?

"Perhaps I even went too far when I suggested the special significance of the murder weapon."

"Do you think that's why you were attacked?" Oscar asked. "I didn't get to ask that yet."

"I can't think of any other reason. He didn't ask for money; he just came at me with the knife."

"But that just drew attention to what you had to say about the murder," I pointed out. "Even whatever channel was on the airport television today ran video of you talking about it on TV4."

She shrugged. "I can assure you that people don't always act rationally."

"I hope that you are recovering well," Mac told Dr. Bloomie.

"Thank you. My physical injuries were minor. I suppose I should thank my ex-husband for dragging me to kung fu lessons. But it's strange to find myself living through the sort of post-traumatic stress that I've seen in so many patients."

"In light of her injuries, I am surprised to see Dr. Bloomingdale here," Mac told Oscar. If he was trying to put the chief on the defensive, it worked a little.

"I offered to meet with her at her convenience in her home or office, but she preferred to come downtown," Oscar explained.

"The media are staked out outside both places," Dr. Bloomie said. "I didn't want them to see the chief visiting me in his police car."

"Didn't they follow you here?" I asked.

"No. I saw to that. I traded cars with my maid. She went home in my Mercedes convertible and a scarf around her head. I left fifteen minutes later in her Fiesta."

"Brava! Ingenious!" Mac boomed.

"I don't feel very ingenious, Professor McCabe. I'm regretting that I ever gave in to Brian Rose's request for an interview on the Bartlett case."

"Perhaps your regret is well placed," Mac acknowledged. "However, I am not convinced that what you said put you in danger. Perhaps the killer believes that you know something that could identify him, something that you did not say on television or in the press."

"But I don't!"

"You are quite confident of that?" Mac said with a question mark in his voice.

"Absolutely." Her tone brooked no possibility of doubt.

Mac tried again. "Are you being held back by ethical constraints—patient-therapist confidentiality?"

"No, that's not the issue. It's true that I can't talk about anything I may have learned about a patient during therapy, but even if I could I don't know what I'd tell. I don't know anything about Noah that would be helpful."

"Apparently somebody thinks you do," I said.

"I have wondered whether perhaps you know more than you think you do," Mac said. "Indeed, I have wondered that about myself. I have a feeling that I heard or saw something important in the early stages of this case, but I do not know what it was."

I'll never let him forget that he said that.

Dr. Bloomie shook her head vigorously. Not a hair fell out of place. "No, Professor, I don't have any deeply repressed memories that you can bring out under hypnosis. If I thought I did, I'd hypnotize myself."

Cute.

Obviously, she was familiar with the *1895* case. Maybe she'd read my book! This didn't seem the time to ask.

"Maybe it was spilling to Mac and Jeff on Saturday that got you cut up on Monday," Oscar suggested. *The wish is father to the thought.*

"But I didn't spill anything! And who would know that I talked to Professor McCabe and Mr. Cody—other than them?

Hey!

"In this town, everybody knows everything."

Not exactly. Oscar still didn't know that his boss, the mayor, had once been married to Noah Bartlett and had written the book that Noah held in his hand when he died. Fortunately, he didn't know that he didn't know that.

Chapter Twenty-Five
Worries and Surprises

That evening, after a day of getting back into the swing of our respective jobs, Lynda and I had dinner at Bobbie McGee's. This is a treat we allow ourselves a few times a month. The sign outside that says "GOOD FOOD—COLD BEER—GREAT MUSIC" is more truthful than most advertising.

A lesser man than I might have looked at the long oak bar and imagined Lynda having a Manhattan while chatting up the bartender, Connor O'Quinn. But not I. That didn't even occur to me. I didn't give it more than a passing thought.

"Why are you looking at the bar?" Lynda asked.

"Just woolgathering, I guess. So, how's your sweeps month project going?"

"Awesome! Human trafficking is real, and it's here in our state. Not that that's awesome, of course. But if we do this series right, we have the chance to make a difference on an important issue that affects people's lives. The numbers on trafficking are squishy, like most numbers are. The people who study this stuff disagree on how many victims there are. But they all agree that millions of people around the world are being exploited every day, pressed into involuntary servitude, many of them children. A lot of it is the sex-trade, including here in Ohio and around the Midwest. A few years ago the governor's task force found that more than a thousand kids were trafficked in this state alone, and three times that at risk. That's why they have posters about it at the interstate rest stops."

It hit me then with the force of a hammer blow that slavery in America wasn't just a historical fact for John Gregory Talton and his critics to argue about. Slavery was still alive under a slightly nicer name.

But I didn't get to say that, because just then Bobbie McGee herself, a big gal in a Stetson hat with a healthy crop of wavy brown hair, came over to take our orders. Like every good restaurateur, she's a hands-on manager. Not being a habitué of sports bars for most of my bachelor years, I'd gotten to know her a lot better since I'd become Mr. Lynda Teal.

"Hi, guys. Watcha drinkin'?"

"The usual," we said at the same time.

"One Manhattan and one Caffeine-Free Diet Coke, coming up." Bobbie had recently begun carrying the latter at my request. My urologist, Dr. Trixie LaBelle, tells me I should drink lemonade to help avoid future kidney stones. Sometimes I do, but not at Bobbie McGee's.

Bobbie holds an MBA from the Wharton School of Business, where I suspect she did not wear the Stetson or the cowgirl persona. Roberta is her real name, and so is the McGee—she acquired it when she married former Cincinnati Reds slugger Brett McGee many years ago.

"How's business?" I said, clever conversationalist that I am.

"Okay for now, but I'm a little worried, to tell you the truth. Some Altiora executive plans to open a trendy brew pub on High Street, where the used-book store is."

"We heard about that," Lynda said. "It might go over with the students who are old enough to drink, but I can't believe it will hurt you that much. I'm sure your loyal customers won't bail on you. They like it here."

Bobbie sat down at our table. "Yeah, but one of the things they like here is Connor, my most popular bartender.

I hear that Bexley, the brew pub guy, is trying to hire him away from me. That could hurt."

Now that was interesting.

"When did you hear that?" I asked.

"A while ago, but not too long. Maybe a week or so."

"Before Noah Bartlett was killed?"

Bobbie shrugged her substantial shoulders. "I don't know. Maybe. Yeah, I think so. Why?"

"The timing could be important. If Charles Bexley was at the point where he was trying to hire help even before Noah was out of the picture, he must have been pretty sure that Pages Gone By wasn't going to be an obstacle to his plan. How did he know that Noah wasn't going to come up with the money at the last minute? Suppose he just assumed that, and his assumption turned out to be wrong, and then he had to take action to remove Noah so he could get control of the building he wanted."

"Wow!" Bobbie said. "You mean he might have been the one who . . ." She didn't finish.

A tiny voice at the back of my mind told me that one could say the same thing about Gulliver Mackie, but I told it to shut up. Bexley had the great advantage of having no connection to St. Benignus that I knew of.

"That's a big 'suppose,'" Lynda pointed out, not unfairly.

"I admit that," I said, "but that doesn't mean it didn't happen."

Lynda's gold-flecked eyes reflected a skepticism that did her credit—how many journalists in their thirties were so uncynical? "You really believe that somebody would kill just to get a favorable location for a restaurant?"

"Some people would kill for a few bucks, my sweet. It happens every day."

Bobbie stood up. "I still can't believe that somebody did that to Noah. He was such a nice guy."

"You knew him?" I hadn't thought of Noah as the sports bar kind.

"Not until that night."

"What night?"

"The night before he died. He had dinner here. I noticed him because he wasn't a regular like most of my customers."

Geese bumped all over my spine. "Was he with a woman?"

"Sure was."

"Can you describe her?"

"Don't have to. I recognized her right away. It was that lady who didn't kill her husband a while back—Ashley Crutcher."

Chapter Twenty-Six
Working Out

"Indeed!" Mac rumbled when I called and told him. "Noah's mysterious dinner companion was one of our own, then. It will be most enlightening to hear what Ashley has to say about this. You have done well, old boy!"

My brother-in-law's congratulatory comment was still echoing in my head at six-oh-six the next morning as I worked out on the elliptical machine at Nouveau Shape. It would be nice to think that Lynda and I had stumbled onto the key fact that solved the case.

But then again, it wouldn't.

Connor O'Quinn had tabbed Noah's dinner companion as a suspect. Mary Lou Springfield thought the killer was a member of the Poisoned Pens. So presumably neither of them would have any trouble seeing Ashley Crutcher as a cold-blooded killer, but I did. I'd rather cast Charles Bexley in that role, a man I'd never met. Why was that? Maybe it was because I thought Ashley was nice, or maybe because she'd been suspected once before in a murder she didn't commit.

"Good morning, Jeff."

I almost fell off of the machine when this greeting from Marvin Slade intruded on my thoughts. Had he been reading my mind? Slade, a regular at Nouveau Shape, had attempted to prosecute Ashley for the murder of her husband about a year and a half earlier. He'd secured an indictment, but the charges were dropped when Mac unmasked the real murderer. If he'd paid attention to Mac, who believed Ashley's story from the beginning, Slade wouldn't have looked like such a fool when she was exonerated. Now here she was in the thick of another murder. But Slade didn't know what Mac and I knew about her. At least, I didn't think so.

"Hello, Marvin. How's business?"

Yeah, I know that wasn't quite the right question, but I'm no good at small talk.

Without his power tie, tailored suit, and yellow suspenders, the Sussex County prosecutor doesn't look like anybody special. He wears horn-rimmed glasses and a bad comb-over. What's left of his hair is brown, but the roots are gray.

"Busy, busy. There's never a recession in crime." He smiled like a politician, which he is. If our hands weren't on the exercise gizmos, he would have been shaking mine.

"I hear that Chief Hummel took you and McCabe with him when he interviewed the mayor about the Bartlett murder," Slade said way too casually. "And when you talked to her husband, too. I'm sure you know that's not exactly standard police procedure."

It's hard to shrug when you're pumping away on an elliptical machine, but I tried. "We just happened to be with him that morning right after the body was found. One thing led to another and we tagged along. I guess you could say he sort of informally deputized us for the day."

I hoped I didn't sound defensive.

"I see. Well, I don't mind telling you that I'm watching that case with special interest, Jeff."

Danger! Danger, Will Robinson! Had Slade gotten wind of any of the several connections that his political enemy Lesley Saylor-Mackie had to Noah Bartlett?

"I'm glad to hear that," I said, keeping my voice steady. "Noah was a friend of mine."

"No surprise there, Jeff. I see you as a bookstore kind of guy. I know that Chief Hummel's a friend of yours, too." He shook his head mournfully. "I have to say, I'm not happy with the pace of his investigation. I've deliberately stayed at arm's length from the details since the chief questioned the Mackies. I wouldn't want anybody to think I had a political axe to grind because the mayor and I belong to different parties." *Gosh, who would ever think that?* "But from the outside it looks like this is taking longer than it should. People"—*i.e., voters*—"tend to be uneasy about an unsolved murder in a town our size."

"You know better than I do that good police work takes time," I said loyally. "And I'm sure you want Oscar to come up with a case that will stick in court, not come apart like the one against Ashley Crutcher." *Insert knife, turn slowly.*

Was I just being churlish for the evil fun of it? Or was I subconsciously trying to inoculate Ashley from Slade's suspicion? I wouldn't put the latter past me. Whatever my intention, Slade turned red, although he didn't react directly to my unpleasant reminder of the Crutcher case.

"Sure, sure," he agreed quickly. "We want to make a good arrest. But justice delayed is justice denied." *I hate legal clichés even more than I hate sports clichés, Marvin.* "The chief assures me that this was no burglary, despite attempts to make it look that way. So there was a different motive, which must have been a personal one, right?"

"Makes sense, yeah."

"So the killer had to be somebody that Bartlett knew. Look, Jeff"—politicians like to use your name a lot so you feel important—"this is Erin, not Chicago or New York. How big can the suspect pool be?"

Bigger than you think—I hope.

"I'm sure Oscar will sort it all out in due time." Actually, I wasn't sure of that, but I was defending my friend.

Slade's tone turned a little sharper. "I don't know how you define due time, but I've seen snails work faster. I'm sure Dr. Bloomingdale would have appreciated a resolution of the case before the killer tried to take her out, too."

Dr. Bloomie! Is that where the pressure was coming from?

"Has Dr. Bloomingdale complained to you?"

"Not yet," Slade said darkly. "She's been too busy avoiding the media, but they haven't avoided her. The story is all over the place, with tabloid TV in particular going crazy. We almost wound up with two murders and no solution in sight. That makes us look like a bunch of rubes. I'm sure I'm preaching to the choir here. I don't have to tell you about bad publicity. I've been following your mess with that wacko professor." *Hit me again, Marv; I won't feel it.*

Slade's tone softened a bit. "Since the chief's not doing so hot, what do you make of this case, Jeff?"

What he really wanted to know was what Sebastian McCabe thought.

"I'm no sleuth," I said, addressing the question he asked rather than what he meant.

He snorted. "Don't give me that. A blind man could see that you and McCabe are up to your ears in this, as usual."

Finally he'd said Mac's name and it was cards-on-the-table time.

My legs pumped harder as I thought furiously. What could I tell him? I certainly didn't want to call attention to *Love's Dark Secret* or to Noah's dinner with Ashley.

"We may have asked a few questions," I conceded. "It's hard not to be interested when a friend of yours has been murdered. Our whole mystery writers' group is interested, and everybody has a theory. Want to hear them?"

"Not especially."

Good. Don't say I didn't offer.

"Really," I said, "if we had a good theory, Mac and I would share it with the chief and I'm sure he'd be right on it." If I kept this up, my nose was going to keep growing until it hit West Virginia. Slade looked around the room. We were the only ones there except for a middle-aged woman lifting weights in a far corner. "I'll lay this on the line for you, Jeff. There's a lot of talk around town about the potential value of that building Bartlett's bookstore is in. There's a budding restaurateur licking his chops over the place. It looks like a number of business interests are better off with Bartlett out of the way, starting with his landlord—Gulliver Mackie."

"Yeah, well, looks can be deceiving." I felt myself getting warmer, and not from physical exertion. "We talked about that with Mackie. Noah's death doesn't really change anything on that score because he was behind on his rent. Mackie had the right to evict him under the provisions of the lease. And according to what the bank told Oscar, Noah didn't seem to have a stash of cash that he was going to pull out to save the family farm at the last minute." It didn't seem a good idea to tell Slade that Mo had poked into her late employer's books as well, also finding a dry well.

Slade was silent for a minute, apparently applying his lawyerly mind to what I'd said to see if he could find a hole in my argument.

The Cody brain, meanwhile, was trying hard not to think about Lesley Saylor-Mackie being the first Mrs. Bartlett and the author of the Rosamund DeLacey novels. If Slade happened to read minds, either of those facts by itself would have raised an eyebrow. The two of them together, *plus* the mayor not coming clean about them to Oscar at the earliest opportunity, would be beyond just suspicious to a man like Marvin Slade. They would seal the deal.

"Well," Slade said finally, "I'm glad to hear it. This new brew pub that's in the works should be a big hit, very good for downtown. I'd hate to see the development derailed." That was Marvin Slade, civic booster, speaking.

He got off the elliptical machine. "Where's your lovely wife?"

"Lynda had an early meeting." It was a conference call with the TV stations involved in her sweeps month project on human trafficking, but that was none of Slade's business.

"Tell her I said hi, Jeff."

"She'll be sorry she missed you," I lied.

Chapter Twenty-Seven
Mystery Woman

The rest of the morning flew by as I dealt with media calls related to the student demonstration in the Quadrangle, which began at 10 A.M. What was the college's reaction to this show of support for Professor Talton? *We aren't surprised, Maggie. He's a very popular professor.* Would the demonstration have any impact on how the college handles his case? *What case, Hadley? No disciplinary charges have been filed.* Were the students saying . . .? *I can't speak for the students.*

What with all that bobbing and weaving, I barely had time to think about the former mystery woman in Noah Bartlett's life, now no longer mysterious. But it didn't take a lot of thought to figure out that Oscar, unhampered by my unreasonable prejudice against giving a former suspect another shot at being a killer, would be intensely interested in Ashley Crutcher's presence at Noah Bartlett's last supper.

"Indeed he would, old boy," Mac agreed when I finally came up for air long enough to give him a report of my recent adventures. "The great puzzle is how he does not know it already. The always-efficient Gibbons has been seeking Noah's dinner date since Friday."

"Once in a while, police routine comes a cropper."

Mac moved on.

"It is harder to calculate how the prosecutor might react to a case against Ashley. Once burned, he might be twice shy. On the other hand, he might relish the opportunity to salve the wound to his ego inflicted by the Crutcher case."

That wound had to be especially raw because Ashley worked as a paralegal for Erin's leading defense attorney— Erica Slade, Marvin's ex-wife. Erica liked nothing better than to square off against Marvin in court, dressed to the nines and breathing fire. Maybe I'm loco for suspecting she was probably disappointed that the earlier murder charge against Ashley didn't come to that, but that doesn't stop me.

"I'd like to think that Slade would be afraid to ask a grand jury to indict the same innocent person a second time," I said, "but I'm not sure we can count on that."

"And we certainly cannot count on Oscar's continued failure to learn about Ashley's apparent involvement with Noah, whatever its nature. Are you free?"

"Yeah. I was just about to take my lunch hour."

"Lunch can wait."

That's a first for you, Mac.

We found Ashley holding down the fort at the law office on Water Street, the lawyers being either in court or taking sustenance in one of the nearby downtown restaurants. Erica's practice had grown over the past eighteen months to the point where she now had the help of two other attorneys in the quarters that had originally been St. Swithin's Episcopal Chapel and later a pub called The Sanctuary.

Light streamed in from the stained-glass windows, illuminating the former bar that was now the reception desk. The administrative assistant who normally occupied that desk was also out when we arrived, replaced by Ashley.

"Hi, guys! Don't tell me you need a lawyer."

No, but you might.

"We wish to speak with about the mystery woman who had a dinner date with Noah the night before he was murdered," Mac said.

Her face fell and a look of panic took up residence in her brown eyes. "Why me?" Ashley wasn't much of an actress, which I rated in her favor.

Still, I pointed at her accusingly. "You were that woman. Bobbie McGee saw you with Noah at her place."

Instead of responding directly to my melodramatic outburst, Ashley looked around at the empty room. "Let's talk in the conference room in case somebody comes back from lunch."

We gathered around an oval table.

"I wouldn't call it a date," Ashley began.

"What would you call it?" Mac asked.

"It was more like a business meeting. The bookstore was in trouble. You probably know that Noah was going to lose his lease and a man named Bexley was going to put a brew pub there unless a miracle happened. I learned that from Connor, who learned it from Bexley, who wants him to go to work at the new place. I didn't know Noah all that well—just from being a customer and from the Poisoned Pens. But I knew the bookstore meant everything to him. The reason we went to dinner was so that I could tell him my idea: I thought I could ask Aunt Serena to put some capital into the business and become a silent partner."

"Aunt Serena?" I repeated.

"Serena Mason, my mother's sister."

Even though that explanation was perfectly good English, it took the Cody brain a few moments to fire all the cylinders and process what she'd said. I knew Serena, everybody did, but Ashley had never hinted that she was related to one of the richest women in Erin, and probably the nicest. She may have been Ashley's aunt, but she was everybody else's favorite grandmother. And yet—

"One would have thought that Mrs. Mason was far too astute a businesswoman to invest in such a failing enterprise as Pages Gone By," Mac intoned, stealing my thunder. "Was this to be another of her many philanthropic endeavors?"

Ashley pushed her wavy hair out of her eyes. "Not exactly. Aunt Serena loves books and she belongs to the science-fiction book club that meets at the bookstore, but I thought that with her business smarts maybe she could make the store profitable. If it was just a matter of money, I could supply that from my inheritance. I wasn't just asking for a handout on Noah's behalf. I wouldn't do that."

The pride in her voice explained why Serena Mason hadn't come to the financial rescue when Ashley's husband had been out of work—Ashley never asked, and probably didn't let her in on the state of affairs at Casa Crutcher.

"Noah wouldn't go for it anyway," Ashley added. "He thanked me profusely, but he claimed that he was about to come into a windfall that would save the store. I figured he just said that to save face."

"Perhaps." Mac stroked his beard. "Perhaps not."

"But why the hell didn't you tell us you were the mystery woman that Noah had dinner with?" I snapped. Lynda says I get cranky when I don't get fed on time. "That would have saved us the trouble of looking for her." *Not that we looked all that hard, but we might have.*

Ashley looked contrite. "I'm sorry, guys. I didn't think of that. I was just scared. Connor said that whoever Noah ate with the night before he died sounded like a suspect. I was afraid that somebody might believe that. I've been there before."

"Hey, wait a minute!" My voice rose. "That dinner was at Bobbie McGee's. How could Connor not have noticed either you or Noah—much less the two of you eating together? It's not that big a place, and Connor has goo-goo eyes for you."

"He's off on Tuesday nights."

"Oh."

"So he didn't know he was practically accusing me of killing Noah, if that's what you mean."

That's not what I meant, but never mind.

Mac's face held a certain bemusement at this exchange, as if he enjoyed the irony of Connor O'Quinn nominating his girlfriend-of-the-month for a murder rap without knowing that's what he was doing.

"Do you think that Connor believed it?"

"I doubt it. I think he might have killed Noah himself."

Chapter Twenty-Eight
The Crux of the Matter

Mac raised an eyebrow. "You suspect your paramour . . ."

"He's not my paramour, Mac—whatever you mean by that," Ashley said. "I'd rather think of him as an experiment in interpersonal relations, my first testing of the dating waters since Tim died. And he was good research for the short story I'm writing about a former college athlete."

"Whatever you call him," I said, "why do you think he killed Noah?"

"I said 'might have.' I'm not making an accusation. But I know him well enough to know that he's impulsive, hot-headed, and likes to get his own way."

What a dreamboat.

"He thought this new pub was going to go over big, and he thought he could do well with a gig there—lots of big tips. Bexley even had him sold on the idea that he could use some connection he had to get WSTV, that wine and spirits cable network, to do a show there. But if all of that fell through because Noah managed to scrape up the lease money so he didn't have to move, Connor would be S-O-L, right?"

"Apparently so," Mac sort of agreed, not looking at all convinced that this constituted a murder motive. But Connor seemed promising to me.

"Dr. Bloomie was attacked by a man," I pointed out, "and he was taller than her. Connor fits the bill."

"Ah, yes, Dr. Bloomingdale," Mac mused. "And what do you suppose she knows about Connor that makes her so dangerous to Noah's murderer, Ashley?"

She shrugged. "I didn't think that far."

"The body of the case indicates someone who had reason to kill both Noah and his former psychologist. At this point I do not see a credible argument that Connor O'Quinn had either. Surely the possibility of Connor leaving employment at a settled and popular establishment for an untested new competitor was not so attractive as to warrant homicide." He shook his massive head. "No, I am afraid that will not do."

He smiled and stood up. "Charles Bexley, however, is another story. A man with a dream, especially an entrepreneur, is not easily dissuaded. I think a visit with him is past due."

"Mac, I'm sorry I didn't tell you earlier that I was the one who had dinner with Noah." Ashley actually looked sorry, unlike most people who say they're sorry. "You did so much to help me when Tim was killed. I should have leveled with you."

"Look at the bright side," I said. "If Oscar finds out, you already have a good lawyer."

After lunch, Charles Bexley agreed to meet us in his office at the Altiora Corp., a sprawling complex just inside the city limits and a major contributor to Erin's tax base.

In getting the appointment, Mac may have given the impression that we were beer aficionados. That's half true—Mac is. He may also have given the further impression that we were excited by what we'd heard about his project and wanted to learn more about it. People are always willing to talk about whatever moves them most.

"Engineering is my profession, but beer is my passion," he explained after the self-introductions and the pleasantries were dispensed with.

Bexley was a brawny guy, about my age, with forearms like trees and a thick mustache. The sleeves of his white shirt were rolled up, showing off his hairy upper limbs.

"The only thing I like better than beer is food," he added.

"I empathize deeply," Mac said. "So a brew pub was a natural outlet for your entrepreneurial urges."

"Gastropub," Bexley corrected. "The Speakeasy will be the first gastropub in this part of the state. We're not talking burger and pizza cuisine here. Well, there might be burgers and pizzas, but they will be gourmet burgers and pizzas among many other offerings. We're going to hire a top chef and create a menu like this town has never seen."

"We?" I repeated.

"My partner and I. Nicholas operated a successful gastropub in Savannah for seven years. We know what we're doing. And it's going to be first-class all the way. We've hired Jonah Wittle to draw the plans. I'll show you."

He opened a drawer in a credenza and pulled out a set of prints, which he unfurled on his desk. The drawings of the inside showed open rafters and visible pipes, with a series of brewing vats within sight of the bar and the dining tables. The exterior showed an awning with a Prohibition-themed logo and seating that spilled out onto the sidewalk.

"We plan to brew a full range of beers here, from an India pale to a bourbon-barrel stout—six kinds for starters."

"I certainly would be delighted to quaff a pint or two there," Mac said. *Or anywhere else.*

"It's impressive," I conceded. "But I have to say, I just don't think it looks very *Erin*, if you know what I mean."

Bexley chuckled. "I know exactly what you mean. But that's the point of The Speakeasy. It will be unique, completely different from anything else in town. The kids will love it!"

Mac raised an eyebrow.

"I mean the young adults in town," Bexley amended. "Not your underage students, of course. And I think WSTV will eat it up because of the historic building, the speakeasy connection. Nicholas knows one of the producers from when they profiled him in Savannah two years ago."

"You have certainly invested a lot of time and money in this venture, and to good effect," Mac said. "If you don't mind my saying, it seems that you have gone out on a rather long limb, given that the High Street building in these designs was already occupied by a tenant who had no intention of moving."

"I wasn't worried about that. The landlord, Gulliver Mackie, assured me that the tenant would be no problem."

"He no longer is. That is the crux of the matter."

"What matter?"

"The murder of Noah Bartlett," I said, just to remind him I was there.

Bexley, a gung-ho and generally cheerful sort, had the sort of face that looked especially dour when his mouth turned down, as it did now. Even his mustache looked grim. "I'm sorry that happened, obviously. But I don't feel guilty about profiting from his misfortune because I don't think I did. The bookstore was going to be out of there anyway."

"Perhaps not," Mac said. "Shortly before he died, Noah told Mackie that he was getting a windfall and expected to pay off the loan."

Bexley sat down at his desk. "That's news to me, and I hear of lot of rumors, Mr. McCabe. For instance, I heard you're running around trying to figure out who killed Bartlett."

I wouldn't call it running around, exactly.

"Then my reputation precedes me," Mac said, failing miserably to stifle a smile.

"You could say that. In fact, I thought maybe you wanted to talk to me about the murder when you called. But no, you said you were interested in The Speakeasy. I took you at your word."

"My word is inviolate, I assure you. Everything I told you on the phone was true. I am most interested in your gastropub in all its aspects. If the project comes to fruition, you can expect to see me as a regular patron. However, I must admit that my devotion to food and drink is only one reason for our visit today. A friend of ours has been murdered. In the past Jeff and I have been of some slight help to Chief Hummel in one or two cases. *Puh-leeze. False humility is so off-putting.* "It was only natural that we should try to be of assistance again."

At least Bexley didn't punch him, which I suspect he would have been good at. "I get that, Mr. McCabe. What I don't get is how you think I can help. I never met Mr. Bartlett. I never even had any arm's-length business dealings with him. His landlord is going to be my landlord. That's the only connection.

"Look"—he held out his beefy arms, a pleading gesture—"I just want to create something new and maybe eventually make a few bucks. I'm sorry that it's going to be built on the ruins of somebody else's dream, but that's not my fault. The bookstore was failing before I ever looked at the space. As for why somebody killed Mr. Barrett, I have no idea. If he had any money, I assume he would have paid his rent. Come to think of it, being dead wouldn't have changed that. He could have left the bookstore and this mysterious windfall he talked about, if it existed, to his heir, couldn't he?"

Mac rubbed his beard. "I see no reason why not."

That's one of his greatest weaknesses—he's a sucker for a logical argument.

"Well, there you are then! His murder couldn't possibly have had anything to do with the future of the bookstore building because it didn't change anything."

"But the killer might not have known that," I said. "Not to cast aspersions, but somebody we talked to suggested that Connor O'Quinn might have wanted Noah out of the way because he was counting on getting a job with The Speakeasy."

"Ha!" It didn't sound like a genuine laugh, but it wasn't supposed to. Bexley was making a point. "I did talk to O'Quinn at one point. He was an athlete in college and so was I. But I wouldn't hire him if he was the last English-speaking bartender on earth."

"Why not?" I asked before Mac could.

I hear he makes great Manhattans.

"I told you I hear things. And I hear that O'Quinn has been selling steroids to some kids on the wrestling team at St. Benignus."

Chapter Twenty-Nine
Wrestling with Truth

"Steroids!" Mac said on the way back to campus. "I confess myself shocked."

"Well, actually, I'm not as surprised as you are." I told him about the investigation of doping on campus, as related to me by Ralph. "And since Connor looks like he uses steroids himself, I wouldn't be stunned to find out that he was the team's connection."

I thought Mac was going to wreck the big red boat he calls a car. "By thunder, Jefferson! Could it really be that simple?"

"Simple? Well, sure. Occam's Razor and all that. The simplest solution is usually the right one. But, uh, what particular simple solution do you have in mind?"

"If it is true that Connor O'Quinn is providing steroids to student athletes at St. Benignus, the motive for Noah's murder is staring us in the face. Noah found out and attempted to blackmail Connor. That is where he expected to get money to pay his back rent."

"And what about the attack on Dr. Bloomie?" I asked. "Where does that fit in?"

"We have been assuming that she might have some special knowledge of Noah because he had been her patient not so very long ago. Perhaps that is true and Connor believed that Noah told her his secret. Or perhaps Connor was also her patient and he believed that she deduced his guilt based on what she knew of him. Her insistence that the murder weapon pointed to a mystery writer could have been aimed at him—or so he might have imagined."

I snorted. "Implicating a writer would leave Connor O'Quinn out of it by definition. I bet he couldn't write the prose on the back of a cereal box. I don't think he even knows much about mysteries."

"Perhaps not. He is, however, a member of the Poisoned Pens."

"What about *Love's Dark Secret?* Where does that fit in?"

"That is not yet clear to me. Certainly, Connor had a secret if what Charles Bexley told us about him is true."

"That's a big 'if,' Mac. You've built a scenario based on information Bexley got from a source he won't identify." We'd pressed Bexley on that point, but he'd refused to give up a name.

Mac lit a fat cigar, an act that, in the confines of his '59 Chevy, rises from mere rudeness to the level of cruel and inhuman punishment. "You must admit that his sources of information appear sound. He knew about our inquiries."

Unimpressed, I rolled down a window. "His sources didn't have to be so great. First of all, anybody who's ever heard about you could guess that you would be sticking your nose into this, and most people in Erin have heard about you. Secondly, his prospective landlord could have told him—Gulliver Mackie was the second person we talked to about the case."

"Gulliver apparently did not tell him about Noah's claim to have the money to forestall eviction."

"Why would he? That wouldn't help him a bit. And besides, Mackie didn't believe Noah and wasn't worried about it. Or so he says."

By this time we'd arrived in the faculty parking lot.

"I concede your point that my theory is a house of cards if Connor O'Quinn is innocent of the accusation leveled by Mr. Bexley's informant," Mac said.

"Since Ralph's already launched an investigation of steroid use on campus, I can nose around and see if Connor's name has come up. And if it hasn't, I'll throw him into the mix."

"That is an excellent suggestion. However, I have a source of my own that I would like to employ first. Meet me in my office at"—he looked at his Sherlock Holmes watch—"let us say four o'clock."

After a fun afternoon of fielding media and alumni calls about our student demonstration—alumni had divergent views about Professor Talton—I showed up at Mac's office a little before the appointed hour. He was practicing sleight of hand, dropping coin after coin from an apparently empty hand into a top hat on his desk. Each coin landed with a satisfying clink. I'm good at generating money from investments, but not that good.

"Pull a killer out of that hat," I said, "*then* I'll be impressed."

"Alas, Jefferson, the hat is empty." He held it up to show me the emptiness.

I did my best not to appear impressed, but probably failed. Even knowing that he had to be palming those half-dollar pieces, I couldn't spot the fancy handwork.

"I suppose there's a reason you're not doing something more productive?" I said acidly, if not venomously.

A look of surprise flashed across Mac's hairy face. "Productive? Why, nothing sparks the creative juices more effectively than leisure, old boy. In the last hour I have completely plotted the next Damon Devlin short story and have come up with a thumping good idea for a novel!"

Show off.

"So what's next on the agenda?"

"A former student of mine named Isaac Lamb should be here any moment. Isaac is a junior, an excellent scholar and a member of the wrestling team."

"Ah. Wrestling team. Steroids. You peg him for a doper."

He recoiled. "I would not presume that of Isaac. No, I believe him to be a young man of good character. However, it is entirely possible that the lad may have known about others on the team using steroids."

"Then why not report the teammates if his character is so good?"

"Given his youth, he might have felt compelled to maintain silence out of a misplaced sense of team loyalty. For the same reason, he may have even demurred in the face of an investigation."

"Then what makes you think he'll tell you anything?"

Mac cleared his throat.

"We had a very good rapport when he was in my class on twentieth-century horror fiction. In fact, that class unfortunately inspired Isaac to undertake a rather outrageous Halloween escapade that he would rather Erin's forces of law and order not know about even now. The statute of limitations has not run out."

"So," I summarized, "he might talk because you get along, but if that fails a little blackmail wouldn't hurt."

"Such a harsh term, black—"

"Professor McCabe?"

The young man who stood in the doorway of Mac's office didn't look like a Lamb. He was all muscle and no hair, having shaved his head as well as his face.

"Ah, Isaac. Thank you for coming."

"Sure. What's this about?"

"This is my friend, brother-in-law, and occasional chronicler, Thomas Jefferson Cody."

Was that nervousness I detected, or did Lamb always look like a rabbit at a hound dog convention?

"He's the one who helps you solve mysteries, isn't he?"

An intelligent boy! A remarkable boy!

"Quite so." Mac pulled out one of his sausage-sized cigars. "Care for a Fuente Fuente OpusX?"

"No, thanks. I don't smoke."

"I am not surprised. As an athlete, you would never do anything that might injure your health, would you? Of course not!" Mac lit the cigar.

"I try not to."

"Good! That is one reason no athlete should ever use anabolic steroids. They bulk you up in the short run, but they damage your body in the long run." Lamb's eyes suddenly looked like golf balls. Maybe he was a duffer in his spare time. "The other reason is that it is simply unethical and unsportsmanlike, as well as illegal, to gain an unfair advantage in sports through the use of chemical enhancements."

He could have put that in shorter words, and fewer of them, but Isaac Lamb didn't need a translator to get the point right away.

"I'm sorry, Professor, honest I am." The words rushed out like a waterfall in spring. "I know I let you and everybody else down. This will kill my parents. It was a stupid thing to do, but once I started I couldn't stop."

"Eh?" Mac raised an eyebrow while the Cody brain chewed over what was going on here. Then I got it: We'd struck gold while mining for silver. Lamb wasn't just a witness to steroid sales; he'd bought and used the stuff himself. Mac figured it out faster than I did, and quickly assumed the pretense that he'd known all along.

"Well, we all make mistakes, Isaac. That started with Adam. Tell us about it."

"There was this guy I met—"

"Connor O'Quinn," Mac supplied.

"You know everything, don't you?" He sounded miserable.

"I am hardly omniscient." *Big of you to say so, Mac.* "I know nothing whatever about ice hockey, for example. Now, proceed with your story. We are all attention. Jefferson may even take a few notes."

"I'm going to get in trouble, aren't I?" He asked me the question, as if he couldn't bear to continue looking at his former professor.

"Not as much as you will if you don't talk." I may have channeled Sam Spade more than I should have, but Lamb didn't seem to notice.

"So pray continue with your story," Mac added. "You met him where?"

"At Bond's Gym. A lot of the guys on the wrestling team work out there, even though we have a facility on campus." Bond's is nothing like Nouveau Shape, where I work out. It's so hard-core into muscle-building that even the women exude testosterone. "This was last year. I'd had some injuries, wasn't doing too well. Freshmen in my weight class were beating me. I was afraid of losing my scholarship."

"And Connor O'Quinn told you about some shots that could help you heal and give you a competitive advantage over the other guys in your weight class," I said. I'd read up a bit on steroids through the magic of Google one afternoon after Ralph had dropped the news on me that we might have a problem.

Lamb gave a barely perceptible nod. "He'd been a wrestler himself some years back in his UK days. He said he had a connection to a nurse practitioner in Cincinnati, an old girlfriend."

"And you just went along?"

"Not at first. I knew it was wrong and I didn't want to do it. But he told me the guys I was competing against were taking steroids already. There's practically no drug checking in the NAIA, just some random marijuana testing." From what I'd read, even the bigger schools of the NCAA did minimal testing. A bill in the Ohio legislature aimed at changing that in our state had gone nowhere.

"Are members of your team fellow customers of Connor?" Mac asked.

He shook his head. "I don't know. He never told me."

"An investigation of steroids is underway here at St. Benignus," Mac said. "Have you talked to the investigators?"

"Yeah, but I didn't tell them anything. I didn't want to lose my scholarship and go to jail. Besides, Connor is a pretty tough guy and I didn't want to get in his crosshairs."

"And yet, it is clear that your silence has weighed heavily upon your conscience. It encourages me greatly to know that you still have a conscience. Well, Isaac, I am afraid that you will indeed lose your scholarship and your athletic career. However, you have gained the ability to sleep at night, which seems a fair trade-off to me. Perhaps I can even help you secure some other form of financial aid." From Mac, that was tantamount to a promise. He has more strings to pull than a puppeteer.

"But . . . I'll go to jail, won't I?"

"I think you mean prison. However, I suspect that you can most likely avoid that if you tell the legal authorities everything. Jefferson here is well acquainted with the county prosecutor." *We even shared the sauna once.*

"Slade goes after the big fish," I said. More Bogart. "You're a minnow."

For the first time the pall of gloom partially lifted off of Isaac Lamb and his eyes registered a faint hope that not all was lost. Sebastian McCabe often inspires such confidence, and it is not misplaced.

"Connor O'Quinn will not be as fortunate as you," Mac added. "Dealing in steroids will seem a minor matter compared to the charges against him of murder and attempted murder."

Chapter Thirty
Murder Is No Joke

"You're not joking, are you?" Oscar vaped hard on his electronic coffin nail.

"Was that a rhetorical question?" I fired back. "Because if it wasn't, it was a pretty stupid one. In fact, it was anyway."

Can you tell I was in a cranky mood, even though I wasn't hungry? How would you feel if you were the communications director at a small Catholic college and you had to tell your friend the police chief that one of your athletes was illegally using steroids—because if you didn't tell him, he might pay entirely too much attention to a leading faculty member with secrets to hide?

The hardest part, which we were putting off as long as possible, would be telling Ralph that we'd verified reports of steroids use by at least one St. Benignus athlete. I was already using half my brain to mentally rehearse my speech to the provost, in which I would explain that we could honestly say our internal investigation turned up the malefactor. Even though the *official* inquiry had done no such thing yet, so far as I knew, Mac and I were employees of the college (for now). I could argue that our questioning of Isaac Lamb in Mac's office on company time was official enough.

While that half of my brain was trying to convince myself that I could convince Ralph of that line, the other half was with my body in Oscar's office just minutes after talking to Lamb. The chief had turned out to be a hard sell for the idea that Noah had attempted to blackmail Connor O'Quinn and got blunt head trauma for his enterprise.

"I think I've got a better idea," Oscar said. "I'm going to have Gibbons expand the search for the woman Bartlett was with the night before he died. Nobody that Gibbons talked to remembers seeing Bartlett in his usual haunts, like Beans & Books and the little café at the public library. So I figure it's time to put more troops on the hunt and go a little further afield."

Just don't talk to Bobbie McGee. She doesn't know anything.

While I fought panic, Mac spread his hands. "Surely a killer who was with Noah the night before would have done the foul deed then, not the following morning."

"Not necessarily. I could imagine a scenario where waiting would make sense. Hey, you're the ones who told me about Bartlett's dinner date."

It seemed a good idea at the time.

"On the other hand," Oscar went on, "how much money would a small-town steroids dealer have to pay blackmail with?"

"Perhaps not as much as Noah believed," Mac said. "Whether Connor had a lot of money is immaterial. Noah assumed that he did, and he thought he could tap into it to save his store. Instead, he revealed himself as a threat that had to be eliminated."

Oscar chugged coffee. I was getting jazzed just from the fumes. "So how did Bartlett find out about O'Quinn's little sideline?"

Mac shrugged. "We found out."

That's right—we did! And we got our first clue from Charles Bexley, who said he heard it from a source he refused to identify. It looked like Connor would have to become a serial killer if he wiped out everybody who knew he was the candy man for certain college athletes. Maybe I should have ridden that train of thought to the next depot, but you have to remember that I was only using half my brain.

"Whether you find my murder theory credible or not," Mac added, "we do have the testimony of a young man I trust. You should talk to him yourself, of course. He has already promised to be forthright with legal authorities, in return for avoiding prison."

We were handing Oscar a case against Connor on a silver platter—dealing in a Schedule III controlled substance at minimum, Murder One at best. You would think he'd be grateful. Instead, he said, "Isn't this a job for the DEA?"

"Why let them have all the fun?" I replied.

Oscar called Isaac Lamb's cell number, but the wrestler didn't answer.

"Damn kids," Oscar muttered. "Like my sister says, what's the point of them all having cell phones when they don't answer 'em?"

"They answer their friends," I said, "just not their parents or cops."

Mac checked his watch. Apparently Sherlock's little hand was on the six. "I suggest that a conversation with Connor O'Quinn would not be amiss, Oscar, despite your inability to verify our account of what Isaac told us. Connor should be on duty serving up drinks at Bobbie McGee's."

Oscar stood up.

"No argument?" Mac said.

"Why waste time? You'd talk me into it anyway."

I've said it before and I'll say it again: Oscar Hummel is no dummy.

"How's your mystery novel coming?" I asked.

"Don't ask."

I texted Lynda to let her know I'd be home late.

The three of us walked in and sat down at the empty end of the bar. I couldn't help but think of a favorite joke:

A priest, a rabbi, and a minister walk into a bar. The bartender looks up and says, "What is this, a joke?"

This was no joke.

Connor O'Quinn was all smiles when he caught sight of us. I wondered how he managed to always have a three-day growth of beard, never four or five. He walked over from where he'd been chatting with a couple of older guys, one bald and one gray-haired. "Hi, Chief! I hope you're not on duty."

"Matter of fact, I am, Connor. Guess I'll have to skip the beer." He looked mournful.

"What's up?" The former wrestler's voice sounded almost too casual, but I thought his darting eyes projected something between fear and nervousness.

"We have been talking to a now-former customer of yours," Mac said.

"Got a lot of those."

"This was a guy who bought steroids from you, not beer or booze," Oscar said, taking back the conversation.

"Steroids?" Connor gave a hollow laugh. "That's bad stuff. I don't know what you're talking about."

"That's lame," I said. "Is that what you told Noah Bartlett when he tried to blackmail you?"

"Blackmail?" I have to admit that he looked like I'd been talking Urdu.

"That's why you killed him isn't it—because he was blackmailing you?"

Mac and Oscar may have had in mind a more subtle line of questioning, but my Mike Hammer approach had its effect. Connor's mouth fell open and he looked around wildly. Before I knew what was happening he was running, which was stupid. Even more stupid, yours truly was running after him in a low-speed pursuit in and out among the tables that stood between the bar and the door.

At least I didn't embarrass myself by yelling, "Stop that varmint!" or the equivalent. Every eye in the restaurant was glued on us—I caught that in my peripheral vision—but nobody made a move to stick out a foot and trip Connor. It's as if they were all paralyzed by the surreal scene.

Mac and Oscar, either of whom might have suffered a fatal heart attack in the act of giving chase, wisely stayed put. But they knew he wouldn't get away.

Connor flew out the door with me at his heels. I almost ran smack into him—safely in the hands of Lt. L. Jack Gibbons, Oscar's assistant chief.

"I want a lawyer," Connor yelled over the sound of handcuffs snapping around his wrists.

Chapter Thirty-One
Bargaining with the Devil

"Erica Slade says her client didn't kill Noah Bartlett," Lynda observed at breakfast the next morning, Thursday. She was looking at Johanna Rawls's story in the *Erin Observer & News-Ledger* as she ate a bagel with cream cheese (eighty calories per two tablespoons).

"Of course he didn't. He's her client."

"She doesn't claim that all of her clients are innocent."

Lynda had me there.

"But that's only because some of them confess before they lawyer-up. Not much she can do then. If your old boyfriend's so innocent, why did he run?" I was still a bit sore from the obstacle course race at Bobbie McGee's, despite Lynda's solicitous ministrations of an analgesic heat rub the night before. My almost-daily forty-five minutes on the elliptical machine hadn't equipped me to be a marathon man. If Oscar hadn't posted Gibbons outside just to humor Mac, I'd probably still be running. No, scratch that; Connor might be running, but I'd be fallen in a heap somewhere.

"Erica doesn't deny that Connor was selling steroids," Lynda countered. "I bet she's working on a plea bargain for that one based on selling out whoever got him the 'roids." *In other words, an even bigger fish.*

"No bet. You didn't hear it from me, Lyn, but Mac's former student said that Connor's supplier was an ex-girlfriend who is a nurse practitioner. That's a juicy tidbit that Lamb should be able to offer up as part of his own deal if he can get to Slade with it before Connor does."

Oscar had finally made contact with Isaac Lamb on Wednesday evening. Tall Rawls's story had touched on that only lightly: "Sources say a St. Benignus student who purchased steroids from O'Quinn is cooperating with police." Any fear that Lamb had of telling what he knew about the older man's pharmaceutical entrepreneurship had to have been dissipated by knowing that Connor was now Oscar's guest in the City Hall jail. So far he was only charged with selling steroids, but publicly identified as "a person of interest" in Noah's murder.

Lynda regarded me with suspicion in her eyes. "Did you know what was going on in the wrestling program when I told you the stories we were considering for sweeps month—including steroids in college sports?"

Uh-oh. I cannot tell a lie.

"I knew there were rumors," I admitted. "But the in-house investigation didn't get anywhere until Mac talked to that former student."

I guess she decided to give me a pass on that, because all she said was: "Well, I'm sorry now that we didn't do the steroids story. The timing would have been perfect."

"Don't be sorry. Doping is a big story today, and Johanna got a nice chunk of it, but human trafficking is a lot more serious problem."

That was even true.

Besides, Ralph had been texting me anxiously about wrestlers on steroids all morning; a series of TV reports might have induced a stroke. Somehow he didn't find comfort in my newspaper quote: "St. Benignus officials have been carrying out our own investigation of reported steroid abuse in the wrestling program. We will fully cooperate with law enforcement authorities and share with them what we have learned." No need to point out that we'd already handed Oscar our chief witness, Isaac Lamb.

Lynda sighed. "I guess you're right. That's a trap we fall into in journalism—devoting too much attention to the urgent at the expense of the important. Still, steroids are a serious concern in the sports world, and testing seems to be really lax at the college level. Connor's arrest should have our reporters asking some tough questions at the colleges and universities in their areas." I could almost see her make a mental note, which she was not likely to forget.

"Okay, that's enough about steroids for now," she said. "Let's get back to the part where I pointed out that Erica says Connor didn't kill Noah Bartlett."

"Oh, yeah." Finished with my raisin bran, I stood up. "Most murderers don't confess, except on TV shows and in mystery novels, so I'm not worried about that. Now that there's a suspect, maybe Oscar's troops can find some DNA evidence to link him to Noah's body. And maybe Dr. Bloomie will be able to identify her attacker when she sees him in a line-up, even though she couldn't remember anything about him in her PTSD state right after he sharpened his knife on her arms and legs."

"Maybe," Lynda conceded. She popped the last piece of bagel—cinnamon with too much sugar—into her mouth as she stood up. "I have to say that I never would have figured Connor O'Quinn for a killer. But he's full of himself and a guy who cuts corners, so I'm not surprised about the steroids. He probably used them himself when he was wrestling."

"I can see that you developed a strong impression of the man from dating him once." *The jerk.*

"More like once and a half. The second date ended in the middle. When I made it clear that I wanted him to take me home—alone—he turned sullen, but not violent."

"You make Connor sound like a real gentleman." Forgive me if my voice dripped acid. "Maybe Erica should call you as a character witness at the trial." I could almost see the two ex-spouses, prosecutor and defense attorney,

licking their respective chops as they prepared for another
round of Slade vs. Slade. "Meanwhile, I'm facing a day of
media calls about steroids at St. Benignus, plus another
round of Professor Talton. The beat goes on."

"Another video?"

"Not that I know of, but new stories keep popping
up around the country as different papers and stations hop
on the merry-go-round. CNBC was the latest. This is death
by a thousand cuts. I have an appointment to talk to Ralph
about all this stuff at 10 A.M. Pray for me. And if I don't
come out alive, marry a rich man."

"I already did." She moved into my arms for a
spousely kiss. "Hey," she said a few minutes later, "is that a
smartphone in your pocket or are you just glad to see me?"

"Both. Life is not an either-or proposition."

I went back to what I was doing before she so
rudely interrupted us.

And my phone belted out Carly Simon's "You're So
Vain." Damn that Mac!

"Ah, Jefferson, I hope I haven't interrupted one of
your morning rituals."

You could call it that. "A gentleman never tells."

"Oh. Well, please apologize to dear Lynda for me. I
am calling to ask you to meet me in Professor Talton's
office in one hour."

I bristled. "I should show up in my own office once
in a while, you know. It's just not fair to Popcorn to leave
her with all the work." *Never mind that she does it better than I
do and never complains.*

"I quite understand, old boy. However, I think you
will agree that the outcome of our efforts yesterday was
worth the time and trouble. In fact, Dr. Bloomingdale has
asked me to appear with her on the evening news tonight to
discuss the case live with a reporter. Surely that will be good
publicity for St. Benignus."

"Surely. And it won't do you any harm, either." It must have been sweet for Mac to get the request to go on TV with Dr. Bloomie, given that she and Mac were competitors of a sort in solving Noah's murder. I supposed it would be kind of a victory lap for him. But he didn't acknowledge that. He just said:

"If all goes well with Professor Talton, I believe that we will be able to present Ralph and Lesley with a satisfactory resolution to that problem as well."

"Such as?"

"Just relax and enjoy the show. It will be more fun that way. You are there as my witness in case anything goes awry."

I wasn't buying it. "That might be good enough for Dr. Watson, but not for me. If you want me there, you'll have to tell me why."

So he told me. But I'm not telling you. Just relax and enjoy the show.

"By the way, your favorite journalist is questioning your deductive genius," I told Mac on the way over to Talton's office.

He raised an eyebrow.

"Lynda believes in Connor's declarations of innocence. She thinks he's merely a self-absorbed criminal, not a killer."

"Indeed? Her opinions are not to be taken lightly. Upon what does she base that judgment?"

I explained.

"A long-ago rebuff calmly received is a rather thin reed to unravel the case against Connor O'Quinn," Mac said. "And yet—" He rubbed his beard thoughtfully.

Something rebelled in the pit of my stomach. "There's not a chance I ran after him for nothing, is there?"

"Of course not! The steroids charge is solid. I am sure it is only a matter of time before first-degree homicide is added. The blackmail, the Maltese Falcon as a bludgeon, it all makes sense. I suppose that Dr. Bloomingdale could argue that she was right about the murder weapon, and Mary Lou could say the same about the killer being a member of the Poisoned Pens. Yes, it fits. There are, however, a few loose ends to be tied up before I can feel entirely comfortable about this solution."

"Such as how Noah found out about Connor's side job," I said, just to show I was paying attention.

"Precisely that, and at least one thing more: For several days I have been trying to remember something I heard after Noah's death that struck a discordant note on my ears. It was out of place or wrong, an incongruity that caught my attention for just a moment, like a fleeting butterfly. Perhaps it was something that Mo said shortly after the murder, or perhaps not. I do not like that feeling of something missed, Jefferson. I do not care for it at all."

On that note, Sebastian McCabe lapsed into a moody silence that lasted until we walked into James Gregory Talton's office.

Talton made a show of looking very busy when we entered. Even at his desk he was wearing his suit jacket. But maybe that's because he knew we were coming. The mass of salt-and-pepper beard didn't hide the smug satisfaction on his dark face. He had no idea what was coming.

"You may sit down, gentlemen." He made it sound like a generous concession to grant us some of his time. "You should have put out a press release on yesterday's student demonstration, Cody. That's quite positive news for the college, I would think—strong support for an embattled faculty member."

Thanks for the advice. That will go into the appropriate file.

"But I assume you didn't come here to talk about that. McCabe, you said you have some news for me that you'd rather talk about in person. Good news, I trust. What is it?"

We sat down, unbidden.

"Ever since one of your controversial lectures showed up on YouTube, James, I have been intrigued by the question of who posted it. The YouTube account name was a meaningless handle, 'TrueAmerican.' Whoever this true American was, he or she seemed to have a real animus toward you. Who and why? Jefferson did not seem to think it mattered, and there was no real reason to believe that it did. I am not of a bent to leave mysteries unsolved, however."

"No?" There might have been a level of skepticism embedded in that monosyllable, but it was hard to tell for sure what Talton was feeling at that moment.

"No. So I pursued the matter until I had the answer. I now know who shared those videos with the world—and so do you." Mac pulled a cigar out of his breast pocket. "You did it yourself, James."

Talton's attempted chuckle rang hollow. "How did you reach that ridiculous conclusion? And put that cigar away! This is *my* office."

Mac obeyed him with a sigh, sticking the cigar back in his coat pocket. "I reached that conclusion by paying attention. You claimed that you were unaware those lectures were recorded. And yet in both you were looking right at the camera as you spoke. That was unmistakable once I began looking for a clue in the videos themselves. With an entire room of students in front of you, you were looking at the camera. That cannot have been unintentional. You must have asked a trusted student or guest in the classroom to unobtrusively record your lecture. And then you made sure it went viral."

Talton didn't panic, as Connor had. If he were any cooler, he'd have had frost on his whiskers.

"And why would I do such a thing?" he asked in a steady voice. "All of this controversy has made my life miserable."

Mac slowly shook his head. "On the contrary, James, it has made you a celebrity just as you intended. You were quoted in the *New York Times* and the *Wall Street Journal.* You appeared on *Speaking Out with Barry Winslow* on Prime News Network. Not coincidentally, your most recent book, *Henry Clay: American Icon*—which you mentioned repeatedly during that highly promoted national appearance—has soared in the Amazon rankings. Not long ago you were an obscure professor at a small Catholic college in Ohio, with a modest reputation among your peers as a solid historian. A Google search of your name this morning turned up more than twelve thousand references."

Talton frowned. "Is that all?"

"I originally assumed when I noted your increased fame that you exploited an opportunity that came to you unbidden. In reality, you created the opportunity with that video. There was zero risk to you in calling attention to your opinions in such an unconventional manner. Though it is offensive to some, your view of our nation's history is unquestionably within the bounds of academic freedom. And you have tenure."

Talton stared at Mac for a while, as if considering his options. Then he showed the ace in his hand. "You won't tell anybody how those videos got online. That would be embarrassing to St. Benignus."

Mac nodded. "True enough, James. However, it would also be embarrassing to you."

"Well, I have to admit that I'm not sure how my new employer would react to my enterprise. It might not be positively."

Mac raised an eyebrow.

"I've decided to leave St. Benignus, although I hope that my years of dedicated service will be reflected in emeritus status. My YouTube performances caught the attention of the American Century Foundation just at a time when I knew they were hoping to hire an African American.

I disdain political correctness, but I don't mind benefitting from it. I knew such positions were lucrative, but I had no idea *how* lucrative! I've also signed a contract with PNN to provide trenchant commentary on a regular basis."

I wanted to scream. But there was an upside to this: If Talton left for greener pastures (green as in the color of money), he would no longer be our problem.

"I'm sure the many students looking forward to taking your classes will be disappointed, as will your current and former students," I said. *First the ego stroking, then . . .* "How soon can you announce your departure?"

"It all hinges on that emeritus status." Talton smiled. "Perhaps you can discuss this with the administration on my behalf. That might make things easier than if I made the request myself. I suspect I'm not very popular with Father Pirelli and Dr. Pendergast right now. I am assuming, of course, that you will keep the origin of those videos to yourselves." *Assume anything you want, asshole.* "Do we have a deal, gentlemen?"

It felt like we were negotiating with the devil. I ignored Talton's outstretched hand. "I have an appointment with the provost in a few minutes," I said. "If anybody can swing something like that, he can." *And may you choke on it.* "We'll get back to you."

I couldn't wait to get out of there.

"I have to hand it to you," I told Mac as we strolled down the hallway. "You solved a mystery where I didn't think there was one. And right after putting the finger on Noah's murderer. You're on a hot streak!"

Mac's smile looked almost rueful. "It is pleasant to think so. Still, I wish I could put my finger on what I heard and no longer remember . . . something to do with Noah."

"Maybe you'll figure it out before you go on the news tonight. You still have a few hours to tie up loose ends."

Chapter Thirty-Two
Loose Ends

Speaking of the devil, Ralph was waiting impatiently for me when we arrived at his office a few minutes after the ten o'clock time of my appointment.

"We regret our tardiness," Mac said.

Somehow Ralph gave the impression that he was looking down his sharp nose at Mac, even though he was seated at his massive desk and we were standing up. "You weren't invited, McCabe."

We sat down.

"His presence will be helpful for our discussion," I explained. *Why am I starting to sound like Mac? Is he contagious?*

"I sincerely doubt that." Ralph sat back. "Very well, then. The purpose of this meeting is to discuss the use of steroids by some members of our wrestling team."

"No, it isn't," I said.

Ralph was too surprised to interrupt as I continued my correction.

"The purpose of this little confab is to discuss the media coverage of that steroids use and the negative attention to St. Benignus College that will result. Right?"

"Obviously, that's what I meant. When the Athletic Department began investigating the reports of steroids on campus, I had hoped that they were inaccurate—or that if the reports were true, that we could announce our findings and our disciplinary measures at the same time."

"That would have been the ideal," I agreed. "That would have made it clear that we take this stuff seriously and are willing to deal with it. We lost that opportunity because things moved too quickly. When one of Mac's students confessed to us that he used steroids, and named his supplier, we had to take that information to the police. Every citizen who has knowledge of a felony has a legal obligation to report it. Failure to do so is a crime."

"Given that a student was involved, and that St. Benignus was involved, it would have been nice to tell me as well," Ralph said acidly.

"We erred," Mac said. "That is undeniable. In the rush of events, certain that Connor O'Quinn was guilty of murder as well as selling steroids to at least one of our students, we neglected our duty to you. We sincerely apologize."

I tried to look sincere. Sebastian McCabe was not about to out-humble Jeff Cody. "I'm sorry, Ralph. It won't happen again." I hope I didn't sound sarcastic, because I actually meant it.

Ralph drummed his fingers on the desk for a moment, enjoying our humiliation to the fullest. "Well, now that the barn door has been closed, where do we go from here?"

"My former student, Isaac Lamb, stands ready to tell what he knows," Mac said. "He is also ready to take his medicine, including expulsion from the wrestling team. Connor may also be cooperative in return for a lighter sentence on the drug charges, hoping to fend off the far more serious murder charge. That means that all of this should be wrapped up relatively quickly as far as St. Benignus is concerned."

"And that means the media will lose interest quickly." I was soft-pedaling a little here. Well, actually I was soft-pedaling a *lot*. I was sure the St. Benignus wrestling team would come up in Connor's murder trial because concealing his sale of steroids was the motive for the murder. But I didn't see any reason to burden Ralph with that until it happened. And the MSM (Main Stream Media) wasn't the only problem; ignorant third parties would be sharing their ill-informed opinions on social media for weeks. But this was no time to cure Ralph's cluelessness on that score.

"Today's story in the *Observer* is not beneficial to the college," he sniffed.

I stifled the urge to point out that Johanna Rawls's job is to report the news, not to make us look good. Instead, I said: "She used a quote from me about how we've been carrying out our own investigation and are cooperating with the police. That shows that we're serious about dealing with the problem."

"Your quote is in the eleventh paragraph."

Ralph is very good with numbers.

I tried a different tack. "You should just be grateful that it wasn't an employee of St. Benignus who was pedaling the steroids."

Ralph grunted. "I suppose I should be. Still, I expect to hear from alumni and donors. A few of them have already been quite vociferous about Professor Talton."

What an opening!

"Ah, on that point, Ralph, I believe we can set your mind at rest," Mac said. "James will very shortly cease to be an issue for St. Benignus."

"What do you mean?"

"He has received financially rewarding offers to join a think tank and to appear as a regular commentator on PNN. He has accepted both."

Ralph's steely eyes brightened. "You mean he's leaving us?"

"There's just one catch." I couldn't help enjoying myself as I prepared to pee on his parade. I'm not proud of that, but there it is. "Talton wants to be granted emeritus status."

Ralph blinked. "Good grief! Whatever for?"

"Ego, one supposes," Mac rumbled.

Wow, that was a moment: Sebastian McCabe tutoring Ralph Pendergast on the subject of ego.

Ralph shook his head. "That's a decision for the board of trustees. I sincerely doubt they will want to bestow the honor on a man whose recent activities have not brought credit to the college."

"Don't play games with us, Ralph." I was tired of messing around. "You're a creature of the board. They forced you on Father Pirelli and they're the ones you suck up to. I'm sure they'll spot you this favor."

His feathers appropriately ruffled, Ralph did a pretty good job of sputtering. Mac swooped in to play "good cop."

"I really think you would be wise to accommodate James's request, Ralph. His achievements as a serious scholar justify it. You might get a few protests from alumni and outsiders, but that will fade quickly. Consider the alternative: He has tenure, which means it will be almost impossible to force him out. If he stays at St. Benignus, he will continue to be a figure of controversy."

Ralph hates controversy. Maybe you've noticed.

"But you said he accepted job offers!"

"I am reasonably sure that think tanks and cable networks are replete with individuals who also labor in the groves of academe. In other words, he could do both. And his commentaries on PNN are not likely to be innocuous. If I were you, I would begin calling members of the board post-haste."

Ralph put his head in his hands. He didn't like it. But he would have to accept it.

We stood up and left the office without further conversation.

"Well, Jefferson," Mac said as we headed back toward our respective offices, "that worked out far better than I expected when I began pursuing the question of who posted the videos of Professor Talton's lectures. As I recall, you were skeptical of my endeavor."

I was a bit nettled by the reminder, so I downplayed Mac's achievement. Hadn't I thrown him enough laurels for that already? "I'm glad to have Talton off my plate, but it's not the worst PR problem I ever had with a faculty member. The Title IX cases are a lot worse, especially when it involves a faculty member and a student."

"Indeed, everyone rightly condemns the breach in professional ethics committed by someone who takes, er, romantic advantage of someone in his or her charge."

Mac suddenly stopped dead in the middle of the sidewalk outside of Gamble Hall, an elephant-caught-in-the-headlights look in his wide brown eyes. "Professional ethics! No, that could not be. And yet . . . Yes, of course it could! Why not? In fact, it must be."

"I hate to interrupt this fascinating debate you're having with yourself, but what is it now?"

But Mac wasn't listening. Mentally, he was somewhere else. So I waited him out for what must have been a solid minute, which is longer than it sounds.

"By thunder, I have it!" he said at last.

"Good! What do you have?" *If you say "a thumping headache," I will kill you slowly.*

"I remember the apparent incongruity that has eluded me, the false note that I have been trying to remember for days. However, that might not have been what he actually said. It could have been a paraphrase. I must find out for certain."

Well, that's clear. "What are you babbling about?"

"It may be nothing, Jefferson—a mere slip of the tongue. But perhaps it is the key to it all. I must ask Mo a clarifying question. Then I will know for certain."

Chapter Thirty-Three
Live at Six!

Obviously, I thought, Mac had found the nail for Connor O'Quinn's coffin. But would he tell me? Not on your life. He had to go all mysterious first, as usual. And then he was going to spill it all on live television. I would get the details at the same time as everybody else. I told myself that he had his reasons, but the slight still chafed.

Live interviews seldom happen during the evening news, but this was a special case: TV4 Action News was understandably hot to get Dr. Bloomie's take on a murder in which she had been intimately involved as the intended second victim. But she was in Chicago Wednesday night and most of Thursday taping *The Shrinks*. So TV4's news director came up with the ratings-boosting idea of a live interview with Mac included. The station had been touting it on Twitter and Facebook all day—"Live at Six!"

Since my über-extroverted brother-in-law had been about as communicative as the Sphinx regarding his late-in-the-day brainstorm, I was eager to get the answer to questions such as: What did Mo know about Connor, or maybe Noah, that Mac had to ask her a "clarifying question" about? And what about Ashley, Connor's casual girlfriend—did she know anything about the bartender's side trade in steroids? And how did Noah find out about that business? And most importantly of all: What did Noah mean to indicate by grabbing that copy of *Love's Dark Secret* off the shelves before he shuffled off this mortal coil?

Tune in tonight—Live at Six!

Lynda and I decided to watch at Bobbie McGee's, along with Popcorn and my sister, Kate. I guess we were drawn to the sports bar for much the same reason that people watch ballgames there—the thrill of the spectator sport shared with other spectators. Or maybe it was because Connor had worked at Bobbie's. Whatever the reason, we all met up at Erin's most popular watering hole a few minutes before the appointed hour of the interview.

"I'll have a Caffeine-Free Diet Coke." That was Lynda ordering, not me. I almost fell off my chair.

"No Manhattan?" Surprise doesn't begin to describe my shock.

Lynda looked at the menu, in an apparent attempt at studied casualness. "I'm channeling Jeff Cody. No calories."

She's probably gained a pound, I thought, although it must have been evenly distributed over her shapely form because I couldn't tell. And I'd studied the subject at some length. I ordered a Hudy Delight, knowing that the low-cal beer would have irritated Mac.

"Mind if we join you?"

The way Lesley Saylor-Mackie and her spouse looked at us, "no" wasn't really a viable response.

"Of course not," Lynda said.

"Isn't this a conflict of interests, Gulliver?" I said, needling the mayor's husband a bit. "You're going to be the landlord for Bobbie's competition."

Mackie shook his football-captain head, smiling. "It doesn't exactly work that way with eateries. They may compete to a degree, but they also feed off of each other— no pun intended." *Why do people always say "no pun intended" when they obviously intend it?* "A sports bar and a gastropub are different animals with different clientele. Nevertheless, if The Speakeasy is jammed, some of that crowd will spill over here. Restaurants are great for downtown development because they actually do better when they're near other restaurants."

"If you say so." *Not that I really needed a lecture in the economics of the restaurant biz.* I turned to Her Honor the Mayor. She was dressed casually, for her, in charcoal slacks and a white blouse, with earrings and jewelry in the same theme colors. Somehow she managed to make it all look elegant. Maybe the clothes make the man, but in this case the woman made the clothes. "Did Ralph fill you in on the Talton stuff?"

That was probably an indiscreet thing to say in front of civilians. So sue me.

Her mouth turned downward. "Don't remind me. Of all the—"

"Shhhh," Lynda said. "Here it comes."

Apparently I'd talked over the opening intro by Brian Rose. He'd already tossed it over to his ever-perky brunette co-anchor, Tammie Tucker, who was in mid-sentence. After seventeen years in television and probably an equal number of facelifts, she still had the jaunty enthusiasm of a teenager. She annoyed me.

". . . exclusively tonight that our own Dr. Bloomie today identified that suspect, Connor O'Quinn, as the man who attacked her at her home on Monday."

Tammie was talking into a hand-held microphone with a solemn-looking Dr. Bloomie and Mac standing at her right. The good doctor was dressed professionally but expensively, with her normal compliment of jewelry, as though she'd just walked off the set of *The Shrinks*. Mac wore a blue bowtie with white polka dots.

The anchorlady thrust her microphone into Dr. Bloomie's face. "What was that like for you, coming face to face with the suspect?"

Dr. Bloomie shuddered. "It was awful, Tammie. Everything that happened to me that terrible night came back to me when I saw that man. As a psychologist, I'm very familiar with the phenomenon of flashbacks after a traumatic experience, what we now know as a manifestation of Post-Traumatic Stress Disorder, but this was the first time I'd ever experienced it myself."

Tammie drew the microphone back to herself. "And of course that man, twenty-nine-year-old bartender Connor O'Quinn, has also been named by Erin Police Chief Oscar Hummel as a suspect in the murder of bookstore owner Noah Bartlett. We also have with us here Sebastian McCabe, the well-known mystery writer, who we understand actually solved the murder of Mr. Bartlett as he has so many others." She looked serious, no easy task for Tammie. "What can you tell us about that tonight, Professor McCabe?"

Never shy, Mac is particularly not shy in front of an audience, even one that he couldn't see. "I regret to say that my friend Noah brought about his own death. Desperate for money, he blackmailed the wrong person."

"Connor O'Quinn," Tammie said confidently.

But Mac shook his head. "No, I was wrong about that. I am pleased to have this opportunity tonight to publicly apologize to Mr. O'Quinn for my erroneous conclusion and whatever harm it may have done to his reputation. I am thankful that he has not yet been charged with murder. He has a deeply flawed character, but he is not the murderer of Noah Bartlett. Nor did Noah attempt to blackmail him."

Lynda stared at me. I shook my head. *No, I don't know what he's up to. But when this is over, I am going to maim him.*

Everybody else, at our table and on the TV screen, was staring at Mac. After a moment of stunned silence, Tammie spoke into her microphone. "If not Connor O'Quinn, who then?"

Mac turned to Dr. Bloomie. "Do you wish to answer that?"

Years of softball questions in front of the camera hadn't prepared the TV psychologist for that. Her voice was edgy as she said, "How would I know?"

"Because you are the answer, Dr. Bloomingdale. You killed Noah."

Lesley Saylor-Mackie, sitting next to me, sucked in air like a vacuum cleaner.

When it came to fight or flight, Connor had chosen flight. Dr. Bloomie was in the fight camp.

"What?" Her voice was full of fury. "That's ridiculous, absurd. I only knew Mr. Bartlett as a patient."

Mac looked her in the eyes. "The truth is quite the contrary, Dr. Bloomingdale. I submit that you knew him in a Biblical sense—that is, you two were intimate. If I were more astute, I would have suspected as much from your strong reaction when I alluded to your relationship with Noah. You hastily assured me that it was only professional, when that is all that I meant. As Scripture tells us in the Book of Proverbs, the guilty flee where no one pursueth.

"Noah was a handsome man who came to you for help four years ago—right after he returned to Erin and right after your husband left you. The intimate relationship that resulted is perhaps understandable, given the weakness of human nature. However, it is a violation of canon 10.05 of the *Ethical Principles of the American Psychological Association*. I quote: 'Psychologists do not engage in sexual intimacies with current therapy clients/patients.' That is quite clear. There is no wiggle room. Perhaps that is why one of you broke it off. Or perhaps it just faded away when Noah completed therapy.

"At any rate, you were no longer involved with each other at the time of his murder. The damage, however, had already been done. If this relationship were revealed, it most certainly would result in both professional sanctions and the loss of your highly rewarding television career. That is why Noah felt confident that you would be willing to make a cash payment to him in order to avoid exposure. You demurred in a most definitive fashion. You bashed his head in."

"I should have known," Saylor-Mackie breathed, practically in my ear. "I should have seen it all."

"That is the meaning of the clue that you were so eager to turn our attention away from—the book that Noah Bartlett was at pains to clutch in his hand as he lay dying, *Love's Dark Secret.* It wasn't Noah's dark secret that he wished to call attention to, but yours—the secret that would ruin everything for you if it were revealed."

"This is just insane," Dr. Bloomie said, apparently so unnerved that she lapsed into the very unprofessional vocabulary ("insane") that she'd refused to use in her interview with Brian Rose. "There isn't a shred of truth in what you just said. It's a tissue of fabrication. All of it."

"Do you have any proof of this very serious allegation, Professor McCabe?" Tammie spoke with an edge of panic in her voice. The producer must have been screaming into her ear. A hometown heroine and marquee name on the station had just been accused of murder.

"That will be for a jury to decide," Mac said coolly, looking at Dr. Bloomie rather than at his interrogator. "However, let us examine the indicators of your guilt, Dr. Bloomingdale, starting with the signs you were once more to Noah than just his therapist. You are commonly known by your television sobriquet of 'Dr. Bloomie' or simply 'Bloomie'—but not to Noah. His assistant, Mo Russert, told us that Noah said, quote, 'Sydney helped him a lot.' Something bothered me about that even before I could put my finger on what it was.

"This afternoon I finally saw the incongruity: Why would Noah, as a former patient, not call you Dr. Bloomingdale? Or, less formally, Dr. Bloomie? When you first met Mo, you said, 'Please call me "Bloomie." Almost everyone does.' I had never heard anyone else use your first name by itself. So I asked Mo whether Noah had actually referred to you as Sydney, and she assured me that he had. She is quite certain that is how he always denoted you."

"Not exactly a lover's pet name," I muttered.

As if he had heard me, Mac said, "Although many people have a relatively relaxed relationship with their medical professionals, it seems highly unlikely that a man whose only relationship to his female therapist was a professional one would refer to her in casual discourse by her first name rather than her universally known nickname."

"That's your proof?" Dr. Bloomie made it sound more like an accusation than a question.

I hope not.

"You find it less than convincing? Well, no doubt a diligent effort by Chief Hummel's troops will turn up someone who saw the two of you together in an intimate setting. However, the title of *Love's Dark Secret* is not the book's only significance as a clue to the murderer. There is also the plot.

"I initially accepted the natural assumption that Noah would not have read a romance novel, and therefore would not know in any detail the storyline. Later, however, I came into some information that led me to believe he would have had a reason to read it. I need not reveal that reason at this time, or perhaps ever." I looked at Saylor-Mackie. Her hazel eyes glistened. Of course Noah would have read her books after they became friends again, and probably told her so. "The object of the heroine's affection in the book turns out to suffer from what is now known as dissociative identity disorder. She convinces him to seek therapy from a psychologist named Dr. Allyson Macy. That character—an attractive but not youthful woman—was clearly based on you, Dr. Bloomingdale, and Noah saw that. In clutching that book, he was telling us that you killed him."

"Wow!" Popcorn breathed.

"So Dr. Macy was based on Dr. Bloomingdale?" Lynda said. "I would have totally gotten that if I'd read the book."

"Who wouldn't?" Kate said.

Not being much into department store shopping, I wouldn't. But I didn't raise my hand. Mac hadn't figured it out either, until today—and he *had* read *Love's Dark Secret*. We'd noodled around the possibility that Noah's novel-in-the-making was a roman à clef, but we hadn't considered the idea that Noah's dying message pointed to a character in the romance novel based on a real person. Noah had recognized the inspiration for Dr. Macy, but he may have had a little hint from the author. Said author remained silent as Mac explained the clue contained in her book.

Dr. Bloomie didn't say anything, either. She just stared daggers at her accuser. Maybe she was anticipating her lawyer's advice.

"You made a mistake when Mo Russert asked you to meet us at Pages Gone By," Mac told her, continuing to build his case. "You claimed to have never been there before, and yet you entered via the seldom-used back door, which opens onto an alley—the same door employed by the murderer.

"Perhaps it was my reference to your relationship with Noah on that occasion that made you believe, wrongly at the time, that I suspected your culpability in his death. Or perhaps it was reading *Love's Dark Secret*, which you bought from Ms. Russert that day. Up until then you doubtless assumed the book in some way pointed to you as Noah's murderer, but you must have been shocked at how close to home it hit. Or so it would have seemed to you as you read it with your guilty knowledge.

"Whatever the reason, you decided to stage an attack on yourself to divert suspicion. Perhaps you were inspired by a genuine attack on a suspect in another murder in Erin. Your reference to my use of hypnotism in that affair demonstrates that you were familiar with the case. I am confident that the emergency room doctor who treated you can testify as to how superficial the wounds were."

It hit me that in a weird way James Gregory Talton had done something similar—he had staged an attack of sorts on himself, although for a very different reason.

Tammie aimed her microphone at Sydney Bloomingdale, but Dr. Bloomie didn't give her a chance to ask for a reaction. "Okay, this stops right now. Get that camera out of my face." The way she said it made me think that if the cameraman didn't obey she might crown him with her heavy bracelet.

"So there you have it, Brian—"

Lesley Saylor-Mackie stood up, tears streaming down her face now. "You bitch!" she yelled at the television above the bar. "He was my first love." Her husband quickly rose to put his arm around her while Lynda, Kate, and Popcorn made sympathetic murmurs.

"He was also a blackmailer," I mumbled, more or less to myself. "That never ends well."

Call me a hard case, but it was the truth.

Chapter Thirty-Four
Easter Morning

More than an hour and a half later we were still at Bobbie's when Mac stopped by for a victory lap. The Mackies had gone home and Bobbie had joined us to lament the loss (temporary, she hoped) of her most popular bartender even before The Speakeasy opened.

"How did you figure it all out?" Popcorn asked.

Lynda rolled her eyes. She loves Mac like I do, sometimes even defending him to me, but she knew he was just waiting for somebody to ask the question.

Mac sipped his dark brew and surveyed the wreckage of our table—empty plates, half-full beer glasses, and the unaccustomed Coke in front of Lynda—for a moment before responding.

"Jefferson turned the light on for me." I tried to look modest. "Something he said about another matter we were involved in caused me to utter the phrase 'professional ethics' in regard to lapses of a romantic nature. As soon as I said those two words, I was suddenly able to grasp what had eluded me for so long—Noah Bartlett's unprecedented, to my knowledge, use of Sydney Bloomingdale's first name. A patient on very friendly terms might well call her 'Bloomie,' but 'Sydney' sounded more like a lover. I immediately saw the implications of that. With this in mind, I considered anew the plot of *Love's Dark Secret* in search of Noah's dying clue. And I found it in the character of the striking Dr. Macy, whom I now recognized as a stand-in for Dr. Sydney Bloomingdale."

"How could Noah and Dr. Bloomie possibly carry on without half the town knowing about it?" Kate wondered.

"I bet they met out of town—in Cincinnati or across the river in Kentucky," Lynda said. "Even people who recognized Dr. Bloomie wouldn't give Noah a second look."

It was time for somebody to bring Mac back to earth. I nominated me. "You do realize that you didn't offer anything approaching proof, don't you?" I said.

"Perhaps individually each of those indicators of guilt is a thin reed upon which to build a gallows," he conceded. "However, as Sam Spade said in the climactic scene of *The Maltese Falcon*, look at the number of them. I was hoping that my verbal barrage, plus the pressure of being live on television, would cause Dr. Bloomingdale to blurt out an admission."

"Fat chance," Kate said. "That's one cool customer."

"I loved her on *The Shrinks*," Lynda offered.

"Alas," Mac said, "I would not count on Dr. Bloomingdale's continued participation in the program."

Sure enough, the production company announced the next day that they were suspending Dr. Bloomingdale and "reassessing her role in the show."

"They're only doing that because she might be up for a murder rap," Lynda mused when we saw that reported on the overhead television. It was Friday morning and we were racing each other on the exercise bikes at Nouveau Shape.

"Well, sure."

"I mean, if Noah had spilled the beans on her she might have been defrocked, or whatever it is they do to psychologists when they have affairs with patients. But would it really have hurt her TV career? Look what happened to Martha Stewart when she got out of jail—she took up where she left off. I'm not the only one who still buys her magazine. So it seems to me that Dr. Bloomie could have refused to pay blackmail and still not gone down in flames. She didn't have to kill the poor guy."

"I see what you mean. All she had to do was hang her head, admit that she made a 'serious lapse in judgment' or some such weasel phrase, and apologize to the viewers. She might have survived. She might have even gotten a ratings boost from having her face plastered on the covers of all those supermarket tabloids." I sighed. "I wouldn't be surprised if Aristotle O'Doul makes that argument as part of his defense if she comes to trial."

Dr. Bloomie hadn't even been charged yet—Oscar was still looking for the smoking gun—but she'd already hired the country's most famous defense attorney. Aristotle O'Doul is who Erica Slade wants to be when she grows up.

O'Doul had already threatened to sue Mac for defamation of character, but it was a hollow threat. True, the video of my brother-in-law confronting Dr. Bloomie had gone viral, racking up a number of views that left James Gregory Talton's controversial lectures in the dust, as well as being picked up by all the TV networks. And, true, Mac had no solid proof of his accusation and no confession. But defaming a public figure is almost impossible, and Dr. Bloomie was certainly a public figure.

The coverage of all this in the *Erin Observer & News-Ledger* was excellent, by the way, thanks to a warning call Mac had placed to Tall Rawls shortly before air time. Lynda was most appreciative of his thoughtfulness.

Lynda and I didn't see Mac again until we went to Chez McCabe for brunch and an Easter egg hunt more than a week later on Easter morning. Lynda had painted her fingernails to look like colorful little eggs for the occasion. The McCabe children, ages sixteen, fourteen, and eleven, are too old and too sophisticated to be hunting Easter eggs. But Mac isn't.

We drank mimosas and ate an egg casserole whipped up by Mac. Lynda skipped the champagne, saying she didn't feel well. She'd said that too often lately. If it kept up, I was planning on dragging her to the doctor.

"I am pleased to tell you that a new bookstore, Mo's Mysteries & Marvels, featuring fantasy and science fiction as well as mysteries, will be opening later this year in the first floor of the old firehouse on Water Street," Mac said as he tucked into the casserole. "She decided not to stand in the way of Mr. Bexley's new venture. Besides, the old location had bad memories for her as the site of Noah's murder."

"But the business was failing," I said. "How can Mo—oh, I get it. Serena Mason bailed her out."

Mac shook his leonine head. "Not Serena, but I have it on good authority that she does have a silent partner."

From the twinkle in his eye I had no doubt as to the identity of the partner, but I sure doubted his ability to remain silent for long. Before I could rag him about that, the doorbell rang.

"I'll get it." Brian, the eleven-year-old, was out of his chair before anybody could stop him. Less than a minute later, Oscar Hummel stood in the dining room arch, smiling like a jack-o'-lantern with teeth (although they may be dentures).

"I've got her," he said. There was more than a note of triumph in his voice—more like a whole symphony.

Mac cocked an eyebrow. "Dr. Bloomingdale?"

"Who else? Did you ever notice a gold bracelet on her right wrist?" I had, and Mac notices everything. "Gibbons watched a lot of archived episodes of *The Shrinks* on the Internet. It hit him that she wore that particular piece of jewelry in every episode—and also on her TV4 Action News interviews. He figured she must never take it off. We know that Noah Bartlett's killer was right-handed and there was lots of blood . . ."

"And some of it hit the bracelet!"

"Right." Oscar was in too good a mood to protest having his thunder stolen by Mac's exuberant deduction. "The DNA testing by BCI[7] was conclusive. I got the results on Friday afternoon. Slade called yesterday to tell me he's taking the case to the grand jury. I wanted to give you the good news in person. Happy Easter."

"How did you get the bracelet to test it?" Lynda asked.

"Judge Rafferty signed a court order based on some other evidence. First, the security camera at Speedy Sal's convenience store a couple of blocks away from Pages Gone By, on Water Street, caught Dr. Bloomie's car parked in the alley during the likely time of the murder. Then, the YouTube of Mac's confrontation with Dr. Bloomie brought forth a citizen from Newport, Kentucky, who is willing to swear she saw the good doctor—her favorite on *The Shrinks*—with Noah Bartlett at Belterra Casino in Indiana about two years ago. She recognized Barlett's photo from news reports. Oh, and Mayor Saylor-Mackie offered to provide proof that the character of Dr. Macy in *Love's Dark Secret* was based on Dr. Bloomie, but I told her that shouldn't be necessary." He smiled slyly. It never hurts to have a little something on your boss.

"Well done, Oscar!" My brother-in-law pumped the lawman's hand. "Truly this was your finest hour."

The chief beamed. "Like I keep telling you, Mac, it's routine, dogged police work that solves cases. Do you think I should give up the treehouse story and make this case into a mystery novel instead?"

---

[7] Ohio Bureau of Criminal Identification and Investigation

Mac and I looked at each other. How could we be both polite and truthful, given Oscar's lack of talent in the field of literature?

"I think it would be better if I tell the true story of Dr. Bloomie," I said. "I'm sure Mac could help you with your writer's block on the mystery."

"Perhaps." Mac looked dubious. The man was not made to be anybody's ghostwriter or writing partner. "That is a discussion for another time."

"Yeah, well, I'd better get a move on," Oscar said. "Popcorn's in the car. She says I have to go to church with her. I just thought you'd want to know about the case. Keep it to yourself, though. We're not arresting Dr. Bloomie until tomorrow. It is Easter, after all."

He departed amidst much bonhomie.

"So," Mac said when he'd come back from seeing Oscar to the door, "Easter morning is an ideal time to celebrate a new beginning." He raised his champagne flute in the direction of Lynda and me. "Am I among the first to congratulate you two?"

My eyebrows formed a question mark. "For what?"

"Damn you, you show-off," Lynda snarled at Mac. "I haven't told him yet."

Mac's bearded jaw sank. "My profuse apologies, my dear Lynda! I assure you that I had no intention of spoiling a surprise. When I noted that you shunned spirits that evening at Bobbie McGee's—a sports bar!—that had me wondering. I thought perhaps you had given up adult beverages for Lent, a degree of piety quite beyond my reach. But when you continued to be abstemious this Easter morning even to the point of refusing champagne, I felt confident that I knew the happy reason."

"Ha! In other words, you guessed and you got lucky." She regarded me with eyes wide as the moon. "I've suspected it for days, darling, enough to be cautious, but I only confirmed it this morning—right before we left for church. I was waiting for a quiet moment to tell you."

Of course, by this time even Dr. Watson would have caught on, but I was no less thrilled to hear the big news from her very own lovely lips:

"We're pregnant, *tesoro mio.*"

A Few Word of Thanks

It's time to round up the usual suspects. Jeff Cody and I want to thank my wonderful team:

Ann Brauer Andriacco, for her constant help and encouragement, as well as her readership;

Kieran McMullen, my sometime co-author, for some crucial forensic and procedural advice;

Deacon Ken Ramsey, a newcomer to Jeff's band of co-conspirators, for providing the DNA evidence;

Jeff Suess, for proofreading and final preparation of the manuscript; and

Steve Winter, for applying his engineering eye to the text.

Special thanks, as always, must go to Steve Emecz for being the world's most easy-to-work-with publisher and Bob Gibson at Stauch Design for producing yet another outstanding cover.

About the Author

Dan Andriacco has been reading mysteries since he discovered Sherlock Holmes at the age of nine, and writing them almost as long. The first five books in his popular Sebastian McCabe — Jeff Cody series are *No Police Like Holmes*, *Holmes Sweet Holmes*, *The 1895 Murder*, *The Disappearance of Mr. James Phillimore*, and *Rogues Gallery*. He is also the co-author, with Kieran McMullen, of *The Amateur Executioner*, *The Poisoned Penman*, and *The Egyptian Curse* mysteries solved by Enoch Hale with Sherlock Holmes.

A member of the Tankerville Club, the Illustrious Clients, the Agra Treasurers, the Vatican Cameos, and the John H. Watson Society, and an associate member of the Diogenes Club of Washington, D.C., Dan is also the author of *Baker Street Beat: An Eclectic Collection of Sherlockian Scribblings*. Follow his blog at www.danandriacco.com, his tweets at *@DanAndriacco*, and his Facebook Fan Page at: www.facebook.com/DanAndriaccoMysteries.

Dr. Dan and his wife, Ann, have three grown children and six grandchildren. They live in Cincinnati, Ohio, USA, about forty miles downriver from Erin.

Praise for the earlier
Sebastian McCabe—Jeff Cody mysteries

"You're in the hands of a master of mystery plotting here. *Rogues Gallery* is a delightful read, hard to put down, and highly recommended. And did I say fun?"
—Screenwriter and novelist Bonnie MacBird

"The villain is hard to discern and the motives involved are even more obscure. All-in-all, this (*The Disappearance of Mr. James Phillimore*) is a fun read in a series that keeps getting better with each new tale."
—Philip K. Jones

"*The* 1895 *Murder* is the most smoothly-plotted and written Cody/McCabe mystery yet. Mr. Andriacco plays fair with the reader, but his clues are deftly hidden, much as Sebastian McCabe hides the secrets to his magic tricks under an entertaining run of palaver."
—*The Well-Read Sherlockian*

"I loved Dan Andriacco's first novel about Sebastian McCabe and Jeff Cody, and I'm delighted to recommend (*Holmes Sweet Holmes*), which has a curiously topical touch."
—Roger Johnson, *Sherlock Holmes Society of London*

"*No Police Like Holmes* is a chocolate bar of a novel—delicious, addictive, and leaves a craving for more."
—*Girl Meets Sherlock*

Also from MX Publishing

MX Publishing is the world's largest specialist Sherlock Holmes publisher, with over a hundred titles and fifty authors creating the latest in Sherlock Holmes fiction and non-fiction.

From traditional short stories and novels to travel guides and quiz books, MX Publishing cater for all Holmes fans.

The collection includes leading titles such as *Benedict Cumberbatch In Transition* and *The Norwood Author* which won the 2011 Howlett Award (Sherlock Holmes Book of the Year).

MX Publishing also has one of the largest communities of Holmes fans on Facebook with regular contributions from dozens of authors.

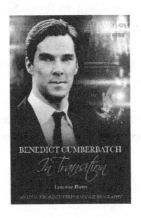

www.mxpublishing.com

Also From MX Publishing and Dan Andriacco

London, 1920: Boston-bred Enoch Hale, working as a reporter for the Central Press Syndicate, arrives on the scene shortly after a music hall escape artist is found hanging from the ceiling in his dressing room. What at first appears to be a suicide turns out to be murder . . .

The first in the Enoch Hale trilogy including *'The Poisoned Penman'* and *'The Egyptian Curse'*.

www.mxpublishing.com

Also from MX Publishing

Our bestselling short story collections 'Lost Stories of Sherlock Holmes', 'The Outstanding Mysteries of Sherlock Holmes', 'Untold Adventures of Sherlock Holmes' (and the sequel 'Studies in Legacy') and 'Sherlock Holmes in Pursuit'.

www.mxpublishing.com